Made for Love

Alissa Nutting is author of the award-winning collection of stories *Unclean Jobs for Women and Girls* and the
novel *Tampa*. Her work has appeared in the *New York
Times*; *O, The Oprah Magazine*; *Elle*; *Tin House*; *Fence*;
and *Bomb*, among other venues. She is an assistant professor of English at Grinnell College, and lives in Iowa
with her husband, author Dean Bakopoulos, and their
blended family of three kids.

ALSO BY ALISSA NUTTING

FICTION

Tampa

STORIES

Unclean Jobs for Women and Girls

Made for Love

ALISSA NUTTING

WINDMILL

1 3 5 7 9 10 8 6 4 2

Windmill Books
20 Vauxhall Bridge Road
London SW1V 2SA

Windmill Books is part of the Penguin Random House group of companies
whose addresses can be found at global.penguinrandomhouse.com.

Penguin
Random House
UK

First published in the United States by Ecco, an imprint of
HarperCollins Publishers in 2017
First published in Great Britain in paperback by Windmill Books in 2021

www.penguin.co.uk

A CIP catalogue record for this book is available from the British Library.

ISBN 9781786091536

Designed by Renata De Oliveira

Typeset in 10.43/15.523pt Berkeley Oldstyle Book by Jouve (UK), Milton Keynes

Printed and bound in Great Britain by Clays Ltd, Elcograf S.p.A.

The authorised representative in the EEA is Penguin Random House Ireland,
Morrison Chambers, 32 Nassau Street, Dublin D02 YH68

FOR DEAN—
WHO CAME TO GET ME,
AND DID

1
___

HAZEL'S SEVENTY-SIX-YEAR-OLD FATHER HAD BOUGHT A DOLL. A life-size woman doll. The kind designed to provide a sexual experience that came as close as possible to having sex with a living (or maybe, Hazel thought, a more apt analogy was a very-very-recently deceased) female. Its arrival crate bore an uncanny resemblance to a no-frills pine coffin. It made Hazel recall the passage from *Dracula* where he ships himself overseas via boat.

The ravaged crate now sat in the middle of his living room, surrounded by an array of tools, both legitimate and makeshift. One of the items on the floor was a can opener. Getting the doll out by himself had required tenacity. There were small pieces of chipped wood everywhere. They made it seem like the crate had harbored an animal that had escaped and was prowling the house.

The mechanical crawl of her father's Rascal mobility scooter announced his arrival behind her, but Hazel's eyes had locked upon the crate. It was big enough for her to climb inside. She could sleep in it. Now that Hazel was technically homeless, she was looking for "available bed" potential in everything she saw.

So could I sleep inside that, or upon it? suddenly seemed like a great question to ask about everything in sight. Maybe the crate would bring the best sleep of her life? It might feel nice to sleep without any extra space, especially after years of trying to sleep with the most space possible between her and the other person in her bed, who was always Byron. In the box there'd be no room to fidget around. No trying to attempt the best position since only one position would be possible. Maybe she'd be able to just lie down and shut off. Recharge like one of the thousand electronic devices Byron owned.

"Owned" was a simplification. He'd also invented them. Byron had founded and built a technologies empire. His wealth and power were a terrifying glimpse of the infinite.

She'd left Byron for good that morning, along with all forms of available funds or identification. Hazel understood that things were not going to end well for her.

Her father would let her stay with him, wouldn't he? It was selfish to ask for asylum—there was nothing harmless about Byron—but she liked to feel she had no other choice. Marriage to an eccentric tech multimillionaire had been kind of isolating.

Her best option was not to think about how she was putting her father's life at risk. But she didn't want to think about the current situation in her father's living room either. There was actually nothing she wanted to think about, so she decided to administer a series of firm bites to her bottom lip and really try to focus on the pain.

"Haze!" Her father's voice was a celebratory roar void of embarrassment. "How the hell are you! I didn't hear you come in."

"I let myself in," Hazel said. Walking up his driveway, Hazel had felt presumptuous entering her father's home with a suitcase, but now, seeing the sizable detritus his newest guest had brought with her, she found some comfort in the fact that she wasn't putting him out luggagewise, even if her presence might be endangering his life. She hadn't come with a giant casket, for instance!

Instead of greeting him, Hazel went to the window and peeked out of the blinds to make sure she hadn't been mistaken. "I didn't see your car parked anywhere so I figured you weren't home."

"Sold it!" her father barked. "I'm not going to need to leave the house much anymore. I'm entering a sort of honeymoon phase with Diane here."

"You sold the station wagon to buy a sex doll?"

Her father cleared his throat over the low purr of the Rascal's motor. The throat clear had been a signal between them for as long as Hazel could remember, a reprimand. It meant she'd used improper terminology and offended someone. For example, Shady Place, the retirement community where her father lived, was a trailer park for adults over fifty-five. Except calling them trailers was frowned upon. Hazel had made the mistake of using the word "trailer" just once when talking to Mrs. Fennigan, her father's garden-obsessed neighbor. *Your flowers are like supermodels!* Hazel had said. *Except in only good ways that aren't entangled with the violent forces of sexism! When I look at the front of your trailer, I feel like I'm watching an action film starring colors instead of people. The cones and rods in my eyes are starting to ache a little, actually*—and the woman had immediately stopped pruning, turned around toward Hazel with the clippers, and started taking tiny steps in Hazel's direction while opening and closing the clippers in a deliberate way, as if they were the jaws of a giant insect. Her father had conspicuously coughed, grabbed Hazel's arm, waved to the neighbor, and pulled Hazel away. *Manu-*

factured homes, he'd whispered sharply, *you call them manufactured homes, what the hell were you thinking, who the hell raised you?*

"Not a doll. This is *Diane*, Hazel," her father said. "I'm going to have to ask you to acknowledge her personhood. Come on, turn around and say hello. Don't be shy."

Hazel took a deep breath and told herself to be a good sport—she was about to ask him if she could move into his house, after all—but when her eyes took in the entirety of the situation she couldn't stop a petite scream from leaving her mouth. Diane was "riding" on her father's lap; the weight of the doll's torso had tipped it forward against the Rascal's handlebars and the two of them were positioned in such a way that he could very realistically be enjoying her right then. They were both wearing bathrobes. She recognized the faded fleece butterfly print on Diane's; the robe had belonged to Hazel's dead mother.

Hazel knew her father couldn't be expected to pick up on the desperate nature of her drop-in visit, but still. She was finished with pretending objects were human. Byron treated his electronics like lesser wives.

"I'm sorry, Dad. I'd prefer to opt out of this particular delusion."

He chuckled, setting his red flesh in motion. Her father was short and ruddy and his complexion was so fraught with broken capillaries that in a certain light his cheeks seemed sculpted from venison. He had a convincing air of physical exhaustion about him at all times, though slightly less so now that he used a scooter due to a botched knee replacement. Pre-scooter, complete strangers often approached him to offer him bottles of water. *You look thirsty!* they'd say.

He was also covered with bright white body hair, which gave a wrongful impression of cuddliness. It reminded Hazel of a type of cactus named "old man cactus," a metaphor gifted from nature. The plant had an inviting, shaggy white coat of fuzz, but the hairs were radial spines concealing a painful layer of central needles below the surface. "I told you she was a firecracker."

It took a moment to realize that her father was talking to Diane, not to her. She sighed. Mostly out of disappointment that she wasn't in a better position to be judgmental. Showing up at her father's home and putting him at risk was indecent. She had no idea what Byron would do when she failed to return that night.

Hazel stared at the gaudy clip-on earrings her father had applied to Diane's earlobes. What was that line Byron quoted when he allowed himself to have a tiny amount of alcohol and his dialogue began to sound lifted from a community-theater rendition of Plato? *Man's greatest desire is simply to bring things to life*? "Christ, Dad," Hazel said, which surprised her. "Jesus" and its synonyms weren't her usual exclamatory go-to's. But if this wasn't a time for a quasi-swear invoking the religious vocabulary of resurrection, when? "Okay. Fine. Thank you both for having me. How's that?"

"You haven't gotten old yet, Hazel," her father said. "You have to find happiness wherever you can get it."

"So should I call her Diane or Di or Mom?"

"Hazel! She's not trying to be your mother. Play nice already. Will you have a drink with us? I feel like celebrating."

Before she could answer, he'd reversed and begun accelerating toward the kitchen. The Rascal's top speed was just fast enough to make Diane's long red hair flow back in the breeze.

"I feel like celebrating too," Hazel called out, "in the sense that I'd like to completely withdraw from the realities of life." She wasn't sure if her father could hear her or not, over the sounds of the Rascal and the hum of the open refrigerator door; she supposed it didn't matter. "I've never been addicted to drugs or alcohol, so it wouldn't be a relapse . . . is there a name for the first time that a person gets really high on a lot of things, dangerously and possibly fatally high, in one's early thirties? I certainly feel like doing that, though I won't, because I'm afraid of an accident—not dying so much as managing to live but severely damaging my brain. Imagine the Frankensteinian attachments and implants Byron would attempt with me smiling and drooling the whole time. That's probably his greatest fantasy—me as part computer, part vagina, part breasts. I've got to speed up this divorce paperwork! Just kidding. It's pointless for me to file anything; there's no way I could possibly protect myself from Byron in a court of law. Wow, do I wish there were. If I somehow managed to half-kill myself, it would be a real purgatory to have Byron helming my power-of-attorney wheel."

"We can't hear you!" her father called out from the kitchen. "One second!" As the headlamp of the Rascal grew brighter, easing toward the living room through the dark tunnel of the hallway, Hazel thought she spied her father give Diane's earlobe a playful bite.

The basket of the scooter held a six-pack of domestic beer and a box of Ritz crackers. Hazel walked over and opened a can, opened another can for her father. "Is Diane a drinker, Dad?"

He gave her a wink with a glistening eye; he seemed to be on the brink of happy tears. "I drink for the both of us."

"Cheers, Pops." Hazel lifted her can and her father did the same. Somehow they formed an awareness that neither was stopping; they both chugged to the bottom and didn't lower their cans until both were empty. He opened another, accelerated just enough to reach it over to Hazel.

"Cheers is right. I'm particularly giddy. It's like a wedding day, but we skipped the boring part and got right to consummation."

Hazel felt what she hoped was a belch rising. "Can I have another beer?"

"I'm serious, Hazel. I know how this must look, but I'm three years away from the average male life expectancy. What was that TV show where contestants had sixty seconds to run around a grocery store and shove as much crap into the cart as possible? That's where I'm at, lifewise: if I don't grab it off the shelves right now, I'll never get to. There's no more procrastinating. Here, let me show you something."

And that's when the bathrobe was lifted. With a quick flip of the wrist, her father relieved Diane of all modesty.

"Oh. Her breasts are huge." Hazel realized she was whispering this with a tone of grievous acceptance, the way she'd report one friend's cancer to another.

"The station wagon was practical," her father acknowledged. "But I won't be missing it."

"How are they sloping upward like that?" Hazel asked. The doll's breasts hung as though Diane were upside down doing a handstand. Her nipples literally pointed toward the ceiling.

"I could hypothesize, Hazel, but I'd have to get a little spiritual on you."

An ambulance went by, its loud wailing pausing the conversation. It seemed to make her father recall a previously forgotten point. "That's another thing," he added. "Do you remember Reginald and his wife, Sherry?"

Yes, Hazel confirmed, she was not imagining it; there was an overall conical shape to Diane's breasts that was aesthetically energizing—she wondered if she could admit this while still continuing to loathe sex overall to spite Byron. When the trouble had first started, she'd thought it might be enough to just begin despising sex with *him*, but she soon saw that was just not going to cut it. Hazel knew that it would seem, to one who might be an amateur at marital rancor, that her masturbating while thinking about someone else would be a victory for her—pleasure, orgasm, the thrill of a mental affair—and a loss for Byron. Not so. She'd tried this for a while, and realized that she was becoming more in touch with her sexuality than ever: she was constantly thinking about sex, longing for sex; her body was turning into a Mardi Gras float except instead of throwing out beads it was tossing heavy vapors of pheromones to anyone close enough to smell, which often included Byron. He was delighted. It didn't even matter that they weren't having sex, because she was oozing it; Hazel had a glow and everyone who saw her, she was quite sure, attributed it to Byron fucking her with sovereign competence. That's when she realized: If one wanted to make a house inhospitable, closing off the vents to one room would not be enough. The power must be cut completely. So she shut everything down. And frankly, now, Hazel was a little disturbed by how the first thing in years to stir those embers was a hyperbolic set of plastic tits.

"Reginald?" her father barked. "You know, Sherry's husband. Navy man? Prominent teeth? They usually brought a quiche to the neighborhood potlucks."

"Drawing a blank, Dad. Why?" Curiosity really seemed to want Hazel to reach out and give Diane's left hooter an inquiring squeeze. She wondered if it would feel like those memory-foam mattresses. If she pressed down firmly, would the shape of her fingertip linger?

"I know you kids don't like to hear it, but people don't stop having sex just because they get old." Suddenly Hazel felt quite lucky that she didn't remember what Reginald and Sherry looked like. She felt like she'd won something. "So Reginald and Sherry, you know, they're both retired and fornicating around three in the afternoon on a Tuesday. Suddenly Reginald's ticker gives out. Now you've got to understand the physics of this thing—Reginald's barrel-chested and hearty. Sherry's an osteoporotic twig. He collapses on top of her and she's trapped beneath her husband's corpse. Feels like she's being suffocated, can't move. It was like that for over a day. Finally, their son comes over. Because he's a good son and calls every day and she wasn't picking up the phone."

"I'm not good on the phone, Dad!" Hazel interrupted. "And if you're telling this story to inspire me to call more, I'm not sure this particular narrative's prize of getting to be the one to roll your dead nude parent off your live nude parent is the penultimate carrot to dangle, in terms of incentive." For the moment, she decided to refrain from adding that there would be no more calling at all now since she no longer owned a phone.

"It wasn't an indictment. Though I do sometimes think of the many weeks my corpse would have to abide, should I die suddenly, before you'd get a whim to drop by again; just telling the story though. Anyhow, this kind of thing gets into your subconscious. Every date I went on that was there in my head—I'm thinking, 'This lady is way too nice for me to die on top of. She doesn't deserve that.' But Diane here . . . I can die on top of Diane all I want."

Hazel noticed the conversation was failing to lead into a natural segue about how she'd just ended her marriage. She opened another beer.

"All bets are off," he continued. "I don't have to hold back! Of all the ways to go, isn't extinction via sex the best you can think of? Let me tell you something about monitoring your heart rate while you're trying to jerk off: it's for the birds."

"Are you saying you're trying to commit suicide using Diane?" she asked. Hazel began to look at the five-foot four-inch silicone princess a little differently now: *Penthouse* pet from the waist up, Dr. Kevorkian from the waist down. Although the robe had fallen to Diane's waist, her greater mysteries were not visible. "Do these things come with pubes?"

"None of your business," her father snapped. "But yes. And I'm not saying I'm intending to die via intercourse. I'm just saying that I'm going to die, and I'd like to have intercourse many, many, many times before I go, and if that happens to be my chariot out of the natural world, I think that would not be the worst ride to hitch."

"Okay, Dad." Hazel eyed the remaining beers.

"Go ahead, they're yours. I'm already high on simulated love-making. Diane exceeded my wildest expectations. I wasn't hoping that it would feel great; I just wanted it to not feel painful—I was worried there'd be, you know, an irritating seam maybe, or that her hair would have a strong manufactured plastic odor, to the point of it seeming like I was undergoing some kind of aversion therapy. Boy was I an idiot. She smells like a new car!"

"I guess that's fitting, seeing that you traded in your old one."

Hazel noticed her father eyeing her empties, his fingers going up into the air one by one, counting. "You're sure thirsty tonight, Haze. Have I noticed before how quickly you drink?"

Her father wasn't the type who liked to feel encroached upon; Hazel knew she needed to make it seem like her moving in was at least half his idea so that he'd feel okay about it. "Well, I'm glad you're set in terms of romantic love," she began. "Speaking of people who might notice if you died though—as in someone who would be in a position to realize your passing on the very day that it occurred—do you ever think a roommate might be nice? Some supplemental human companionship for playing cards, conversing, shooting the breeze?"

Her father let out a hard laugh that caused Diane to plunge sharply forward. Hazel was shocked to find her own arms extending out with worry—she felt instinctually moved to catch the doll and make sure it didn't fall.

"Are you loony? Living alone is the greatest thing that ever happened to me! And now that I've got Diane, that takes it to a whole new level. We can have candlelight dinners naked. I can use her abdomen as a plate! That is something I've never done that I will not mind doing—eating a ham sandwich off the chest of a beautiful woman." He stared once more at Diane's breasts, his brow crumpled with admiring scrutiny. "She's a goddamn miracle. What's the saying? 'Today is the first day of the rest of my life.'"

"A miracle," Hazel mused. In a way, the crate on the floor did resemble an opened tomb, Diane a modern-day Lazarus delivered from stasis to take her place amongst the living.

It was then that her father saw it. He twisted uncomfortably in the seat of his Rascal, his movement pushing Diane's extended arm slightly to the left and into the horn, which gave a resonant, protracted toot.

"Hazel?" he asked. "What's with the suitcase?"

2

"YOU'RE LEAVING BYRON?" HER FATHER HAD BEEN REPEATING THIS
for over a minute. When outraged, his voice became a mythic roar,
to the extent that it seemed odd he wasn't holding a trident. He
suddenly looked naked without one. "But Byron's a genius! Every
time I leave the house, all I see are Gogol products!" This statement
was almost a whine, high-pitched, with a hysteria that made Hazel
think of overzealous infomercial entrepreneurs. She remembered
one disturbing commercial where a man with a machete was chopping up a mattress, or trying to, while screaming, *Pick up the phone!*
Pick up the phone! But she couldn't recall if it was the knife being
sold or the mattress. Was he cutting the bed to show how effective
the knife was? Or the mattress's layers? Or was it a kind of guilt-
inducing sales tactic: we won't stop harming beds until enough of
you phone in an order?

"I understand it's surprising news," Hazel said. Her father had placed a protective arm around Diane's waist and drawn her in close: his posture suggested that Hazel was not so much his daughter in an hour of need as a hopeful suitor who'd been flirting with his girlfriend at the bar and was being told to back off or agree to a fistfight.

"But, Hazel," he continued, his voice finally lowering, "do you know how much money Byron has?"

"Listen," Hazel begged. "I know you want to have a private sexual revolution with Diane and I am all for it. I have noise-canceling headphones." This was a lie. She certainly used to have these and so many other gadgets, but she'd made a point of not packing a single product from Byron's company.

It killed her to admit that the Serenity Combination Head Massager/Internet Browser did sound excellent right about now. The device, no bigger than a set of earmuffs, expertly rubbed users' temples while a beam of light projected images of any search term spoken aloud. Back when Hazel was in college, there was a thin grocery-store-brand chocolate cookie that she'd gotten addicted to; the plasma donation center where she'd sometimes sell her fluids for drug and cheeseburger money gave them out as a post-session bonus. They tasted a little biscuity (Hazel's dorm roommate refused to eat them, saying that the cookies seemed designed as treats for an imaginary species somewhere between "golden retriever" and "human toddler" on taxonomy charts). But there was something gratifying about the base simplicity of their flavor. And due to their exceptionally granular surface, they performed the bonus duty of polishing Hazel's lips as she ate. When she wore the headphones, Hazel liked to zone out to close-up stills of this cookie's exterior. She zoomed in on them hundreds of thousands of times until the pictures looked like photographs of some faraway planet's chocolate terrain.

"He made you sign a prenup, right? You walk away, you get a mere pittance?"

The question inspired Hazel to look down at her father's hand, then at Diane's, and yes—there were rings; they must have had an informal union of sorts that morning.

"It's super complicated and legal," Hazel replied. She figured this would shut him up. Complexity was like kryptonite to her father—there was no difference in his mind between "elaborate" and "convoluted." *Steer clear of fine print* was one of his favorite sayings, which Hazel supposed could be good advice, but he had a super-inclusive interpretation of fine print that made it hard for him to eat at restaurants. He also had a phobia of lawyers. Her mother used to exploit this; Hazel could always tell when her parents were fighting because there would be a courtroom drama loudly blaring on the TV.

And it was true; the prenup was exhaustive. It had caused her father's lawyer phobia to rub off a little on her too. She'd signed it in one of Gogol's conference rooms and still remembered when the legal fleet arrived with the document: they'd all appeared to be wearing the same suit and moved nearly in tandem, like synchro- nized swimmers. It was one of the only times she'd ever seen Byron not looking at a screen of some kind; he'd watched her sign each page. There'd been an interpreter of sorts seated next to her, telling her the essence of what each major paragraph was saying—mainly noncompete clauses so technology companies couldn't hire her and glean insider secrets—though the interpreter also worked for Gogol. Hazel had been welcome to bring her own attorney, but since she wasn't entering the marriage with any money or assets of her own, she hadn't seen the point.

The settlement she was supposed to get in the event of a divorce would be a lot of money to most people, and had seemed like a lot to her at the time of signing. She actually hadn't paid much attention to the amount—was it just under a million?—or to anything else. Hazel remembered thinking this exact thought: *There is no way I can lose*. She'd come to realize that she could, and had. Byron would never allow a divorce.

"He's bad enough to give up the lifestyle you must be accustomed to now? How is that possible? I don't see any bruises on you!" Her father's anger momentarily caused him to hold Diane in a more precarious fashion, like she was a full grocery bag he was clutching while berating a small pack of children. Then he gripped the doll around her waist and locked his fingers together.

It was a little mesmerizing to Hazel, the way he maneuvered the doll against his body like a pair of skis or a similarly unwieldy piece of large sporting equipment. His current grip made Hazel remember a documentary about old-growth forests she'd watched with her father once—protesters were chaining their arms around trees to try to prevent them from being logged. *What's the problem?* he'd asked, pointing to the screen. *Saw right through their arms if they feel so strongly about it!* "It's a harsh economy out there, squirt. You've got zero job experience in the field of that degree you never finished. You're cute, I mean I think you are; your dad thinking you're cute is no uphill battle. But, Hazel. I've seen the TV office sitcoms—you're too old now to compete with 'intern cute.' Is he cheating on you? I'd imagine that's tough, but you might consider looking the other way. It seems worth it for a lifelong ride on the money train. What a voyage! Why interrupt it?"

"Well, Dad. The train got a little inhospitable." Had she just polished off the last of the beers? She had. Hazel knew she was drunk, but for the moment this was a secret her internal self was managing to keep hidden from the rest of the world. It had been such a long time since she'd gotten tipsy. Her speech and posture actually seemed to have forgotten how to be drunk. Was it possible to get drunk in your mind but not in your body? Byron had always refused to have beer in the house, which was Hazel's drink of choice. There was a microharem of top-shelf spirits, carefully cultivated for guests, but she never partook. They seemed hexed to Hazel, like potent gentrification elixirs: She feared they'd begin eating away at her tacky proclivities the moment they touched her lips. Drinking them would make her less *her*, somehow, so she usually just abstained. That had been one of the central ironies of her marriage: She'd loved their courtship because it had made her feel like she was someone else, and that had been all she'd ever wanted. Until she married Byron and had to be someone else full-time. Then all she wanted was to go back to being herself and hating it again. "If only it were a simple case of infidelity."

"What do you mean?" he asked. "You've been together nearly a decade. Can't you work this out with him? You know your mother and I loved each other, Hazel. In our way. But if we'd been concerned with joy and self-actualization and all that, we wouldn't have made it. It's all about excitement and thrills with your generation. If you're not having fun, you want to throw in the towel. Have you even considered lowering your standards in terms of general happiness? Did you think about how lucky you are that he married you in the first place? You were a nobody!"

She felt her mouth curl into a defeated smile that would definitely creep her father out, and that was good; that was a smart instinct on behalf of her face. Her father was the type who had to be a little creeped out before he'd shut up and listen. "It got really bad. You don't know the half of it."

This did quiet him. He glanced into Diane's eyes for support, shrugged. "Okay. Let's run with that. Maybe I don't. But look around you, kid. This is a long way to fall. There's one bathroom. A single bathroom. This week? I do my business at night. It's different all the time though. Wildly variable with little advance notice. If I get a heads-up forty-five seconds before showtime it's a good day."

Her father was a hard man to read. For example: there was a time in college, pre-Byron, when she'd decided to live rent free in an anarchy squatter house so she'd have more money to use for monthly minimums on credit cards and could buy more clothing at the mall. The toilet there was a white bucket that got knocked over constantly because most people who used the white-bucket toilet at the anarchy squatter house were not wickedly sober. Would telling him that she'd once used that toilet make him feel better about letting her live there with him now? Or worse?

"How long are we talking here, Hazel? What's your time frame to get back on your feet? I think you should swallow your pride and ask for a little bit more dough from the guy if need be, just to set yourself up."

"You don't understand; this is what I'm telling you. I'm not even taking the prenup money. I can't leave him and take his money at the same time, Dad. Money's a way to track me and know what I'm doing."

Hazel felt herself pretending to take a drink from her empty can; she wasn't sure why. But she went along with it and soon had the firm opinion that there was a drop left inside she could get to if she just tilted the can right. Then a little later came the realization that she'd been trying to get the drop for several seconds, maybe longer. Maybe both of her hands were pawing at the can's bottom and she was handling the can a little roughly and her father knew that she was drunk now.

She came up for air and crumpled the aluminum can, hoping the sound would be cathartic, but it could not have made a more alarming noise. It was the sound of property damage occurring several yards away.

"Dad," she continued, "I haven't thought too far ahead. That's probably not a grand surprise." She'd meant to plan a little more, but she'd also come to the understanding that there was no point in planning because she had to leave Byron without taking anything. Plus she'd gotten pretty scared that morning. There had been blood, and that was that. "I guess I just figured on staying till I can make it on my own."

"I could die before that happens!"

"What about a year? Could you give me a year? That seems like a pretty modest ask in terms of length of time to start a completely new life, right?"

Hazel looked at her father and had to sit back down. She was expecting to see the cheeky sails of his rage-face puffed full, or maybe even what she and her childhood best friend used to term his "thermometer head," an Easter-egg-dye scarlet rash that moved from his forehead to his face to his neck to his chest in clear gradients and always told them, with sundial clarity, just how pissed he was and how in trouble she'd be.

Instead he was looking at her with soupy eyes that seemed to have burst. As if they'd tried to hold in all the pity he felt for her but had buckled under the weight.

"Dad . . ."

The moment she spoke his hand flew up in a sporting gesture, catching her thought and stopping all play. He leaned into Diane's robe and wiped his eyes, blew his nose a little too loudly. Was that a generational thing? Hazel wondered. She'd never felt entitled to blow her noise to the point where it made an unpleasant sound. Not even in front of family.

"All right," he said and nodded. "Stay if you want. Slide all the way back down the ladder." The crushed beer can was lying on the floor by her foot; Hazel gave it what she thought was a small tap but it leaped theatrically into the air and landed inside the coffin like it had been trained to do so. "This is no longer the honeymoon evening I'd envisioned. I'll be honest about that. Could Diane and I have a little privacy first? Before we never have any again? Maybe there's a neighborhood bar you could walk to."

Yeah, there probably is, Hazel thought, *but I'd rather not amble about when Byron is so into the idea of killing me.* He was far more likely to have goons pull up in a van and abduct her from an alleyway than to bust down the door of her elderly father's home and cart her away in front of the neighbors. The conversation with her father seemed to be winding down, though, and Hazel knew this information was a pretty flammable log to throw on a dwindling fire. Better to approach it in a more generalist fashion. "So you'd like me to walk alone to a bar in the dark and then walk home even later at night when it's darker still and I'm more inebriated, all so you can scream sans guilt during conjugal play with a doll? If I'm following what you're saying."

"Don't be dramatic."

"It's not dramatic! Do you know how frequently women get assaulted?"

"Well, if that happens to you tonight, I'll really owe you one.

How could I make that up to you? Maybe by letting you stay in my house for a year for free?"

Hazel felt the back of her neck prick with warmth—she was flushing. She knew he thought she was spoiled. There were ways in which she was a coward, sure, and he knew those ways, and that's why her father thought he was right about this. Well, so much for his comfort then. "Yeah? Stupid me for leaving him? He wanted to put a chip in my brain, Dad."

With his right hand, her father revved the engine of his Rascal, as though to inject more horsepower into his head—he was thinking. Eventually he shuddered and buried his nose in Diane's hair. When he looked back up, he said, "Chip? Like a tracking thing?"

"Sort of. Like a file-share thing. So I'd be wirelessly connected to a chip in his brain and he would be wirelessly connected to mine. We would meld. The first neural-networked couple in history."

"Jesus. Is that what kids are up to nowadays? I'm glad I'm near the grand exit. Brain melds. Not for me. Your mother and I didn't even trust French kissing."

"No, Dad. It's not what *anyone* is doing. It has never been done. He wanted me to offer up my still-living brain for research and development, essentially." She hadn't consented, but of course her consent wasn't going to stand in his way. Nothing ever did. Plus, Hazel was convinced he was in the process of making her sick so that she'd go, of her own volition, to their private medical facility and check herself in, which would be the beginning of the end. For the past few weeks, she'd been having increasingly severe headaches; this morning she'd gotten a nosebleed in the shower. It was the first nosebleed of her lifetime. The blood had gone down the drain and was detected by their SmartFilter, which did in fact even know the blood was from her nose, which did in fact set off an alert, which caused Byron's video-calling face to appear on the screen-wall of their bathroom. It was nearly a purr the way he said it, his stony-blue eyes radiant with cold power: *Hazel, don't you think you should go see the doctor?*

"Yikes," her father said. "Sounds like things took a turn. Did you at least get to spend a lot of his money?"

Yes and no, Hazel thought. Totally, yet not as much as most would. Plus, she'd increasingly stopped leaving the compound, or bringing things in. It was hard to explain, but buying something and taking it home, or having it shipped there, wasn't the same as encountering it in the actual world. It was like a King Midas situation, except instead of turning to gold everything that entered Byron's house became wildly uninteresting. "You know, when I realized I was going to leave eventually, I thought it might be fun to try overindulging on richness before I went out. Spend so much money I got sick of spending money. I figured I could order really strange things that would be funny to leave behind. Like hundreds of thousands of cans of soup? But I got so scared that I stopped caring about anything besides leaving as fast as I could." His house was intentionally in the middle of nowhere, as were Gogol's most important ancillary buildings and the microcity that served its worker elite. Without a job or an appointment, there was no reason to come across its perimeters. Most regular employees worked in one of its city branches, but cities made Byron paranoid. Nearly everything made Byron paranoid.

Hazel began rubbing her face in thorough circles with both of her hands. "And did I ever tell you he liked using the phrase 'global domination'? He did. Heavily. Who, besides crazed sociopathic dictators, comes home to his partner after a meeting and says, 'I love the taste of global domination! Want to taste it? Give me a kiss!'

I felt like I lived with a cartoon villain. Worst of all, since I had no idea how to respond, I'd go along with it like I was proud of him. 'Cheers to you, global dominator!' I can't count the number of times I raised a water glass in his direction and said that."

"All right, well. Sorry your marriage was a shit show, kid. Sounds like you need another drink even more than I thought." He returned his face to the sanctuary of Diane's hair and began mashing around in it, lifting up individual pieces and almost polishing his cheeks and chin with them. "Scram for now and I'll see you in the morning."

Hazel felt a deep sigh building inside. She wanted it to be her father's fault if she walked out the door and got kidnapped or worse by Gogol thugs, but it wouldn't be, and her father knew it wouldn't be, and he would therefore fail to feel the inordinate amount of guilt she'd like to think he'd feel for sending her out of his home when she really didn't want to leave. "Sure, Dad. I'll go to the bar. Words every father longs to hear his daughter say: I'm off to the tavern until way past your bedtime."

"You have to actually go," he specified. "No pretending to leave and sitting on the steps for a few minutes and coming right back in." The Rascal beeped its loud message of backward motion; he performed a turnaround maneuver and the new couple sped off to the bedroom. "I know," Hazel could hear him whispering to Diane, "I'd say she's lost it too."

Hazel grabbed her father's house key from the wooden dachshund key holder that hung by the front door. The keys dangling from the dog's belly made them look like oversize metal udder caps were milking the creature to death. The dog's wide glued-on eyes were begging Hazel to rescue it from a life sentence of indentured lactation.

Hazel liked the feel of her father's key in her hand, the way its teeth hurt her palm if she gripped too tightly. Entry to The Hub, Byron's special name for their domestic compound, was controlled through a combination of voice and retinal detection. Certain rooms required a fingerprint and a keypad code; their cars were controlled via remote.

Little things like physical keys made Hazel feel as if she were going back in time, which she realized was exactly what she wanted to do. Get away from the futureworld she'd lived in with Byron, away even from the technological present. From now on she wanted no part of what Byron and his cohorts liked to call the Bionic Revolution, though they frequently slipped—was it a slip?—and said Byronic.

The more she could live a strictly manual and basic life, the more distant she'd be from him, and that was a hopeful thought: there was a way to feel like she was reclaiming herself.

She was having less hopeful thoughts too. It was a humid night and she was sweaty and anxious and really did not look her best. This somehow made the thought of a stranger coming to kill her even sadder than it had to be.

HAZEL SUPPOSED SHE COULD TRACE THE BEGINNINGS OF HER father's desire for companionship post-widowerhood back to an excited midnight phone call she'd gotten from him several years ago.

It was nearly 2 AM when she received it. "Hazel!" he'd repeated into the phone. "Hazel! Hazel! Hazel!" Like her name was a word he'd just managed to learn.

Coming out of a dead sleep, her brain hadn't been awake enough to distinguish alarm from enthusiasm. She'd been convinced her father was having a stroke.

"Let me call 911, Dad," she'd instructed; "I'll have a helicopter meet you at the hospital." The ER he'd be taken to was a little over a two-hour drive from The Hub, but it had a helipad, and Gogol doctors could start working on him during the flight to the medical facility adjacent to The Hub. It was state of the art to the point of hilarity. Concealed speakers throughout the premises pulsed a series of soothing yet definitively upbeat ambient sounds—it really seemed like a noise that could keep death at bay, the way certain low frequencies drive off vermin and insects. *I tell you what,* one patient said in a promotional video; Hazel thought she remembered Byron saying he was an oil baron. *It's like you get to time travel to the future and go to the hospital thirty years from now, this place. I had a quadruple bypass two days ago and it was the most relaxing thing I've ever done. I can't wait to have another!*

"Hazel! Hazel! Hazel!" her father had continued. "It's not an emergency. I mean it is, but not in a medical way. I had what those artist types call an epiphany."

At that point, a large blinking question popped up on the bedroom wall in red neon letters; it had been sent by Byron's Sleep Helmet, detecting her alert state of increased stress. *WAKE BYRON?* it asked. The helmet didn't automatically roust Byron when she woke in the middle of the night with a racing pulse because every single dream she had at The Hub was a nightmare, and if the helmet woke Byron every time she sat up in bed gasping in panic he'd never get any rest. So the helmet made it her choice.

She'd never once decided to wake Byron.

When Hazel slid two fingers to the left in the air, the question went away. "So you're all right, Dad?"

"I'm better than okay," he'd said. "I'm going to start dating strangers! My friend down the street set up a profile for me on a Web site!"

Hazel looked down at sleeping Byron and felt a pang of jealousy for her elderly widower father's new shot at amorous joy.

Since Hazel got married, her capacity for envying others was one of the few areas in which Hazel had experienced growth rather than paralysis, to such an expansive degree that she was able to disconnect and observe it from afar with a sense of pride, like a racehorse set loose and dominating the track: *Can you believe how fast that marvelous beast can RUN?* She felt justified in describing her emotional impoverishment as "gifted." It was definitely in the top percentile.

Hazel tried not to watch Byron's Sleep Helmet, but it was hypnotic. Tiny strips of blue light ran upward from the helmet's base across the main facial panel, parting into separate paths at the top of the head. The glass was dark; it made him look larval and unfinished in a way that made her afraid to disturb his sleep. She'd had nightmares where he'd removed the helmet to reveal a half-formed face with his skin's internal layers showing.

But waking Byron unintentionally would be difficult. Inside the helmet, a soothing delta-wave-beat pattern was interacting with his REM sleep cycle, guiding it along like a set of training wheels to make sure it didn't get disrupted; no light whatsoever could penetrate the helmet's glass. Hazel didn't like to wear hers; it sat on a pedestal on their dresser and seemingly watched her all night in a creepy vigil. When she put the helmet on, she felt like she was practicing being dead, and it was a little too convincing for her taste. It seemed too easy to go along with, was the scary thing. The average user fell asleep in less than two minutes of helmet engagement. "I don't want to be such a convincing understudy that I get the role," she'd told Byron, but of course his gadgets had an answer for everything; they always did: Sleeping inside a sensory dome was the safest sleep possible because it monitored your vital signs. If your pulse were to dip dangerously low, an alarm within the helmet would attempt to wake you; if your vitals were still nonresponsive, it would wirelessly alert emergency medical personnel. And even though she didn't wear her helmet, since Byron wore his, Hazel's safety was covered: their model, the Omega, had been programmed for partner awareness. It monitored all detected life within a set radius. If Hazel experienced a problem, Byron's helmet would know.

The following week, her father had tried three different dates with three different women but gave up when all of them opted to call it a night within the first ten minutes of meeting him. "I've never been much of a conversationalist," he told Hazel.

This was true. She'd sometimes had the urge to confide in him about the state of her marriage, but his style of sympathy was very "back-bar sports commentator on a satellite delay"; had she said something along the lines of, *Dad, I think I made a mistake marrying Byron*, he probably would've talked about something else for a few minutes, to the point that she'd decide he hadn't been listening and had failed to hear what she'd just said, and she would feel partly hurt but partly relieved by this. Then, just as she'd begun to relax and think of something more benign to talk about, his entire body would suddenly bolt to life: *Wowza! Miserable, are you? Huh! Ho! That's a tough one.* Better to avoid this talk until it was unavoidable, she'd decided.

Which had now happened.

It was strange to feel sad leaving his house instead of giddily emancipated. Perhaps this was the first time it had ever happened. During her marriage, she sometimes visited her father just so she could feel better about her life when she left. A trip to his home always made a pretty convincing argument that his gruff personality, heavy flaws, and the shortcomings of her childhood were fixed roadblocks that would prevent her from ever experiencing true joy, so her choices and lack of personal ambition or work ethic or relative sobriety didn't really have to matter. Her mother was at fault too, of course, but dying had reassigned the parameters of her mother's despotic reign. She couldn't actively ruin Hazel's life anymore because Hazel, like all living things, now fell outside her mother's jurisdiction.

Maybe this was partly why Hazel decided to marry Byron after her mother died. It was a way to pick up some of the slack—to make her own life awful all by herself.

3

MEETING BYRON HAD BEEN AN ACCIDENT. ONE OF HAZEL'S GO-GETTER friends in college had been assigned to interview Byron for their campus newspaper. He was coming to graduation to give what he'd termed "a digital commencement speech."

What he'd done had been innovative, Hazel had to admit—she hadn't been at the ceremony but she'd heard about it on the news and from throngs of her matriculating friends who had stayed on course creditwise. Byron had gotten up on the podium wearing a suit and sunglasses, which was what he wore when he wanted to look cool. First he stated that he didn't have a speech prepared because they were all going to write the speech together. He asked everyone in the stadium to think of one word that best described their time at college, and to shout it on the count of three.

Next, he had everyone yell a word that summarized their greatest hope for the future, and then, finally, a word describing what frightened them most about the life changes they'd face after graduation. ("Would you like to guess," Byron had later confided in her, in an almost-flirtatious way, "how many people yelled 'bong water' for all three questions? Another counterintuitive statistic: 'titties' was a more popular answer for what scared people most about the future than for describing their time at college. As in thousands more people. Wrap your head around that. The other surprise to us, particularly to our interns, who are more 'of the people' in their expectations, was how few graduates yelled— excuse my language here, this is a direct quote—'pussy' to summarize their collegiate experience. Maybe 'titty' is easier to yell in front of one's grandparents than 'pussy.' More people actually yelled 'potato chips' than 'pussy.'"

"Did anyone yell 'cock'?" Hazel had asked.

"That's why you should've graduated," he'd said.)

Thanks to a new Gogol vocal-recognition software, every individual voice was able to be heard, analyzed, and statistically ranked for relevance, then an algorithmic speech was composed. It discussed the worth of the university experience, the challenges that lay ahead, and the dreams the students were on course to pursue, all using the most popular answers to heavily resonate with the crowd. It was funny and poignant. It was also a tearjerker due to a new aspect of the software. Onstage with Byron were the parents of a student who had died in a car accident during his junior year. Had he lived, he would've been graduating. Using one two-minute home-video clip, the software was able to anticipate with almost perfect accuracy what his pronunciation of nearly any word would be, and the auto-composed speech was given in his voice while his touched parents wept in disbelief on the Jumbotron and the crowd lifted their hands to their chests in an attempt to soothe their hearts.

The standing ovation at the speech's conclusion was the longest in the school's history, at least those that were digitally recorded—this was suggested and then confirmed by Byron's analytical team, who combed through the footage of every speech and event ever given at the college.

"It was a risk," Byron told Hazel off the record after she'd finished interviewing him.

Her friend Jenny, the responsible/motivated one who was supposed to be getting to interview Byron, had gotten a horrible stomach flu. Hazel was essentially the stunt double.

"Of course we tried it with the parents beforehand and made sure they were good with it. Afterward they told me it was an incredible experience. They felt like they'd just gotten to spend a little more time with him. But voices are complex triggers. Emotions can turn. In trials, many relatives stated to us that hearing the voice of a deceased loved one started to feel unwelcome, violating." Hazel remembered thinking about Byron's voice the whole time—why didn't his voice seem sensitive when he was saying very sensitive things?

Jenny hadn't been shy about letting Hazel know she wasn't her first choice. "But I know you'll do it because you need money, right?"

She sure did. At that point in her life, Hazel had never been married to a millionaire. She'd been waitressing a little at a diner near campus earlier in the semester, but the job turned out to be filled with pressure from men. They'd be in town for the evening and would ask her to take them out and she'd need to decline without losing her tip, which was almost impossible. Or they would say something like, "I don't even think I'm going to get food. I just want to sit here and flirt with you all day," and then the bill would be almost zero because they'd sit there drinking coffee and winking, and even a generous tip on a cup of coffee was not enough to buy the things Hazel tended to use her money for, like electricity or beer. Or they'd say something sad like, "Actually, I was having a really hard day and you being kind to me right now is meaning more to me than you will ever know," and then she'd have to keep faking kindness, extreme kindness in fact; or they'd be in a terrible mood and when she set their silverware down they'd accuse her of having touched their fork with her soiled hands, which she wasn't sure how to interpret—were they implying that she'd been masturbating? That she'd been doing sexual acts with her hands prior to her work shift and hadn't washed them? Did they hope for a confession they could follow with an offer to punish her? In almost every situation, it was awkward to produce a plate of lukewarm French fries and try to move things along, and this was what she almost always had to do. After a month she quit.

"I need to have this interview on my résumé," Jenny had insisted. She'd been delirious with fever, and wildly dehydrated, but still more organized and personable and attractive than Hazel. "It won't really be a lie since I wrote the questions. All you're doing is asking him the questions I wrote and recording what he says. I'm paying you to be an extension of a tape recorder." Hazel just wanted the money, but thought she should feel like it was an amazing opportunity, so she'd told her friend how excited she was. She pretended to love the suit her friend forced her to wear although it didn't fit and made Hazel's torso look like a rectangular plaid couch cushion.

Upon arriving at the gig, she even contorted her face with an expression of feverish enthusiasm. All of Byron's employees stood out—they had a clean sleekness that made them seem more recently showered than anyone else; their tailored clothes looked made of special fabrics (and actually were; there was an in-house catalog of sorts they all shopped from in order to meet hypoallergenic, anti-bacterial office standards plus effortlessly avoid lint, wrinkling, and odor). They all seemed to be thinking much harder than Hazel herself had ever thought. "Hello." She'd smiled and greeted the handlers who were waiting for her on a couch inside a vast lobby. "I'm Jenny Roberts," she'd told them, "and I'm so grateful for this opportunity."

"You are not Jenny Roberts," they'd responded. "You are Hazel Green."

Their scanners had read all the cards in her wallet; they'd gleaned online information to instantaneously confirm her identity. "Okay," she said. "But I am so grateful." Hazel wondered if the scanners could tell that was a lie too.

She explained her friend's predicament and was asked to have a seat. Eventually Byron agreed to see her anyway, despite the deception. He told her later it was because he found her confusing in a fascinating way. *When I looked at you, I was just delighted. I had no idea what to think of you. I could tell you were wearing another person's clothes but I didn't know why. I couldn't imagine who you were or what you wanted.*

Here was the thing: Hazel had not delighted her parents, ever. Nor had she delighted herself. But when she walked into the room and Byron had said, "Hazel Green," her name sounded new coming out of his mouth. Upgraded. Precise and scientific. "I wasn't expecting you. Hazel Green." He said her name like she was a species of rare insect.

Hazel had never intrigued her parents or herself either. But Byron couldn't stop asking her questions—although she was supposed to be interviewing him, things soon took on the feel of him interviewing her.

"Is that a Band-Aid?" He pointed to her panty hose. She'd cut herself shaving before putting them on and hadn't been able to wash off the bloodstain—Jenny had given her only one pair—so she'd tried to cover it with a flesh-colored Band-Aid. "You placed it on top of your stockings," Byron had said, amused. "You're a little remarkable."

"No one has ever said that to me," she told him. "I cannot believe the most important person I've ever met just told me that." He laughed and tilted his head, staring at her like she was someone familiar whom he hadn't seen in a long time. It was satisfying the way she could give him false praise and his attention to her automatically seemed to deepen. Soon she was acting like he was the most enthralling person she'd ever met.

Hazel was twenty-two; he wasn't that much older than she was, twenty-seven, but he felt older by decades. It was hard to explain. Part of it was just success and power; Hazel had never been so close to someone so successful before. Byron's looks weren't anything special—he was a rather plain white guy, tall and thin with long fingers whose tips were oddly circular. When he placed them on the table and slid them back and forth while talking, they reminded Hazel of the suctiony paws of a tree frog. Was he good-looking? Would she like to have his fingers perform an adhesive walk down her leg? She couldn't decide. But she loved how happy she was making him just by appearing to have a great time.

His haircut creeped her out the way freshly hedged lawns sometimes did, making her feel like life was already over and she'd arrived on the planet too late: people had tamed everything wild, which was the same as destroying the wildness since taming it turned it into something so different. *We pretend when we want to forget things are dangerous*, she thought, though she immediately failed to apply this concept to herself or reflect upon why she was pretending to be super taken with Byron when she wasn't.

One of the only things Hazel knew herself to be great at was concealing her true feelings, so it made sense for her to showcase this talent front and center whenever she needed to impress others. It was a skill she'd learned early on. Sitting there with Byron, she began remembering how she'd often wanted to scream when lining up for the bus at elementary school because everything felt so artificial. No one was okay, but it was not okay to say that. There they were, ages five to ten, most of them in brightly colored clothing with cartoon backpacks that seemed designed for a utopia in an almost-mean way. They were all emotional messes, especially Hazel. She watched the news with her parents at night and hardly slept because of it. She had a hard time playing in large groups of friends because her own house was so quiet that recess overwhelmed her—she was romantic and would've preferred just one special friend, but this was not how social dynamics worked. One of her classmates had a brother with cancer. Others were mean, shy, hungry, sad. By the age of nine, Hazel sometimes had a fantasy daydream at school where the teacher walked into the classroom and yelled,

ISN'T EVERYTHING HORRIBLE? DOESN'T THE PAIN OF THE
WORLD OUTWEIGH THE JOY BY TRILLIONS? WOULD YOU
LIKE TO PUSH ALL OF THE DESKS INTO THE CENTER OF
THE ROOM AND BURN THEM IN A GIANT BONFIRE? THEN
WE CAN RUN AROUND SCREAMING AND WEEPING AMIDST
THE SMOKE IN A TRUTHFUL PARADE OF OUR HUMAN
CONDITION. SINCE YOU ARE SMALL STATURED, CHILDREN,
IT MIGHT HELP OTHERS TO FEEL THE FULL BRUNT OF YOUR

AGITATION IF YOU WAVE STICKS AND SHRUBBERY OVER
YOUR HEADS ALL THE WHILE. WE DON'T WANT TO KILL
ANYTHING WE DON'T HAVE TO KILL; EVERYTHING LIVING
THAT WE'VE EVER SEEN OR KNOWN WILL DIE WITHOUT
OUR INTERVENTION, OURSELVES INCLUDED; THIS IS A
PSYCHOLOGICAL LEAD BLANKET THAT EVEN OUR MOST
PERVASIVE MOMENTS OF COMFORT CANNOT CRAWL OUT
FROM UNDER AND ONE UNEXTINGUISHABLE SOURCE OF
DESPAIR, SO WE WON'T BE PERFORMING ANY RITUALISTIC
SACRIFICES; THAT'S NOT THE DIRECTION WE WILL GO IN
JUST YET; HOWEVER, ASSISTANT PRINCIPAL LAWRENCE IS ON
THE PROWL FOR A ROAD CARCASS WE MIGHT BE ABLE TO
USE AS A REPRESENTATIVE PROP BECAUSE NOWHERE IN OUR
AUTUMN-THEMED POSTER BOARD DÉCOR IS MORBIDITY
OR DECAY SYMBOLIZED. OUR SCHOOL BOARD MEMBERS
CANNOT AGREE ON HOW BEST TO ACKNOWLEDGE THE
BOUNDLESSNESS OF HUMAN CRUELTY. IN OUR SOCIETY
SOME OF YOU ARE FAR SAFER AND MORE ADVANTAGED
THAN OTHERS; AT HOME SOME OF YOU ARE FAR MORE
LOVED; SOME OF YOU WILL FIND THAT CONCEPTS LIKE
FAIRNESS AND JUSTICE WILL BE THIN, FLICKERING
HOLOGRAMS ON THE PERIPHERY OF YOUR LIVES. OH,
LOOK, CHILDREN—I SEE MR. LAWRENCE IN THE DISTANCE
DRAGGING A PORTION OF A HIGHWAY-SLAUGHTERED DEER.
LET'S GO HELP HIM LUG IT INSIDE AND BE REMINDED THAT
WE TOO INHABIT BODIES MADE OF MEAT-WRAPPED BONES;
LET'S MEDITATE ON THIS CORPOREAL TERROR.

Whenever her mother had asked, Hazel always told her, *School is great.*

Byron didn't seem to feel any corporeal terror. Hazel felt like he must know all kinds of calming, existential secrets that she didn't, which only strengthened her urge to win his favor so he'd share them.

At the end of the interview, Byron took her right hand and clasped it between both of his. *This superrich person really likes me*, she realized. Her adrenaline spiked and she felt an invigorating wave of accomplishment surge over her; her chest filled with a sensation befitting the visuals of an effective mouthwash commercial. An outbreak of goose bumps bloomed over her body.

In hindsight, Byron's cold skin might have had something to do with this. Or maybe it was his parting words to her, addressing a subject she hadn't told a single person about.

"I'm so sorry," Byron had said, "that your mother is dying."

THE DAY AFTER INTERVIEWING BYRON, HAZEL WOKE TO HER PHONE ringing. This was a surprise since it had been shut off for nonpayment for over three weeks. Who calls on a dead phone, besides a dead person/ghost or a spiritual higher power, and which possibility was more frightening?

Her immediate thought was that her mom had just died and was calling her from the beyond. "OH. Shit," Hazel muttered. It was early for Hazel, around 9 AM, and she was hungover, which her deceased mother would totally be able to detect from Hazel's voice.

Her mental lexicon of images of possessed phones began to flash through her mind—demonic tongues coming out of the receiver and licking the person's earlobe with green saliva, retractable needles stabbing through the handset's speaker holes the moment the unsuspecting recipient placed the receiver against her head.

Hazel put on an oven mitt then picked up the phone with the gloved hand. She held it out in front of her at a distance for a moment. Better to let the haunted device make the first move.

"Hello?" Hazel heard a voice say, a male's voice, which let her sigh with relief. It wasn't her mom's fresh ghost. All other deadies felt easier to handle.

"It's Byron Gogol."

"You died?" Hazel exclaimed. In the silence that followed, she realized there could be another explanation and tried to backpedal. "I mean my phone was dead. I mean it hasn't been working," Hazel said. She hoped this made it sound like the problem had been a service or a technical failure. Jenny had just given her money, but Hazel planned to spend it on liquor and convenience-food items.

In truth she didn't want to know of her mother's passing, and her mother had already stipulated that there would be no funeral. *Let's not do good-byes,* she'd insisted the last time Hazel was home. *Come give me a firm handshake and we'll agree to see each other later. A gentlemen's agreement.* And Hazel had, though she'd wanted to acknowledge the grappling voice in her mind, half her women's studies professor and half—who? Octavia Butler? Hazel liked to imagine every thought she had that felt feminist was coming into her brain directly via Octavia Butler's spirit—*Neither of us is a man, Mom. Also you certainly are not gentle.*

"But I guess my phone is working now?" She knew that wasn't a charming thing to ask, so she tried to think of what might charm him. "It's great to hear your voice," she said.

"I wanted to hear yours, too, so I took care of your bill. Would you like to go out this evening?"

Some facts about herself, facts she now realized Byron clearly knew, like how she was broke and about to flunk out of college, couldn't be camouflaged. But her words and expressions didn't have to match reality. He'd like her more if she seemed to adore him already, so she did. "This can officially be my only-Byron phone," she said. "I won't tell anyone else it's back on. If I answer and it's anyone but you I'll just hang up." Then something less contrived slipped out. "But how did you know my mother is dying?"

Already, though, she was imagining dinner, an upscale affair maybe involving a piano, or pianos. Fancy restaurants probably did not stop at one piano. She had nothing to wear. She did buy clothing on credit cards (and occasionally shoplifted, easing her conscience with the knowledge that the company used sweatshop labor. She told herself that stealing sweatshop-labored garments and wearing them was somewhere on the family tree of protest for human rights.). But most of her clothing was intentionally distressed—holes, skunk-spray patterns of bleach, faux cigarette burns, patches. *Christ*, her dying mother had said the last time Hazel returned home. *Christ, Christ, Christ. Were you recently assaulted? What kind of a look is that! If I saw you walking down the street, I'd stop the van and ask if you needed a ride to the police station. You know what those jeans say to me? "I was gravely wronged. I have a report to make." And not in a good way!*

Her clothes didn't match the grand degree of agreeability and optimism she wanted Byron to think she possessed.

"I'm sorry if that felt like a violation," he said. "My team had to investigate you yesterday before we spoke. They're pretty thorough, in terms of electronic records. In terms of most things."

Hazel wondered if he worried about her being too sad to party with him, or whatever the evening plans were, due to the maternal situation. How best to convey that she wasn't fraught with grief without seeming like a monster? "We've reached a point of acceptance with her condition," Hazel said. She borrowed this language from a hospice pamphlet titled "Reaching a Point of Acceptance With Your Condition." It had sat on their coffee table for weeks, unopened, then was finally thrown away when her intoxicated mother refused a bottle of Ensure by karate-chopping it down with the side of her hand and spilling it everywhere. "What should I wear tonight?"

"I'll send you something," Byron said. "Be ready at eight." Then there was the dial tone. Hazel decided to call the library and inquire about the current balance of her fines, always hefty. She had no plans to pay, but she wanted to call someone since her phone suddenly worked.

What he sent was a gray leisure suit and slip-on shoes, made of the same fabric as his workers' clothing and his own. It was both sensual and androgynous, hugging her small breasts but also changing the parameters of their shape into something more concave and winnowed, like two tiny abdomens. The shoes were incredibly comfortable, so much so that they gave her the disconcerting feeling of having no feet at all. She walked slowly in them, filled with the suspicion that she wasn't doing it right.

"Walking feels like not walking, in these!" was the first thing she planned to say to him that evening. "Best shoes ever!" She'd drunk a few personality beers before the car arrived, thinking Byron would be in the car that was picking her up, thinking they were about to go to dinner and her buzz would soon be diluted by food. But the car had only a silent driver who made her sign a form declaring her physical person was harboring neither secretive recording devices nor undisclosed biological specimens. A screen in the car played looped footage of select portions from Byron's speaking engagements. Hazel pressed every button she could find in an attempt to change the channel, finally opening the partition by accident. "Please don't touch anything," the driver said to her without looking back. Then the partition closed.

WHEN THEY ARRIVED AT THE HUB, AN ESCORT TOOK HER THROUGH A ten-minute labyrinthine walk back to a mood-lit room where Byron sat in a hanging black chair that looked like a hollowed-out alien egg. He was absentmindedly typing on something in his lap that appeared to be a sheet of glass while watching something in the corner of the chair that also looked like a sheet of glass. There was a large bowl on the table in front of her that Hazel eagerly walked toward, hoping it was filled with nuts or another snack food, but it was filled with small white rocks alight in a bed of blue flames. She had to pee so badly.

Byron smiled and stood up as Hazel walked into the room. *So this is how it feels to have someone be really happy to see you*, she thought. "You look stunning," Byron said. "Don't you love these clothes?"

"I've never felt anything like them!" Hazel exclaimed. "They make me hate my skin for not being made out of this material. And the comfort level of these shoes. My feet feel totally seduced. Every time I take a step I expect the shoes to start whispering dirty things to me in French."

Byron was very pleased. "We're on the same page. I'm curious to know—what do you think of the house?"

His smile was beaming, anticipatory. Hazel realized that he wanted her to continue the statements of awe. Her performance of being dazzled was her ticket of admission.

"I'm just trying not to hyperventilate," Hazel said. "I won't move my head to the right or the left because I'm already overwhelmed. If I indulged my peripheral vision too I would probably faint." She swallowed and decided to make a risky move. "I missed you," she added.

Byron's face went blank and Hazel chided herself for overreaching. But after a moment he said, "There's something I should tell you."

Hazel felt her cheeks flush. She'd pushed too far, too soon. Or had she?

"I feel the same way, Hazel," he said. "I think you and I should talk about the future."

"I'd love that," Hazel said, a placeholder phrase to conceal her shock. The future? *Why focus on the negative?* her father would say anytime she brought up her future. Or her past, or her present. What did he mean? "This is embarrassing," she said, "I think it's my excitement, being here. . . . Do you have a bathroom?"

Byron winked. "Wait till you see. Here, Fiffany will take you." Byron pressed some sort of button inside the egg and a female worker appeared. "Are you menstruating?" she asked Hazel in a low whisper. "Only select facilities are calibrated for this possibility."

"I doubt it," Hazel answered. She was a bit of a denier when it came to her cycles; all her underwear were stained. Unless she was bleeding profusely, she took a very laissez-faire position on the whole thing. She felt that giving her period the cold shoulder made it end more quickly each month than rolling out an assortment of absorbent products to give it the grand welcome.

The woman's eyebrow rose. "Right this way."

"Are there any vending machines or anything?" Hazel asked, hoping for some charity. She didn't have any money, and hadn't brought any credit cards. If a tech millionaire couldn't pick up the tab for a snack, who could?

"We're more into vitamin packing." The woman reached down to her pant leg and produced a small wrapped package of pills, seemingly from a fold in the cloth, like a magic trick. Hazel blinked.

"These are drugs?" Hazel asked, hopeful.

"Bioengineered kelp," the woman corrected. "Let me give you a second packet. They might help you sober up a bit."

"Oh good," Hazel said, although this immediately made her decide she'd pretend to take them but not swallow. "Do you have any water?"

The woman held open a door and rolled her eyes. "They dissolve. Sublingual." At Hazel's blank stare, she rolled her eyes again. "You put them under your tongue."

Hazel stepped into the room. It was pitch-black until the door closed, then a single beam of light shot down from the ceiling to illuminate a toilet. It looked like the toilet was floating in the middle of outer space. Squinting, Hazel walked over and sat down on it, disturbed to find her pee didn't make a sound; what did make a sound was a whoosh and a rush of heat between her legs upon her urine stream's conclusion. Like she'd just been wiped dry by a sunbeam.

The light turned off and another light illuminated a sink across the room. She stood and pulled up her pants then tried to feel in the dark for a button to push to flush, but the entire toilet seemed to have disappeared. "This place is wild," Hazel said aloud. Just that morning she'd been considering either purchasing a used toaster at Goodwill or doing a series of intentional Dumpster dives in search of one.

Led back to Byron, Hazel entered to find him pointing a determined finger at the wall, sorting through supersize projections of her. There were various images from throughout her life—yearbook photos, theme park pictures taken of her during a roller coaster's descent. "Do you know how interesting you are to me, Hazel?"

She giggled a little. Part of her had the urge to run from the house or compound or whatever it was—what the hell was going on here, after all?—but a larger part of her felt curious and lucky. Jenny would be dying right now. Already Hazel imagined telling her: *Giant pictures of my face!*

"I'm going to be direct," he said. "Efficiency is important. My schedule and lifestyle largely prohibit traditional dating, so here it is: I'd like to pursue a romantic relationship with you. The connection we have is undeniable. I was thinking we could agree on an initial six-month commitment? What do you say?"

"Commitment?" Hazel asked. It was one of those words she'd of course seen in advertisements and books that held great meaning for others but had no application to her own life, words such as "vacation" or "insurance" or "long-term goals." Certain parts of the English vocabulary had always existed in the margins for her that way, like a religion that she didn't believe in but appreciated knowing about.

"Nothing legally binding, of course. We have to establish trust, so I'll take you at your word. But I ask that for the next six months, we date exclusively. Then we'll evaluate our relationship."

"Evaluate?"

"Decide where we want to take things. If the relationship should advance, maintain, or . . . well, as we say in business, dissolve."

"Under our tongues," Hazel said absentmindedly, recalling the kelp packet. "Oh," she said, looking up to find Byron's full attention directed upon her, a nascent smile upending his wide mouth. "Sorry, I was thinking of something else."

"Is that your way of accepting?" Byron asked, suddenly looking both aroused and amused. "Are you suggesting that we kiss?"

She hadn't been. But then he was upon her with hot, delicate lips that seemed to insist she needn't notice him kissing her—it was the kiss equivalent of a late-night waiter discreetly sweeping up around the table as guests finished eating. For just a second her mouth flowered open and his wet tongue slid its width across hers, and then she was being guided from the room, suddenly in the arms of the escort. So quick was this transfer, she asked the handler just to verify. "I kissed Byron a moment ago, right? Not you?" She also wanted to ask, *What about dinner?*

"We did not kiss," the woman said, urging Hazel down into the car parked out front. "Byron will be in touch." And he was.

The Hub later came to seem like more of an allegation than a residence to Hazel. Not because they didn't spend a lot of time there—they did. Hazel hardly ever left, in fact, and though Byron spent most of his days a few minutes away at the central office, he equated travel with risk and kept his off-premises trips limited. He came home to sleep every night around ten with the regularity of a programmed machine.

But even on that first visit, "living" felt like a generous term for what happened inside The Hub. Yes, it was an impressive, sprawling structure. It was sleek and spotless and clinical; every wall of every room was sentient with touch and recognition technology. It didn't seem real to her then, and never started to. One of Hazel's only hobbies in their marriage was walking through the house very open-eyed and just slightly openmouthed. She was a little convinced that The Hub was a holding tank for death, an exact replica of the place where souls go immediately after departure. She never mailed a physical letter during the tenure of their marriage, but if she had, in the space reserved for a return address she would've written something to the effect of, "Where I live is where the deceased go to cool down to the afterlife's new room temperature."

SIX MONTHS LATER TO THE DAY, BYRON PROPOSED AND HAZEL'S mother was dead. Most of Hazel's ideas of marriage had more or less imploded on her last visit home prior to her mother's passing. "Where's Mom?" she'd asked her father, not expecting his answer to be traumatic.

"She's at Bernie's," he'd said. Bernie was one of her parents' widower friends who lived nearby. "She's been sleeping with him for a couple of weeks now. It's one of the things she wanted to do before dying. A few rolls in the hay with other partners. We were virgins when we married, you know."

Hazel did not know, and thinking about her mother having sex was like thinking about a refrigerator having sex, or a stove. It seemed to Hazel that beneath her clothing, her mother didn't have genitals so much as a central heating coil or an evaporator fan.

"She's having an affair?"

Her father propped his glasses a centimeter more upright on his nose, turned the page of his newspaper, resumed his wince. He couldn't read anything without making a severe cringing expression that implied he was bracing for impact, like a driver about to have a deer come through the windshield of his pickup. "Don't be silly. It's just intercourse. This is bucket-list stuff."

"But doesn't that bother you?" Hazel paused, unsure of how far to take the conversation. She supposed, though, that she wanted to have some idea of just how weird things were getting. Was it time to cut off all contact? "Are you . . . taking on other partners too?" She steadied herself against the countertop, held her stomach. Her parents' prudishness was like a natural law she'd taken to be a fundamental aspect of existence, one of the cohesive forces of the universe. Now Hazel felt the curtain of order slipping, primal chaos beginning to rumble forward. "Are you swingers?"

"Jesus, Hazel." Her father put the paper down, sipped his coffee. "I'm not a communist. No, there's no reason for me to fool around now. I'm not in any hurry. Plenty of time to sleep with other women once she dies."

Hazel took a seat at the table. "It doesn't seem like a betrayal?" She opened up a package of cookies and started stress eating then realized they were shortbread laxative biscuits. Laxatives and extramarital sex—that was the summary of what was going on with her parents.

"Eh, she feels shortchanged by the cancer thing. If it softens the blow, so be it. It's free and doesn't put a single demand on my time. Honestly, I feel lucky that her final wishes have been so cheap. When Jim's wife got cancer, he had to take her on a European cruise. I could tell you stories all day about friends' wives who turned into greedy leprechauns when they began dying. Suddenly they're obsessed with gold! They want gold this and gold that. Caleb's late wife, after her first round of chemo, she couldn't get enough gold. Then she wrote into her will that she wanted to be buried wearing all her jewelry. He couldn't pawn a single piece of it after she croaked."

Hazel's bowels gurgled. "Are you sad Mom's dying?" she asked.

Her father nodded. "You know I don't like change."

IN HINDSIGHT, OF COURSE HER COURTSHIP AND UNION WITH BYRON was suspect. Now she could admit she knew on some level that she shouldn't have gone along with Byron's proposal and acted like she wanted to marry him. He was just so successful, though. And he found Hazel to be such a pleasant curiosity. At least the Hazel she pretended to be with him—universally cheerful, up for anything, with no preferences of her own. It was easy to get along with him because she acted like a mood ring, always agreeing with what he found great and what he found intolerable.

She'd once heard a news story about a man who'd kept a secret family locked inside his basement, a second wife whom he'd kidnapped and three children she'd birthed and raised in captivity. All while his first wife and their children lived upstairs. Hazel could imagine, somewhat, the possibility that maybe the upstairs children didn't know. But the upstairs wife? The case came up in one of her psychology classes, and the general consensus was how could she not know? There were some holdouts—maybe the wife was just a really trusting person and so on, and wasn't it plausible that she believed he kept the basement triple padlocked for boring reasons, like being super protective of his carpentry hobby space? Other students piped up with stories about the wives of prolific serial-rapist torture murderers. When their husbands were finally caught and found to have murdered dozens of women, often over a series of decades, some wives claimed to have never suspected a thing. But weren't these husbands probably great liars? her classmate friend wondered. Their professor cast his own vote. He looked a little like a Beethoven/Einstein hybrid, the latter's wild hair with the former's serious gravity. Everything he said sounded prophetic and metaphorically dimensional; a statement like *Please shut the door because I can smell the lunchroom and do not wish to* seemed a rumination on the greater impossibilities of privacy. He'd looked at them and said, "Everyone knows everything all the time." *Huh?* they'd all thought at first. But yeah, okay, Hazel later reasoned. Maybe not all the time, maybe not everything, but on certain levels, subconscious and whatnot, she gathered that people did probably know a lot more than they let themselves acknowledge.

Which now seemed applicable to her own situation. Sure she'd wanted to believe the narrative that she was inexplicably lovable: one encounter with her and a calculating, domineering technology genius was swept off his feet. No strings attached. She did believe he'd been fascinated by her; maybe he still was, a little bit. But he'd assumed that choosing her meant she would perform feats of active gratitude on his behalf for the rest of her life. Which actually, Hazel was fine admitting, was probably a fair thing for him to expect, given who he was. So many women would've been able to fall under his spell. Hazel saw them all the time—his assistant, Fiffany, was the clearest example—and had assumed that she too would eventually fall. Why wouldn't she? She'd accomplished nothing, and was in the midst of a few life pickles. Hastily leaping into something new was her preference. Byron also likely found it great that in terms of science and engineering, she did not have a clue. He wanted someone he could astonish. And use.

This was the secret gut knowledge that she'd had and didn't listen to. She should've bowed out the day of the engagement. Her ring had several nano computer chips embedded between layers of the band. One was actually placed into the center of the diamond itself—for Hazel's "safety" the diamond's interior housed a GPS and various other internal monitors. Immediately after he'd slipped it onto her finger, she'd gotten a text message from the ring's sensors explaining that her heart rate was too rapid; it instructed her to sit down, place her head between her knees, and begin slow, deep breaths. "You should," Byron insisted, and she had. "I'm just so happy," she'd said. But not really. It was a panic attack.

Her life was going to be so different from what she'd thought. This had felt sad and she wasn't sure why, because she'd always planned on having a terrible life. But familiar terrors: loneliness, paycheck-to-paycheck ennui, unsatisfying dates with people a lot like her whom she wouldn't enjoy because she did not enjoy herself. In a life with Byron she had no idea what to expect. But Hazel reasoned that Byron's proposal was a *phew, that was close!* situation. She'd found a loophole to all the warnings her parents had ever badgered her with, their insistence that she'd have to clean up her messes. Her student loan and credit card debt felt crippling to her, but it was an inconsequential amount to Byron—he'd pay it. She'd partied too much, been lazy, and was about to flunk out of college. Readmission would be a long and tough road. But college was silly to Byron. "I dropped out to devote myself to my start-up full-time," he told her. "Wouldn't you say I'm doing okay?" Her mother had just died, and now, instead of having to move back home at a time when her father would be even more emotionally unpleasant than usual, she was going to be moving into a futuristic mansion the size of a small village. Maybe her father would even be forced to stop disapproving of her on all accounts since she'd landed such a successful husband. "You rescued me," she'd joked to Byron, and he'd replied, "You rescued me too. You're the first and only woman I ever thought of marrying."

"Same," Hazel said, but marriage with all sorts of people had long been one of her most obsessive thoughts. The first person to actually ask her had been the mechanic at the oil-change place when she was fifteen. He'd proposed to her on the spot after a ten-minute conversation and she'd felt that she liked him enough: he had a thin scar on his cheek that looked like a cat whisker, and though the stitched name on his uniform said "Jake," he assured her that was not actually his name. As for his real name? *I haven't totally decided*, he'd said, but he promised to pick one before the wedding so he'd have a name to put on the certificate. In the meantime he told her to call him Been-Jake, if she wanted to, or said she could come up with her own name for him. Hazel had loved this because she'd never named anything before.

ONCE, AS A CHILD, HAZEL HAD TRIED TO NAME THE FAMILY CHRISTMAS tree, but she was overruled. She'd gone into the kitchen to tell her parents ("I named the tree! Piney!") and found them both at the table weeping. A woman named Phyllis had just died; she was a friend of theirs Hazel had never met who lived several states away in a region of the country Hazel had never traveled to.

"Well, if we're naming the tree this year," her mother had sobbed, "we're going to name it Phyllis!" This had caused a fresh round of vocal grief on her father's part, which in turn triggered another from her mother. "I love that idea," Hazel lied.

The tree's namesake status proved to be a deflating element of that year's holiday—it wasn't right to have celebratory lighting and ornaments strewn all over Phyllis, her mother insisted; it was not okay to place presents below her branches that weren't direct offerings for the departed. The bulbs and ornaments were removed and a black linen scarf was draped in their stead. On Christmas morning, rather than open up gifts, they prepared a meat loaf and put it beneath the tree, along with a can of Dr Pepper and a *TV Guide* opened up to the "Cheers 'n Jeers" page: a few of Phyllis's favorite things. Then they'd sat on the sofa together as a family and watched the steam of the meat loaf dissipate. When it appeared to have cooled down, her mother said, "I feel like we just saw Phyllis's spirit leave the earth and ascend up to heaven."

"Are we going to eat?" Hazel asked.

Her mother sighed. "After seeing that, I'm really not hungry. The symbolic transition from life into death reenacted before us, wow. Now that's a true Christmas gift. Just a very solemn one. I think I'm going to go lie down." Her father had agreed, and after they'd left the room, Hazel did something she knew would be frowned upon but also didn't see the harm in—she went up to the tree and ran her finger along the ketchupy spine of the loaf's top then tasted it. It was candy sweet. She started to go in for another, but felt something on the back of her neck: the energy in the room had shifted from neutral to judgmental. She spun around and saw her father standing in the doorway, eyeing her in disgust, shaking his head. But then he left, and she tasted another bite anyway. The meat loaf was present; his scorn had left the room.

4

IT HAD NOT BEEN ONE OF HIS MORE SUCCESSFUL BREAKUPS, THOUGH it had been a successful payday. Elizabeth, sweet mole-covered Elizabeth (this had been Jasper's secret name for her, Moley Elizabeth), had recently written him a check for $38,000, the entirety of her current 401k, allegedly to be put toward Jasper's first year of medical school. It was a safe bet, he'd convinced her: when he graduated and became a doctor, he'd be able to pay her back with interest, though it wouldn't be of any real consequence at that point, his money versus her money, because of course they'd be married by then—*I don't want to propose until I can properly provide for you; otherwise I'd ask this very second!* It had cleared; the money was officially his; the breakup text was sent; the cell phone destroyed; a new cell phone purchased. Moley E. was rather resourceful though, he had to admit—she had somehow (no use in thinking about how, though she had probably called in a favor to her very boring friend Dana, who worked for one of Gogol's data-research divisions) found not just the motel he was staying in but also his actual room.

Now she was repeatedly thumping against his window with *energetic commitment*; the thumps were not simple fists against glass, which he could have ignored, but wall-shaking slams. In fact she was hurling her full body against the window again and again, and had been doing so for such an extended period of time (two entire episodes of *Law & Order*!) as to seem indefatigable. From previous close calls with other women, in earlier years before he'd fully mastered what he was doing, Jasper knew how the fuel of heartbreak and rage could turn an average body into a superhuman engine. Finally, he moved the curtain back to watch her run from the balcony to the glass of his window, which she did some three or four times before she noticed him watching her through the protective layer of glass. His gaze had the air of a disinterested psychiatrist looking in at a mental patient locked in an isolation room.

She did look pretty insane at the moment because she was sweaty and disheveled and blood was drizzling across her face from a small gash near her scalp. Plus she was so angry. Her eyes seemed enormous and helium-filled. She had jettisoned the weighty cargo of logic and reason. Moley E. was flying high.

"You sociopath," she began. "Give me back my money or I'm calling the cops."

It was best to stay calm, unaggressive, at this point. This was easy because he knew things were going to play out just fine for him no matter how big a scene Liz chose to make. Although he never appreciated police involvement, it didn't concern him the way all the women, the way Moley E., thought it might. "It's not illegal for me to break up with you, Liz," he said through the window.

This was when their mental gears began to shift; he could liter-ally watch the realization occur. First they looked away and down, thinking. Then all the taut muscles in their faces began to slacken and drop, and not all at once—it was like watching a large tent be disassembled, the structure regressing into formlessness as pole after pole was removed. The money had been given in a single wire transfer. Gifted. There'd been no false guarantee of investment, no paperwork trail of a scam. Elizabeth began to weep. Jasper closed the curtain.

"You'd better look over your shoulder for me your whole fucking life," she screamed. Now she was crying, and that was for the best— she would probably prefer to cry in her car than outside his motel room, and her sadness was an indicator that she'd soon begin proc-essing the grief. Thinking of how he'd never again be running his tongue along her mole-speed-bumped torso. How the only reason he'd done it in the first place was to get her money.

Not that it had been a horrible experience for him. Jasper didn't know how to feel about the fact that he liked having sex with these women, with nearly any woman—he always enjoyed it. He kind of didn't want to enjoy it *so much*. He wanted it to feel more like work, like what he did was closer to prostitution than to fraud. But the sex with them was effortless; he never had to fake arousal. He liked to consider himself a feminist in this way. Though he understood he didn't *fully* align with what he considered to be their set of ideals, he knew they were all about body acceptance, and he had always accepted every body. He had a talent for getting turned on. This was the gift he'd been given in life. And it was silly for people not to make a living off what came easiest to them.

He also, due to his wavy, Greek, shoulder-length hair and goatee, strongly resembled a European Jesus, which was an asset.

When people stopped him in pharmacies or at the gas station and said, "Who do you remind me of?" he'd answer, "God's only son, perhaps?" and at first they'd laugh but then they'd nod and grow excited. This sense of him feeling familiar was key in his line of work. The trustworthiness factor was everything.

A romantic relationship in which he didn't have a secret agenda held little appeal. In fact, the thought of vulnerability disgusted him. The grief of his father's multiple divorces had warped the man, like water damage to wood—he was still the same person, essentially, just blurrier. Not quite level. In any given situation, there was always a danger now that emotion could get the best of him. He could bend and give way without notice.

On television, a TV program was re-creating the graphic skiing death of a famous actress; they'd rigged a crash-test dummy upright onto a motorized sled, and were showing a montage of the mannequin crashing into a tree with such force that the cap and wig they'd outfitted it with flew off. The camera zoomed in when it landed in the snow, perfectly somehow, spread out as though a living woman had just melted in that very spot.

A light switch came on in Jasper's brain. Why didn't he go somewhere colder? The same things he loved about beach communities—seemingly designed for transient living and those who preferred to stay anonymous, in addition to having a guaranteed population of working professionals and wealthy residents—possibly went for winter-weather resort areas as well. He'd grown up in the South and had never dreamed of leaving the humid heat, but maybe a break from the heat was just what he needed. Particularly after Elizabeth. With that one, simply crossing the state line might not be enough for her to lose his scent.

He scratched gently at his balls; he hadn't shaved them for a few days, not since the breakup. They always caused a pleasant response in women. "So soft!" Moley E. had exclaimed the first time. "I didn't know they were like that without hair. I always thought balls felt more like elbow skin." She'd pinched his scrotum between her thumb and middle finger, rolling it like satin finery. "It's like your balls are made out of rose petals." This exclamation had made him feel sad for her somehow, like he was spoiling her forever. In a few months, when she'd somewhat recovered from the shock of loss—both of her money and of her illusion of love—and found a new boyfriend, Jasper supposed that boyfriend would have hairy balls. Unusually hairy, even. It seemed fate was like that. It would be a tough transition for her, though maybe, Jasper had reasoned, that would be for the best. Maybe from now on, hairy balls would feel like safety to her. Maybe anything that wasn't smooth would. Maybe she'd purposely start to buy low-thread-count sheets that scratched, single-sheet toilet paper with no quilting. In fact, before they'd even finished having sex the very first time, Jasper had already begun to decide it was Elizabeth's fault that she didn't realize what a foreshadowing his smooth balls were—that she couldn't see it was all going to slip through her fingers so easily.

JASPER HAD BEEN IN THE SAME LARGE BEACH TOWN FOR NEARLY A year now, and in his line of work that was too long. For a few years he'd been uncharacteristically diligent at holding himself to a six-month deadline then relocating. Self-control didn't come naturally to him; he found schedules boring, but the money responded well to this routine—it was eerie how he was able to chart out the courtship, the committed and loving relationship, and then the con into three symmetrical parts, like acts of a play. The formula paid off but it grew dull. Eventually he noticed he was staying longer, letting things get more heated, thinking about trying to fit in a second con with those who seemed particularly gullible.

Instead he'd kept up the same pace but had dropped more lines into the water, and clearly he was getting distracted—Moley E. finding him was proof of that. He'd grown sloppy. A year in the same city was careless, which was why it had been exciting.

He needed to go. He'd take in one last sunset by the ocean and pack up.

The sun was sliding low, toward the waves, seemingly melting down a little smaller and thinner as it went, but the day's heat was still tightly packed in the air; someone needed to lift a giant lid off the sky. He walked farther and farther into the water until the waves crested up against his shoulders and chin, then he relaxed and went limp, floating. Soon there were only the ocean and the sun, the unmoving heat and the endless drum of the water. He closed his eyes and felt flattened between these two forces. He loved the lobotomized feeling he got from putting his ears beneath the water, hearing nothing of the world. His groin began to swell with a half-hearted erection.

Then something struck Jasper in the face. Hard. So hard his entire body slammed down beneath the water and hit the ocean floor.

He should panic, he knew. But moving wasn't easy. In his head he heard an affectless female voice, a somewhat arousing one, begin saying the word "suffocation," repeating it with clear enunciation, like a word in a spelling bee. He could imagine that might be death's style—to talk in a sexy voice that made people want to give up and quit fighting.

Gradually his limbs came back online, tingly and a little painful, as though they'd all fallen asleep. He managed to sit up and push himself to the surface. Jasper took a few relieved breaths. What the hell was all that?

Then the water next to him parted with an unexpected ripple; his eyes startled open and were hit with saltwater from his drenched hair. The stinging blindness that followed brought true fear.

Had she followed him to the beach?

"Elizabeth?" he called out worriedly. His stomach was churning. "Honey, I'm so glad you're here. You're right, we need to talk." He tried to scan for threats with his cloudy vision, but the motion of the waves made it impossible to tell in what direction he should look. Then he felt an unmistakable thigh graze: something was moving in the water around his legs.

Jasper stumbled back. Dread and self-pity were knotting in his chest. Something had just nosed his groin. He pictured Elizabeth in scuba gear, kneeling on the ocean floor holding a length of piano wire. About to attempt castration.

He needed to get to shore.

Jasper started pumping his arms, then the sensation of being painfully and forcefully goosed came over him. Something launched his body several feet forward in the water; his head submerged. He came up coughing. "Moley E., please!" he howled, then howled again in raw distress—he had accidentally cried out her secret-joke name.

If she hadn't been certain whether or not she was going to go through with it and actually take his manhood, now he had convinced her. It was coming any instant. Then he'd have to end his life in a eunuch suicide, all because of his big mouth. If only he'd said, *Liz, please,* instead. If he'd just said it tenderly enough to her, he probably could've turned things around.

He felt himself pulled beneath the water again. This time weighty, repetitive thrusts striking across the sides of his torso kept him there. Nearly a minute passed before his mind decoded the culprit—it was a giant fish? Lack of oxygen was dimming his vision to pale pink at the edges. But he could see that his assailant wasn't Moley E. or a shark or some similar monster from the depths. No, it was a dolphin. He was sure of this on a visual level—definitely the exterior of a dolphin—but why was it assaulting him? He was being gyrated to death.

The first effects of asphyxia began setting in, and Jasper welcomed them—he needed a break. With fondness, he recalled an ample-chested dental hygienist who'd helped him into a nitrous oxide mask a few years ago. He'd been practicing his career for about three and a half years at that point and told himself he couldn't afford to be giving someone whose degree came from a vocational college a second look (*You are limiting your income!* was the exact thought-phrase of how he liked to scare himself away from such temptations), but she'd grabbed his bicep with her hand and had a firm confidence about her, and this had kicked off a pleasantly indulgent line of thinking on his part: wouldn't it be nice, just as a quick detour, to be with someone who took charge of everything and gave him a break from running his acted show? She'd bent in closer to him, close enough that he could smell cigarette smoke beneath her mint gum and jasmine perfume, and said, *Breathe in deep and have fun with this. It'll take you on a mini vacation.* He'd breathed as deeply as he could and felt himself smiling, chuckling, grabbing her arm, saw her lifting up his mask just a little so he could speak, saw her tongue draw across her lips to moisten them as she smiled back, all expectation, heard himself ask, in a slightly too-high-pitched voice, *How much do you earn a year? After taxes? I don't think you make enough for me to flirt with.* She'd placed the mask back down over his mouth, roughly, and that had been the end of their dalliance.

Jasper felt his lungs spasm; his eyes seemed blinded by the overbright light of the lamp above the dental chair beaming down. A wave crashed.

He shook his head and realized a dolphin was circling around him in the water. Its scary hyena chatter reminded him of the Wicked Witch of the West.

Think, he told himself. He had great expertise in sneaking off while paramours were sleeping or distracted. But the moment Jasper began to move, the dolphin stopped its idle swimming and righted its body in his direction like a compass needle. He yelped and fell backward as it moved toward him at full speed, its bottle-nose ramming into Jasper's solar plexus. This happened a few times, each bumper-car–style collision a little more painful than the last, until a new variation occurred: as the dolphin neared him its mouth opened. Jasper shielded his face with his hands—though he wasn't sure if he was going to escape the encounter alive, pro-tecting his moneymaker at the expense of his limbs seemed like a no-brainer choice—then moments later came the rough scrape of its tongue upon his arm, the tearing pinch of its teeth playfully needling him. When he peeked through his arms, watching the dolphin turn around and get ready to return to him for another swipe, there was a moment when the creature's impish eye locked with his own.

It was only a second, but it was unmistakable. He knew that look. This dolphin wanted to have sex with him.

This understanding disarmed and even touched Jasper in a

way he wouldn't have thought possible moments earlier—they were more similar than different, two lotharios of nature out for an afternoon swim. This ironically led him to his next epiphany: he could hit the thing, they could compete! Why hadn't he tried that? Because avoiding conflict was his overall nature. The reason he excelled at his job and at pretend relationships in general.

And because Jasper had never been in a physical fight before. This would be an embarrassing public admission. But he had worked out (a whole lot!) at the gym, and he'd always felt like time spent lifting weights was sort of a flex credit in terms of sparring and masculinity; working out and fighting both earned qualifying points in the same requisite category. There was probably some conversion chart detailing how he could cash in several thousand reps of barbell dead lifts for having landed punches in alcohol-infused bar altercations, the *I think* you *bumped into* me type. He regretted steering clear of contact sports now. He could've done some of those martial arts classes, jujitsu and Muay Thai and all of those. Why hadn't he? His doll face, he reminded himself. Those frightening cauliflower ears would not vibe well in his profession. There were easier ways to maintain abs.

The dolphin lunged toward him and he readied his fists, letting out a yell that sounded higher and more panicked than Jasper would've preferred, and brought his fist down across the dolphin's head. But the creature dodged the punch. It locked its jaw down around Jasper's wrist, attempting to pull him underwater.

Now Jasper was grateful for the athletic digression his mind had just taken—if a beating wouldn't work, he'd wrestle the thing. He managed to put it in a headlock, at which point it went still with confusion and they surfaced together, his left fist clamping its bottlenose shut. It was an interesting position. He remembered a propaganda cartoon from the Cold War era of a soldier riding a giant missile like a mechanical bull.

How could he escape? The thing was frisky! Letting it go seemed like giving it the green light to come back stronger and destroy him. He wondered if he could choke it out. Was that possible with a dolphin? Maybe then when it went limp, he could push its body behind him in one direction and charge toward shore in the other.

Jasper took a breath and held its chest in tight against his torso, readying to squeeze tighter still, but then the dolphin stopped flailing. It went completely still and silent, like a car that had just been turned off.

Tell me I did not just kill a dolphin? Jasper thought. Having killed a dolphin felt like a very creepy thing to him, even if it was unintentional and totally in self-defense. That had to bring some type of curse. Other people wouldn't know, but nature would. In the mornings there would always be tons of bugs on his car or something. Dolphins were like what—alpacas? In that violence against them was weird. He didn't know if people went to jail for killing dolphins, but if he were to stand in front of a judge and explain he'd had to, he figured the essence of the judge's response would be very *Dude, really?*

Jasper wondered how often the dolphin's blowhole needed to be above water. He'd never paid attention in science classes, except on days when they got to use fire or watch sex-ed videos. Because of education budget cuts, these movies were always outdated by at least fifteen years, and there was a fetishistic quality to the actors having clothes and hair and makeup from another decade—he and his friends called the erections they got when they watched them "time-machine boners." There was a poster of an artist's reconstruction of a female hominid hanging up on the wall in class that aroused Jasper too. He'd joked to himself that these were also time-machine boners, if he went back in time so far that there were no other people there to stimulate him, just the apelike mammals that served as genetic precursors to the human species. But he was never able to think up a term clever enough to allow confessing this fantasy to his peers. "*Extreme* time-machine boners" sounded like it wasn't just that the amount of time travel in this scenario was way more intense but also his erection, etc.

He looked again at the dolphin, at its eye, and was relieved to see a flutter of movement. He was not a murderer! But it did look unusually sleepy, in a bad drugged-out way. He tried to pull up all his mental-pictorial references of dolphins—the real, the cartoon, the sand sculpture. He'd never seen one looking so drowsy. The thing was in trouble. Maybe it was at its end. Or maybe there was a more hopeful explanation. Did it just need a nap? Did dolphins nap? He tightened his grip upon it, awkwardly holding it like a guitar that was too heavy to play, thinking he could sway back and forth with it in his arms in a type of infant bedtime maneuver. Then when it dozed off he could let go and the dolphin could float out to sea like an unmanned surfboard. Maybe.

"Wait," Jasper said. "No. No!" Somehow he hadn't noticed until now—if it hurt, he wasn't feeling it—but his wrist was bleeding. In a gross horror-movie way. Cone-shaped tooth marks were delivering endless bright blood from his skin. Their punctures seemed bottomless.

Maybe he himself was in trouble, and not only because of the wound. After all, why had the dolphin come at him like that in the first place? Did dolphins get rabies? Did they carry STDs in their saliva?

A brown recluse spider had bit Jasper's father once, just after his mother had left them when Jasper was in junior high. They hadn't thought to worry about preserving the specimen. His father had performed a vigor killing on the spider, giving it several deaths, then had used its juices on the bottom of his shoe to draw a wet smiley face on the cement floor of their garage. It was around 8 AM on a Saturday morning in late spring. His father was eight beers deep and shouting along to Christmas carols on the record player while they changed the oil in his sedan: *Jingle bells! Fuck you, Denise! The whole town knows you're a tramp! Oh what fun . . . Jasper, are we having fun yet?* By noon they were both lying down inside the car listening to the country music station, his father passing in and out of consciousness. Jasper was pretty buzzed himself, having realized about two hours into the marathon of songs that if he opened a beer his dad wasn't going to stop him.

He felt drunk enough to go try and talk to one of the neighbor girls, Savannah, who was always in her front yard in a bikini, usually with another bikinied friend, tanning or play fighting her friend with a hose. *It's like that girl isn't allowed in the house,* his mother said once. Now Jasper's mother wasn't allowed in his house, which was strange. He'd looked over at his father in the car, wondering if he should try to set up a fan to blow in on his dad's head before he left, then saw that his father's calf had quadrupled in size and turned a mottled, vascular blue. A living nexus of sweat was moving across his dad's face; his body smelled like a ripened wet dog.

At the hospital it turned out to be a big deal that they didn't know what had bitten him. Nurses tried showing his intoxicated father different pictures of spiders, but he wasn't helpful. (*So my wife left me,* he'd say. *So she's not coming back.*) The flesh necrotized further than it had to while they experimented. The next day the physician came in to lecture: "If you'd been able to get the specimen into a jar, that would've helped. Also if you hadn't been drunk." A third of his dad's calf looked like it had been eaten away. A close-escape cannibalism type of thing.

Now Jasper thought he felt the dolphin peeing on him. The creature had certainly relaxed.

He looked toward the shore. It would not be prudent to let a dolphin who may have just swapped pathogens with him go, particularly an aggressive-acting dolphin. The creature had to be tested. Who knew what it might've given him? He could put it in the trunk of his car? Tie it to the roof with a rope? Head straight to the emergency room?

Today had been strange. His karma, were he to buy into that for a moment, was not at its brightest because of the whole Moley E. encounter—it seemed like his crime had not been breaking her heart or stealing her money but seeing her afterward at the motel; that had made him feel poorly, and now this dolphin thing. The sooner he reached land, the sooner another day could begin and he could wake up and feel lucky like always.

Getting the thing to the shore turned out to be the workout of a lifetime. He had to groan a lot. It felt impossibly heavy, and he was very tired from their battle, which had gone on for how long? He had no idea. Jasper shuffled and looked down.

The creature's back was glistening like a mirror, so much so that Jasper found he could see his reflection in its gray flesh. With his grimaced face, his mouth open in a labored breath . . . Jasper recoiled. He looked old.

So old that it couldn't be his reflection: he was actually seeing his future. It was right there beneath the surface of the dolphin's slick sheen. It was a troubling revision of the ever-young self-portrait that his mind held fixed inside his ego. Despite the creature's weight and his bleeding wrist, Jasper felt compelled to stare for a while longer.

Why was he seeing this? Was it some kind of message? What did it mean?

When he did finally look up, he and the dolphin were no longer alone. In front of him was a wall of people lining the shore, all of whom were holding out an arm, extending hands upward and toward him.

Each hand held a Gogol cell phone, snapping photographs and taking videos. "You saved the dolphin!" a woman cried out.

Jasper felt his brow grimace, his shoulders tense. "No big deal," he said.

5

AS SHE SHUT HER FATHER'S DOOR, HAZEL HAD THE URGE TO TIPTOE
around its perimeter, searching. Was there a crawl space she could
hide under and thereby continue living for a few more hours? But
this was probably not possible, her continued living. When she'd
placed the thin suggestion in the air a few months ago, "Maybe I
should move out?" Byron had given her a terrifying look. It seemed
almost helpless: *Don't you know what I'd have to do then? Why would
you make me do something so awful?* "Unacceptable," he'd said. For
Byron, this meant the worst possibility it could.

Yet she'd done it. Because maybe there was a slight chance he
wasn't going to kill her? Though probably not.

Of course *he* wouldn't be doing the killing. Not in a hands-on
way. That Hazel could almost find funny: Byron, in his gadgetry-
infused suit straight off the cover of *Wired*, standing behind the
sun-faded American flag above her father's front bushes, doing

something so direct and noninterfaced as placing his hands around her neck to strangle her. Then she might get to laugh in his face as he squeezed her life out because it was so not him. Plus, a few moments after her death, he'd be really embarrassed to have indirectly displayed emotion via physical homicide.

What she needed to be watching out for was more along the lines of a microdrone kill. Some buzzing thing that looked like a yellow jacket and stung her between the eyes with a synthetic poison venom. Hard to convey to her father that this was a realistic, genuine concern. That *was* Byron's style. Full stop.

And really, she didn't want to die. Not in a gung-ho way. Sure, the depression of being Byron's constant audience and test subject had given her an easy coin of nihilism to flip in her hand: heads she died, tails she lived a life of misery. But Hazel hoped now that after so many bad years of internal and external surveillance, of cohabitation with someone she'd grown to hate and fear alike, the absence of sadness might feel something like contentment, or close enough. She did want to live long enough to see what a life of independence might be like, how both her pleasures and problems would feel if she'd never used Byron as an escape route. If she'd been smart enough to say, *Your money is tempting but wow are you strange; I am too but let me just add that something does not feel right here. Something feels aggressively odd on a next-level realm I had not previously imagined, in terms of foreboding discomfort.*

Hazel turned around on the porch and opened her eyes, which she realized she'd been protectively squeezing shut: it might only be a second before someone or something threw a vial of fast-acting acid into her face.

But what she saw playing out in front of her on the street looked like a small-town musical production. A geriatric opus, but a sizable one. The elderly apparently came out at sunset, and the sunset was beautiful. Its light was antiaging. It tinted their gray hair a luminous auburn and endowed their bald scalps with golden, healthy tans.

Everyone stopped in place, as if on cue, stared at her for a moment, and waved. She felt like she'd landed in an AARP mobile-home version of Oz.

The elderly people gathering there in front of her seemed both intrigued and terrified by her relative youth. Off in the distance, she could see more elderly people coming from streets that were farther away.

She felt like she should make a speech, announce a run for office. Finally one broke the silence and simply yelled at her.

"Who are you?!"

"Yeah!" another added. Hazel couldn't tell if their tone was due to outrage or being hard of hearing. Technically, since Hazel was under fifty-five years of age, she was not allowed to stay at Shady Place for an extended period of time, though they had no way of knowing that was her plan. Maybe they could smell the residential intent upon her.

When her father had moved into the park after her mother died and Hazel had married Byron, he did so with a cover story: he told people his daughter lived in Washington and was "into strange politics" and their relationship was very strained. When she visited him with the security escort in the digital sedan, if anyone asked, her father claimed she was the daughter of one of his military buddies who'd died young, and she dropped by some-times to hear stories about their troop. He didn't want anyone to know Hazel was married to Byron. *Boy, would the gold diggers come out in droves then,* he always said. *It would be like* The Godfather. *All day long people would be dropping by, asking for favors.*

Hazel now looked out upon the masses and cleared her throat. "I'm one of Herbert's nieces," she said. If Byron had spy cameras on her and was seeing this, that was good, maybe. Look at all these witnesses with nothing but time on their hands. Lots of bird-watchers among them too, probably: Owners of binoculars. Nosy neighbors. This sea of sagging flesh was a safety net.

"Your uncle never comes to the socials," one woman complained, also yelling. A leashed teacup dog was biting her edema-puffed ankles, but she didn't seem to feel it. Which was good because the dog's owner had dropped the leash and seemed to be taking an upright nap. Hazel could hear him snoring. "Is your uncle blind?"

"I think he is," Hazel said. "I'm pretty certain." Why not?

"You know there are these teenagers," another woman added. "They like to ride their bikes through here and you know what they do? They piss on our lawns. In broad daylight. I can smell it now, can you?" she asked. "Their piss in our grass?"

"I bet it's a gang thing!" another yelled. They were crafting an informal town hall. It occurred to Hazel just then how ironic her risk of imminent death was. What would their reactions be were she to say, *Guess what? Of all of us standing here, I'm actually the most likely to die tonight!*

This was a compelling reason not to stand there playing it safe and let the next few hours be whittled away listening to their teen-urine conversation. She should try to pack in whatever she most wanted to do ASAP. Like her father was doing with Diane. Like her mother had done with Bernie, et al. Was sex what Hazel most wanted to fill her last hours on earth with?

She gave it some thought. She wasn't opposed to a final quick fling, but a beer in a bar sounded greatest. There were just fewer variables. Plus she could go to a really dirty bar. She hadn't been anywhere filthy since she'd married Byron.

Hazel decided to speak to the group in a parlance they'd understand. "So nice to meet everyone, but I'm on my way to a doctor's appointment."

"This late at night?" a man in a ball cap cried out. His hat declared him to be REtired!

"Of course it's gang related," a competing voice offered. Hazel began walking forward. The crowd didn't part for her. They all stood fixed in place and she had to maneuver around them like traffic cones.

HER FATHER'S TRAILER PARK WASN'T NEAR THE NEIGHBORHOOD where Hazel had grown up. She passed a Laundromat and a convenience store and a shop that seemed to sell wigs and custom podiatric items with equal fervor. And then—she couldn't believe she'd never noticed it before when being driven back to The Hub, probably because she'd had her head buried between her legs in the same antihyperventilation posture she'd assumed post-engagement (this posture had become her standard resting position, really)—there was a Gogol outlet peddling used electronics.

The window display held a toothbrush device, a Tooth-Flash 3.0, that was like an automatic car wash of fluorinating antiseptic gel. Hazel had tried it once and gagged the whole time. The brush produced a defensive amount of foam. Hazel felt like she was a large predator who was trying to eat the device because it seemed the brush was filling Hazel's mouth with a lathery toxin as a form of defense. Byron loved these personal products because they made

Gogol seem harmless: how could a company whose home-health line loosely trafficked in dental hygiene have anything to hide?

Hazel didn't know if there even was a bar within walking distance of her father's trailer. She recalled the times when she was young and he'd tell her he'd hidden ten quarters in the backyard and she needed to go look for them. He'd actually hide only six, and she would look until the sun went down and then go inside and get a flashlight and look some more, and when he finally called her back inside or she got tired and eventually complained to him that she'd only found six, he'd say, *Then you didn't look hard enough.* He insisted this even when she finally got wise and made him admit there only ever were six coins. *If you really wanted ten*, he'd argued, *you would've found four more somehow.*

Of course, Hazel could go into the Gogol outlet and search-app for a bar in a matter of seconds, but that was exactly what the enemy wanted. No longer would she ever rely on any of that. Hazel wanted to begin forming her own mental maps, fallible and distractible as they might be—her very own lay of the land. She was going to deprogram herself, she'd decided. Not that Byron had brainwashed her, exactly; she clearly wouldn't have left him if he had.

But it was all very cultish at Gogol, the way reliance upon technology was perceived as a personal strength and the degree of one's reliance measured that person's value. Hazel had once posed a question to Byron: "Say one of your workers walked into your office tomorrow and was a full-on Transformer. This individual, a real go-getter, has managed to sever her brain from her human body and put it inside a robotic frame. Would this please you?"

He hadn't blinked. "I'd make her do the same thing to me right then and there. Same day. If for some reason the results weren't replicable and she couldn't, I'd give her the company. Co-CEO until my retirement, then it would be her show for eternity. I can think of few greater competitive advantages for a technology corporation than an immortal CEO."

"So you'd want to be immortal?" Hazel had clarified, repeating the question with disbelief. "You'd want to be immortal?"

"Why wouldn't I? Technology is only getting better. Thanks, in large part, to me." Then he'd winked at her, and that wink had made Hazel feel like her organs were a house of cards that Byron had just blown down. At the time, the thought of welcoming death was her only fantasy escape from the marriage, and Byron was apparently going to try to stave death off for them both for as long as possible.

But Hazel had felt that she'd made her bad decision and needed to accept the punishments it brought: This was her life, and she couldn't get out of it. She truly probably couldn't, even though she'd now made the overture of leaving. He was going to come for her one way or another. It had taken her a few years to decide to do it no matter the outcome. Knowing something was much different from knowing what to do about something, she supposed.

For example: at present she was ambling along an unfamiliar street and had no cell phone or Internet device or navigation system and she was looking for a bar and her husband whose corporation included multiple armament and surveillance technology subsets probably wanted her dead. She knew these things, but what to do about them still eluded her.

It was then she saw a sign for THE SPOTTED ROSE. The name seemed like a bad euphemism, perhaps an inelegant venereal-disease reference. If Byron found her there, it seemed as good a place as any to die.

6

THE BAR COULD NOT HAVE BEEN BETTER: IT HAD REGULAR TVS, NOT the Gogol TeleGlass Hazel was used to at home, and people were smoking real cigarettes. Loads of them.

Gratitude flooding through her body was a deeply foreign sensation to Hazel. At first she mistook the feeling to be a diarrheal precursor.

Smoking wasn't allowed at The Hub or any of Gogol's campuses, except, oddly, for the doctor at Gogol's medical subsidiary who was in charge of most of Hazel's checkups. When she'd asked Byron about it, he'd said, *Well, I'd prefer she didn't, but she's special. I'm very happy with her research.*

The low-hanging clouds of smoke felt like a chemical bath, in a good way—the bar was a decontamination chamber. Everywhere patrons were anointing one another with exhalations. Here was an opportunity to get as much of Byron's technology off her skin as possible before death. She had learned this much from her husband: the future hated germs. She'd hardly ever gotten *physically* sick when she lived with him. Nothing in the house was cloth except their bedding, towels, and napkins, which still really weren't—they were all made from some slick, antimicrobial fabric that seemed to blend silk and low-density aluminum foil. When she rolled over in bed, it made a crinkling noise that reminded her of opening up a burrito wrapper.

Was this a way she could get back at Byron a little—contaminate herself as much as possible before her slaughter? She could stop washing her hands, make out with strangers bearing cold sores. Maybe germs would be like camouflage against Byron and his employed agents, like covering oneself in mud to elude being sniffed out by a bear. If she got sick or infected enough, their sensors might stop registering her humanity: they were probably calibrated to find someone who'd been living the past several years in great economic privilege.

Sitting down at the bar, Hazel picked up a near-empty glass that had been left behind by a previous patron. "I'd like to drink a beer out of this used glass, please," she announced, a little too proudly. The woman immediately filled it up without dumping out the cloudy half inch at the bottom.

"You doing this because you're in love with him?" she asked.

Hazel's stomach twisted. "With Byron?" She could imagine him watching her with directorial zest on a spy camera as she left her father's house, imagine him removing every bartender at every local bar in a five-mile radius and replacing them with Gogol employees who would ask Hazel about her relationship with Byron immediately after serving her a beer. "The guy who left that glass?" the woman clarified. "You really into him?"

Hazel could not imagine Byron leaving the glass; no programs or images were moving on its surface. "Oh," she replied. "No. I just didn't want a clean one."

The bartender set a lukewarm pint down in front of Hazel; its top few inches of foam seemed to have been excreted by a Tooth-Flash. "If you don't want a clean one, you came to the right place," the bartender said. She was looking past Hazel, winking at someone. "That goes for the glasses and the patrons both." The bartender took out a pack of cigarettes and Hazel started to ask for one, but she saw the woman was almost out. Hazel thought about how when she'd married Byron, she'd been so excited at the thought of leaving notions of scarcity behind—she was sure all feelings about not having enough, any worries of when or even if she might be able to get more of something, would disappear with the type of unlimited money Byron gave her access to.

She had really, really believed in money. It had been the central fairy tale of her suburban childhood. And many of the myths about it had been true, sort of: because of Byron's wealth, Hazel had gone to many hotels in beautiful places.

But Byron would go to work, and she wouldn't leave the room; security never advised it (after the third or fourth trip to a foreign metropolis, their skylines from her hotel window all began to look the same for some reason. "I thought the world would be bigger," she told one room-service attendant, who responded by silently opening her bottle of wine.). She could, technically, buy whatever she wanted, but Byron somehow found time to analyze and comment on every purchase, to the point that she grew to hate buying anything because it was fodder for conversation, and she wanted to talk to him as little as possible. Money had made aspects of her life approach a level of supernatural comfort—the furniture, the bath and shower, the lack of routine inconvenience and struggle. But her marriage, her extremely wealthy marriage, had also been the beginning of her true education in scarcity. Byron had just about smoked her all up. How little she had left, how low she was getting never preoccupied him. He always had a new request for her to summon enthusiasm for, increasingly less palatable than the last. Just use this machine. Just wear this monitor. Just put this chip into your brain.

The man on the stool next to her was wearing a leather cowboy hat and a strange vest with no shirt underneath. The vest looked like skin that had accidentally peeled off his body long ago, and he'd saved it and eventually glued it back on for nostalgic reasons. It took Hazel a moment to understand his outfit because his skin was the same texture and color as the clothes. The whites of his eyes were entirely pink though. He appeared to be in the middle of a secret stage of death, a bonus level most players aren't able to unlock.

The thought occurred to Hazel: she didn't have to get sick to play sick—if her father could have a pretend girlfriend, couldn't she wear pretend lesions? Prosthetic open sores? Maybe that would help her feel less Byron-coated in a more instantaneous way. In the meantime, though, she wanted to try being social enough to tempt contagion.

"Is anyone sitting here?" she asked the man.

He turned and looked her up and down. He was the type of smoker who didn't use his hands once he'd placed the cigarette in his mouth. Keeping ahold of it made him talk with the locked-down jaw and pinched lips of a ventriloquist.

"This doesn't seem like your usual place," he offered. "You in the midst of a personal crisis?"

"Totally," said Hazel. She scanned the liquor bottles lined up on the wall; a few of their labels seemed to tickle a waterlogged lobe of her brain. Gogol excepted, Byron didn't allow branding in the house—it was a bizarre tic, one of the many things that made The Hub seem like its own planet. The food staff removed all outer packaging of foods and beverages; housekeeping discarded any product labels. Images and logos, he said, were visual energy drains. "I just left my husband and moved in with my father," Hazel continued. "I'm destitute."

The man smiled, extinguished his cigarette, extended his palm. "That's my favorite quality in a woman. Pleased to meet you. Call me Liver."

"Is that your legal name?"

"Legal's not my thing."

Liver had tough skin; his handshake was an exfoliant. "I'd like to buy you some strong drinks," he said. Liver heralded the bartender with a sharp whistle; it reminded Hazel of the tropical rain forest birdcall setting on her meditative sound machine. She'd left it behind, of course, along with everything else. Her new sound, she decided, would be no sound. Her new possessions would be no possessions.

"This will make your feet go numb," Liver stated, lighting up a new cigarette. The short jar he slid over to her appeared stolen from a surgical museum. It seemed like a medical specimen had been steeping inside it until the bartender removed it prior to serving.

"I appreciate it," Hazel said, "but I have to stay a little alert. I'm in some trouble and might need to think fast."

"No obligation," Liver said. She noticed there was a spot on the side of his head where hair didn't grow. It was shaped like the round cigarette lighter in old cars. "How long were you married?"

"A robot officiated at my wedding," Hazel said. "Let me start there."

THE ROBOT HAD BEEN AT BYRON'S INSISTENCE. IN MOST WAYS THIS had been a relief to Hazel; it meant the wedding would be a showcase for Byron's programming as opposed to her brideliness. More specifically it meant that tech and industry business magazines would send photographers, and photographers from these venues would not care whatsoever about her unfortunate dress.

Some medical considerations arose during the dress-purchasing process (hives), and they ended up being the deciding factor when it came to selection: she'd chosen the least itchy model without even trying it on, then guzzled enough antihistamine to guarantee she'd pass out on the ride home.

But it wasn't as if she'd gone into the process with her defeatist sail at full mast. She'd had high hopes of finding something beautiful, but had made the mistake of confessing her insecurities about the process to Byron. His solution had been to recruit Fiffany to go dress shopping with her.

Hazel couldn't help but feel woefully inadequate around Fiffany. She was Hazel's age but had already made herself indispensable to Byron at Gogol. Her body was toned and perfect; she was tall, with glowing skin and stylish highlighted hair, and when she laughed it was a baritone speakeasy laugh that attracted people and made her sound like she was ready to stay up all night drinking scotch and telling clever jokes. Plus Fiffany's face was not a deal breaker in any way. Its symmetry was astounding.

This filled Hazel with a panic she couldn't describe, that Byron had chosen his most attractive, traditionally feminine assistant to escort Hazel in selecting a wedding dress. It confused her, too, about how Byron wanted her to be. She'd started exclusively wearing the shapeless, comfortable clothing that made up the standard Gogol worker uniform; that seemed to be his preference. But Fiffany's outfits didn't look like they came from the Gogol product line. Was he hoping that Hazel would become more like Fiffany? He'd told Hazel that Fiffany was too made-up and appearance-obsessed for his tastes, but she wondered if he wished Hazel were slightly more made-up. For their wedding, did he want her to find a dress that could downplay her Hazelity and amplify her Fiffyness?

The dress fittings required her to stand in her underwear, which had a significant grape Popsicle stain on the waistband because she hadn't expected she'd have to disrobe in a group setting. Then she had to hold her hands above her head and close her eyes very tightly. Then she had to be suffocated by fabric for several seconds that felt like minutes (they were trying to lighten the mood, but Hazel did not appreciate the way the sales associates had imitated Viking ship rowers with one yelling "Heave!" and the other yelling "Ho!" as they attempted to squeeze her inside). She managed until she tried on a labyrinthine gown whose peekaboo cutouts had a frightening dead-end effect: every hole that looked like it might be an exit for her arm or head was covered with a screen of translucent lace and her limbs couldn't find their way out.

It was possible she'd begun freaking out in secret about three dresses earlier, but inside this one, her anxiety really found its foothold. Her arms started thrashing around in the creature-dress's central lagoon of ruffles, and then apparently she passed out.

Hazel awoke on the floor to find she'd ripped her way through the dress's midsection. Fiffany had done Hazel the favor of recording the entire incident, and kept replaying it as new sales representatives appeared in the room—they'd heard what had happened but had only now been able to break away from their clients to come see the video for themselves. They laughed deep belly laughs each time Hazel's top half emerged through the ripped dress's stomach. "Born again as a bride!" the saleswomen joked. "If a surgeon came in and gave this dress a C-section," one exclaimed pointedly, arguing her case like a theatrical lawyer in court, "this is the *exact* spot where he would cut. This *means something*," she said, but she didn't say what it might mean, and Hazel was grateful for that, because it couldn't mean anything good. "Do you want to see my C-section scar?" the woman asked.

Hazel didn't. Instead she pretended she had to faint again and sat down.

She charged the ruined dress to Byron's card, along with an exceptionally simple ivory frock that zipped all the way up, required no over-the-head action, and had a velour skort lining. "That one looks . . . roomy," Fiffany said. When Hazel nodded, Fiffany sighed. "I'm saying it's hideous," she clarified. Fiffany's voice had the patronizing tone of someone explaining a harsh truth to a stubborn innocent, an exasperated mother finally giving in and telling her child the more unsavory nuts-and-bolts details of why the sleepy man camped underneath the bridge couldn't come stay in their guest room. "We don't want extra space. We're not buying an RV." Hazel had felt herself begin to blush, but then she saw Fiffany look over her shoulder—Fiffany was appealing to a sales associate behind them for help, and the woman had obviously just heard the entire exchange.

Hazel turned. When the associate looked at the dress, her face became sad. Once, at the zoo, Hazel and several others had watched a shunned chimpanzee in the corner of the primate enclosure sample its own excrement. Afterward everyone, including Hazel, had worn the expression that the sales associate was making now. "I've never sold this style to a bride," she finally remarked. "It's usually the mother of the bride. Or, more commonly, the grand-mother."

Fiffany nodded. "Fixed income and waning eyesight," she said. "That's what this dress appeals to." But just looking at the other dresses gave Hazel a prickling-heat sensation; she felt her hands swelling up. Her ring finger especially was aching with an increas-ing tightness.

"Oh!" Fiffany had suddenly called out. "I'm going to call a medic. Something is happening with your body!" It was true; Hazel was breaking out in a collector's variety of welts. Luckily Hazel's en-gagement ring had already called the paramedics. Fiffany bumped into an arriving EMT on her way out of the room.

Hazel completed the purchase of the dresses from a stretcher, the sales associate going over all the details and making a big display of speaking loudly and clearly, like Hazel was hard of hear-ing instead of bearing an anxious rash; the way the woman held each paper up close to Hazel's reclined head was very deathbed-style. They seemed to be confirming the details of Hazel's final will, which she should have, perhaps, in retrospect, understood to be an omen. Hazel whispered a question to the associate, not wanting Fiffany to hear, and the woman bent over a microscopic amount out of decorum, but it was clear this was as close as she was willing to get to Hazel's hive-swollen face, and it was not close enough.

"I'm so sorry," the woman apologized. "I still can't hear you. Can you speak up a little more?"

"Will you give the dress pockets?" Hazel finally hissed at normal volume. It would be good, she'd realized, to have a place to stash some sedatives on the wedding day.

The associate pursed her lips. "We can do anything you like," she finally said. Her words had the intonation of a sincere apology.

But the dress-purchasing mission wasn't entirely fruitless: six months later, Fiffany and the EMT got married. Fiffany wore a smaller version of the dress Hazel had ripped her way out of. Per usual, Byron was on his device for most of the ceremony, but since Fiffany chose to get married in the Gogol headquarters employee chapel, he did attend, and he did pause for one moment to look up and comment to Hazel when Fiffany walked down the aisle, "Well, she looks just beautiful," he said. "Doesn't she?" He started at Fiffany for a moment with the same look of delight he'd given Hazel in the interview. Then, so casually Hazel might've easily ignored it, he added, "Love the dress." And she hadn't wanted her face to grow hot, but it had. And she hadn't wanted to turn to look at him. She did though; already at this early point in their marriage, curiosity had stopped being a friend to her. Byron was staring at her, waiting for her eyes to meet his, and when they did he gave her a knowing wink.

Of course Fiffany had shown Byron the video. Why wouldn't she? Hazel was surprised to find this felt far more painful than imagining a full-blown affair: Byron and the attractive Fiffany, chuckling together in his office at Hazel's expense, somehow caused her a more vulnerable form of pain.

Fiffany had gotten divorced two weeks later. Hazel told herself it was a crazy thought, but she almost wondered if the wedding had been a show. That Fiffany had done it just so Byron could see her wearing that dress and feel like he should've married Fiffany instead.

FOUR DRINKS LATER, HAZEL WAS FOLDED OVER ACROSS LIVER'S LAP. "Was that sent here to kill me?" she'd ask, then point to something in the bar. "Was that?" She rubbed her finger along Liver's knee then glanced at the sheen on her fingertip. Like an otter's fur, his pants seemed to produce an oil-based protective coating.

This was a digression. She'd been telling him all about the failings of her marriage, Byron's monstrosity, the ways that he'd refused to respect the most basic of personal boundaries, such as her skull. "I mean a *microchip*," she continued, returning to the story. "He wanted to put it up here." She felt her hand move toward her head; a finger—her own? the verdict was out—went inside her ear. Attempts to sit up were unsuccessful. It felt like Liver's pants were magnetic and her cheeks were lined with metal shavings. "Is there a bathroom?"

"Yes, ma'am," he responded. "There is. Big enough to screw in. Small enough to feel romantic. May I escort you?"

Hazel shook her head. "I'll be right back," she said. By which she meant she would never return, not to Liver's lap or to the Spotted Rose. Probably because she'd be dead.

It had been a long time since she'd had alcohol with so many impurities; the inside of her mouth felt lined with grit. But this was good, she reminded herself. She needed to rid herself of Byron's long-standing odor of sterility, and she was succeeding. When she burped it smelled like the world's most fermented peach bobbing in a bowl of lighter fluid.

Hazel felt fawnlike on her walk home, newly born; her legs had forgotten everything. She reached the sanctuary of Shady Place's entrance and decided it was okay to begin to crawl. For a while she dry-heaved into a neighbor's faux-stone wishing-well planter, which maybe wasn't too far off from tossing in a penny, so she decided to leave a wish that could be granted. *Universe,* she thought, *please let me convert to a tangible existence now. One without interfaces and constant monitoring and a shower that talks. Also please let me live long enough to taste an adult life of my very own, even if it's a pathetic one.*

She crawled several more feet before passing out at the foot of Mrs. Fennigan's tranquility fountain. Sleep came to Hazel—she couldn't help it—the moment her brain heard the running water. Like birdcalls, water was one of Hazel's preferred meditation sound-machine settings. Well, her former meditation sound machine.

An ambulance came careening into the park with sirens at full blare, sans consideration for someone who might be passed out on a nearby lawn: one of the street's routine elder deaths. Hazel looked up at the sky; swampy clouds crisscrossed the moon. It was very late. Rocking up onto her knees, she tried standing but found she was still intoxicated. More so, somehow, than she had been when she'd passed out. Her eyes were drawn to the flaccid promise of a garden hose dangling off the side of a trailer a few feet away. "Water!" she announced, then decided she should not speak aloud at present. That had been a misstep.

For a while she just sprayed the hose onto her face, her eyes closed, then she began lapping at the stream—why did her tongue feel so swollen?—still without opening her eyes. By the time she became conscious enough for reason to set in, she realized she didn't know if her pants were wet from the hose or another source, so she spent an additional few minutes soaking them just in case.

It would alarm her father to see her enter his home in the early dawn hours wearing saturated clothing. It just would. This was extra incentive to make it back to the screened-in-porch room before he woke.

After a few failed attempts, Hazel was able to cross to the other side of the street on all fours, but her errant path led her to head butt a lawn flamingo.

Suddenly the moon was wide and full above her head like a spotlight. The flamingo, with its raised, tucked-under plastic leg, suggested the shape of Byron kneeling down on one knee, and memory flooded her. This was how he'd presented her with the microchip that he wanted to place in her brain: Byron had cleverly, in a faux-romantic overture, put the chip inside a velvet ring box, made his proposal regarding their tandem neurosurgical alterations, then had gotten down on one knee, opened up the box's lid, and said, *Hazel Green, will you meld with me*?

He had worn a tux.

Of course this is what his research had told him to do—he was altering a familiar social script in which she was supposed to feel gleeful, flattered, adored; she was supposed to throw her arms around him afterward and say *Yes!*; she was probably even supposed to cry.

When Hazel didn't, Byron's nonplussed solution was to wait it out. He likely assumed the offer was so overwhelming to Hazel, in a good or great way, that she was in shock and needed time to process. Maybe a lot of time, right? Since it was such a wonderful proposition. Byron had stayed like that, on one knee with the box extended outward, for the entire argument that followed; he seemed to have strong feelings that this staged position was the key to changing her mind. He was still like this, smiling, insisting to himself that if he stayed in a classic pose of devoted inquiry a few moments longer everything would fall into place, when Hazel turned and left the room. She was crying and disgusted; he was calling out after her—*Hazel, stop and think for a moment! What is love if not progress? What is love? What is love?*

Now she emitted a wolverine growl and pounced upon the flamingo, tackling it to the ground. Wrapping one arm around its middle, she gripped its long neck like an oar with her other hand and used the flamingo to help prop herself upright and walk along.

Many of the yards they had to pass through were booby-trapped with motion-sensor lights: when they'd walk past these, or through a stretch of particularly clear moonlight, the flamingo's glass eye appeared to power on and glint at her with a furious bewilderment. Hazel worried it had reservations about its forced relocation. "I'll take you back tomorrow," she promised, a total lie. Even if she were still alive tomorrow, she had no plans to return it. The bird was inanimate, yes, and Hazel had never believed in hunting, but having taken it down by summoning her hatred of Byron felt like a trophy kill in a way that pleased her.

"You'll like my dad's friend Diane," she assured the bird. Maybe the doll and the lawn ornament would be able to communicate with each other. She liked the thought of her father having to pretend the flamingo was real if she had to pretend the doll was real.

Plus her father seemed to be in a far better mental space than she was. Acting as though the bird could understand her and was her beloved confidante might be the very best thing. "You and me for a little bit," Hazel told the flamingo. "Let's give it a try."

When they arrived at her father's doorstep, as with any partner who'd helped her drunkenly stumble home, Hazel felt the need to instruct the bird about what to expect inside. "We have to be very quiet," she whispered. "Dad's asleep. There are obstacles we'll have to watch out for, like a large wooden box that you might assume is a coffin but isn't."

She unlocked the door and turned the knob.

Remembering her junior high and high school days, part of her felt like she'd become a delinquent teenager all over again and worried that her father would be waiting up, sitting on the couch with his arms crossed. Diane would be next to him, dressed to the nines in one of her mother's now-vintage outfits, her plastic face somehow remolded to have forehead wrinkles of displeased judgment.

Or worse, that Byron would be sitting there, or someone he'd sent.

That would be the end. But if it was her father, she could simply shut the door, take the flamingo into the backyard, and curl up with it there. It had been a long time since she'd held someone else during sleep. Byron's skin always felt refrigerated, and in sleep his pulse slowed down to a low, controlled speed that seemed akin to hibernation. In the beginning of their relationship, back when she thought that she was maybe almost starting to like Byron, or was right about to almost start, laying her head upon his chest was a difficult exercise in anxiety. After every beat of his heart, there was just enough pause to make her nervous that the next might never come.

Not long after, though, she'd secretly started hoping that it wouldn't.

7

HAZEL CRACKED THE FRONT SCREEN DOOR AND WAS RELIEVED TO hear snores ringing out from her father's bedroom. The last time they'd both slept under one roof was the night of her mother's funeral, when Hazel had gotten so drunk that the thought of getting in a vehicle made her nauseous; she'd slept on the sofa until her father's snoring woke her, then she'd turned on the TV. Her brain was soft from stress, and in this vulnerable state, the program that came on easily pushed through the surface layers of her consciousness straight into a permanent memory—it was an aerobic-exercise show, presumably for effervescent insomniacs. The lead woman's eyes and smile gleamed with unfiltered sadism; her growling chorus of *Burn! Burn! Burn!* made her seem a recent transplant from 1690s Salem—she'd ditched the bonnet and donned a leotard. Full proof of her evil powers came next: the remote control's batteries inexplicably stopped working, and to

Hazel's dismay, the longer she watched the mechanical violence of the woman's kicks, the more hypnotic the program became. In the background, one woman performed at half speed and yet another performed at quarter speed; watching all three at once was an almost-pleasant optical illusion. But the aerobic leader's eyebrows were harshly triangular; Hazel found nothing pleasant about those. They made her feel very unsafe. Their arched points looked capable of perforating the television screen, maybe opening up a spatial vacuum that would suck Hazel in. Then she'd have to perform a kick routine at one-eighth speed for the rest of eternity. During this entire nightmarish fantasy, her father's snores had been a metered background sound track, and hearing them now, Hazel began to feel the woman's kicks as punctuated jolts to her temple. "We should go lie down," Hazel said to the bird. "We've had a big day."

The hollow flamingo was picking up vibrations from her father's snores, which made the bird seem to be alive and nearly purring. Getting down the hall and back to the porch without crashing into furniture would take balance. Hazel thought of tightrope walkers and the balance sticks they used. A factoid she knew from Gogol was the more technical term for tightrope walking: funambulism. It struck her as an odd word for it—tightrope walking seemed scary, not fun. One of Byron's earlier triumphs was the creation of a thick fiber-optic rope that could transmit several networks' worth of information in seconds; the project came to bear the moniker Funambuloptics. It was sold as part of a defense contract for more than twice what the company was worth at the time (which was already more than nearly every other tech company in the world was worth), the reason being that if it were dangled from a helicopter, or hosed in through a window or a pipe, it could capture every particle of information on every computer inside the building without any human being having to be present. In theory, of course. Everything Byron's military-contract units made only worked in theory. Non-theoretical use would violate international law.

Hazel couldn't remember how tightrope walkers held those sticks. Up and out? Squat and close? The snoring sound felt like an oppressive, low ceiling all around her: it seemed like she had to watch her head so she didn't hit it against the noise. Squatting, Hazel picked up the flamingo by its stick leg and clutched it in front of her chest, which didn't feel helpful. Now that she thought about it, everything surrounding tightrope walking felt suspect. Eventually she placed the stick behind her neck and draped her arms over the top of it, as though it were a pink crucifix she'd been affixed to, and teetered toward her room.

At some point they stopped to take a micronap on the floor. Then Hazel found it easiest to take a canine approach, gently picking the flamingo up by the neck with her mouth and dragging it to the foot of the porch's couch, whereby a wash of maternal instinct set in: by the light of the window, the narrow daybed seemed tailor-made for the creature. Hazel turned down the knitted afghan, set the flamingo inside, and drew the covers up to its beak. Its reflective eye was centered perfectly on the pillow. She realized that she too needed sleep and was actually drunk enough to get it; her inebriated brain insisted there was no point in staying awake in a vigil, awaiting Byron's next move. It was going to come no matter what she did, and at the moment, if someone were to kill her, her brain would probably register the death as a happy one stemming from the pleasant esophageal burn below her ribs.

She crawled in next to the bird and wrapped a protective arm across its girth.

WHAT HAZEL *HATED*—AND SHE COULD FEEL HERSELF HATING THIS even as she slept—was how her dreams always turned to Byron. Not in a pleasant-revenge way, not even in a central way. He was just there, the most prominent building in the skyline of her thoughts, unable to be moved or overlooked. She could hear him right now in fact, mid-dream, calling her name and asking her to wake up.

"Help!" Byron screamed.

Hazel opened her eyes and screamed as well, first at the beaked pink plastic head, impossibly small on the pillow next to her, then at the ceiling—it was a nightmare, except it wasn't a dream. There was truly an image of Byron's head projected across her ceiling. She screamed a third time when the image blinked; its eyes were animate. It cleared its throat. "Hazel," the image declared. "It's me."

Though it covered the full width of the porch ceiling, proportion-wise it was not a perfect enlargement. Byron's forehead was stretched out like the top of a hot-air balloon, forming the upper two-thirds of his face. The rest of his features and mouth were compressed into an elongated column that shrank down indefinitely to the micro-scopic point of Byron's chin.

Hazel glanced around the porch, locating herself; her temples throbbed. Hoping he hadn't seen the flamingo yet, she tried a few maneuvers to push the bird down beneath the afghan. "Byron," she snapped, looking upward. It was like her ex was a literal giant who'd come searching for her by prying off the roof of her father's home. "Either kill me now or get off my ceiling." At present he looked so cartoony that she could almost forget he was orchestrat-ing her assassination behind the scenes. And face-to-face, Byron was incredibly nonchalant. He would be right up until the moment he had her murdered.

"You left your mobile device at home. No one's answering your father's phone. How would you prefer I contact you?" From the darting gaze of his pupils, the subtle shifts of his head and manic blinks of his eyelids, she knew Byron was working. His desk was like a hive; a bizarre honeycomb arrangement of staggered monitors surrounded it, and he could somehow, with a variety of designated eye movements, independently respond to or control each one without moving his hands. "We need to talk," he stressed. "It's important. Trust me. You don't want things to escalate."

He shifted his shoulders, which caused a new distribution of his head projection—the wooden ceiling fan now appeared to be implanted in his left cheek, spinning around like the most whimsical birthmark of all time. It was too much to keep up with in her nauseous state. Hazel closed her eyes so she wouldn't get sick.

"Wrong," she whispered, unsure if Byron could even hear her. Where was his face coming in from? She scanned the room for the source before finally seeing it: a thin beam of light streaming through the back window. "I won't ever bother you or speak of you. You can forget I exist. I was like a charity case you took on that didn't pan out. You overestimated my potential. It happens. I'm sorry I failed you but I won't continue wasting your time, effective immediately."

"You don't understand, Hazel. I'd like to be certain you understand before I enact a solution we can't reverse. This isn't a secure connection . . ."

"I definitely do not feel secure, Byron. Isn't this breaking and entering? Your face, you know, breaking in?" She paused. "I know you're going to have me killed. Can we go ahead and agree on a day and time? I won't try to stop it; I just want to know." Hazel saw a quick flash behind Byron's head—someone was there in the office with him. It had only been a second, but she swore she'd just seen the outline of Fiffany's head, that Fiffany's eyes were staring back at her.

"It is in your own best interest to receive some facts. I've taken the liberty of putting some basic electronics in a weatherproof safe in your backyard. Its code is the date of our anniversary."

"I'm not opening the safe, Byron. I don't ever want to use electronics again." She managed to be surprised by the flash of anger that crossed his face—of course this was a personal affront to him. But there was a tiny bit of control and comfort in the fact that while he could kill her tomorrow, maybe he couldn't make her use a cell phone before he did it. "I'm not asking for any of your money, which should prove I'm too insane for you to stay in a relationship with. Why don't we just go our separate ways? My life will be such an insignificant, invisible thing. I'll truly disappear. That's all I want."

Hazel thought back to the beginning of their marriage, when the constant monitoring and sensors started to feel increasingly claustrophobic. She tried to believe Byron's reassurance that it was innocuous—what did she have to hide? what was it hurting?—but increasingly she noticed Byron commenting on her daily activities around The Hub while he was away, the meals a staff member brought her each day changing based on the report of bodily scans she hadn't been aware she was getting. Back then they'd had what Hazel thought to be a normal amount of occasional sex; Byron wasn't the sort of person who could let go with abandon or fully stick his tongue in someone's mouth. But soon not fucking became one of the only barriers Hazel could manage. *Sex with you would be redundant!* she'd yelled at him once when he finally admitted there were multiple cameras and scanners and more in every room including the bathroom, that no second of her time inside The Hub had gone unrecorded. *You're already inside my body with these fucking sensors!* It was for safety and convenience, he'd stressed. It provided necessary data that technology relied upon, technology that would supposedly keep them healthy, happy, and vital. *I don't have a psychology degree, for example*, he'd argue, *but I can have your words and actions processed and analyzed with almost ninety-seven percent accuracy to reveal to me your current state of mind. How many couples can say that?*

Now, Byron snort-laughed. What did Byron ever find funny? She couldn't think of a single thing except how great it was to win. "I need you to do something for me, Hazel. I need you to go get the mobile device out of the safe in your backyard and call me on a secure line. Can you do that?"

"What happens if I don't?"

A ringing filled the room—a phone on Byron's end. His eyes performed a series of spastic blinks; whenever she saw him working, it looked enough like he might be having a seizure to make her feel hopeful, but the flutters and rolls of his lids always turned out to be calculated. "I'm going to need to let you go for the moment, Hazel, but you know how to reach me. I'll talk to you later today. Probably just after noon. That's not an arbitrary time, that's when you're going to want to place a call to me, and the first order of business in our conversation will be a gentle reminder that I did try to warn you. I did, Hazel. You're leaving me no choice."

With that, the regular ceiling came back into view. She glanced toward the back window, hoping the projection box was something he'd had installed that she could break with her hands, or cover by placing the flamingo's cavernous abdomen over the top of it, but the box had retreated.

She made herself a solemn promise that even if he somehow beamed her father's house, with her father inside it, out of existence that afternoon and she found herself sitting all alone on the grass of an empty yard with no other object surrounding her but the safe Byron had dropped off, she still would not call him. She would urinate on the safe, maybe. Then she would walk away to try to find solitude and revel in it. Assuming he let her live.

And maybe he would? Perhaps she'd been too pessimistic. There was clearly something more he wanted from her. Hazel tried to hope he might find a way to get it somewhere else. She knew this wasn't the case though.

Her clothes and hair were still wet. But in the light of the morning they felt different, less soggy and more refreshing, as if she'd simply showered with them on. Hazel removed them and took a moment to relish her nonrecorded nudity, then realized she had to assume Byron was recording video of her if his face had just been plastered across her ceiling.

But she was in the world, having a moment outside Byron's landscape of influence! She reminded herself that she'd existed before she'd ever known Byron, so a resumption of existence without him was absolutely possible. She'd previously come to believe that it wasn't.

The shopping carts at her father's local grocer had wheels that locked up if anyone tried to take them beyond the parking lot, and a part of Hazel had figured that a similar thing would happen to her if she left The Hub's borders without plans to return.

But it wasn't like she wanted to go back to her pre-Byron life either. When she'd married, she hadn't brought any possessions with her because everything she owned was shitty. And when she left Byron, she hadn't taken anything; it all seemed like his stuff. He'd either invented it or paid for it.

Now she put on a T-shirt that she'd gotten free back in college.

It was a thank-you gift for signing up for a credit card that she'd immediately maxed out then never made a payment on; the card's logo was splashed across the front in different fonts. She paired this top with sweatpants that had DROPOUT written down their left leg in a Sharpie marker. She remembered being intoxicated and writing this upon herself one night back when it was clear she would not be rebounding from academic probation. It sounded better than "flunkout."

These clothes now seemed an ill fit for her microdermabrased face and asymmetrical haircut and perfect veneer smile. She'd really prided herself on the way she'd begun to ape dignity as Byron's wife, and he'd sometimes commented, with a surprised tone, on how respectable she looked during the rare occasions when they attended an event as a couple. This getup wasn't the outfit she wanted to die in, not ideally, but maybe if she renounced and removed all external indications of social merit from her physical person, he'd begin to question whether Hazel was worth all this trouble. She couldn't simply drop down to a baseline maintenance of her physical attractiveness; she really had to start looking rough, like she meant it. Maybe Mrs. Weathersby, her father's neighbor down the street, was still hoarding parakeets. If so, Hazel could drop by and ask for a tour of the bird room. She could stay until her clothing was covered with avian dung.

OUT IN THE LIVING ROOM, HER FATHER WAS PUSHING DIANE'S ARRIVAL coffin toward the door by accelerating his scooter and hitting it. He kept backing up then gunning the throttle and hitting it again. She couldn't tell if it was moving a bit each time or if no progress was being made, but it looked like a cathartic morning activity.

"Hello, Dad!" Hazel called. He gave a small wave indicating that he was too busy to chat.

She walked to the refrigerator and opened its door, then the sensation of being watched filled her with nausea—she turned, ready to confront one of Byron's electronics, but it was Diane. It creeped Hazel out how she was able to sense the doll. "And hello to you, Diane." Hazel started to raise the carton of OJ toward her in a gesture of merriment, but froze.

Diane did not appear to be herself. At all.

Overnight, the doll had devolved into some sort of catfish/human hybrid—gone was her foxy, closed smile with the corner lip upturned as if to say, *I know the dirty stuff you want to do and I think you're a sick individual but I must be the biggest sicko of all because I want to try every one of your filthy ideas out*! Now, beneath her prim nose, there were no features at all except a puckered, circular, bright maroon opening that reminded Hazel of a baboon's ass.

"What the hell did you do to her face?" Hazel called out. Diane now looked a lot like the tortured figure in Munch's painting *The Scream*, if the tortured figure were a red-haired female sex doll. Her arms were bent upward at the elbow, hands framing her cheeks; her mouth was a wide cavern of terrible surprise.

"That's her other face," her father said, appearing at the doorway.

Upon realizing he meant *the face I can have intercourse with*, Hazel was torn between true curiosity and a desire to change the subject at all costs.

Curiosity won. "Only the face switches? You don't trade out the whole head?"

"No decapitation necessary." Her father zipped over, pulled some sort of pop tab on Diane's scalp, and lifted it off.

The empty stocking of the mouth hole looked like a prototype of a synthetic digestive organ. Its color was a near-pink gray; it glistened in the morning sun streaming through the kitchen window. When he began to put it back, Hazel had a memory of watching a magician packing his tricks up after the show, stuffing endless feet of colored scarves back into a small black top hat.

"Good talk," Hazel concluded. "Hey, do you mind if I keep that body box? Can I take it back to my porch room?" She'd realized there probably weren't any cameras inside the box, at least not at present, so she could get a few solid hours inside it with the lid almost shut, where no one else would see her. Byron would find some way to have any comforting hiding spot she found networked by nightfall, but at least she'd get to do it once.

"If you can get it back there, sure. It's heavy as hell. The deliveryman asked me if rocks were inside. I said, 'Nope, I ordered a new girlfriend!' and he really cracked up. Had no idea I wasn't joking!" Despite the fact that the top layer of Diane's face was sitting on the table, propped upright against the napkin holder, her father tenderly kissed the doll on the cheek. "I have to go to a goddamn doctor's appointment," he said. "This becomes your social circle when you're my age, Haze, doctors' appointments and funerals. You're either dying or trying not to."

"Always best to keep busy. I'm gonna try moving it. What time's your appointment? Do you want me to come with you?"

"No need. There's a small bus that comes right to my house. The driver's a bit of a talker. Hates his wife. Complains about her the whole time. For his sake I pretend I'm married to an awful woman too."

"Why can't you tell him you're a widower?"

"That's boring. Plus it makes most married men envious. No one wants to hear good things about other peoples' lives, Hazel. If I have any aged wisdom to impart to you, it's that."

"I like hearing good things about you, Dad," Hazel said, because she felt like she should. But she couldn't remember ever hearing something good about her father.

"You might not want awful things happening to your loved ones, sure. But what if I'd been a super-brilliant guy and you'd followed your same trajectory of flunking out of a mediocre college? If you hadn't married up to the financial stratosphere afterward, of course. Wouldn't you have wished I were less of a superstar? Wouldn't my fame have made you feel insignificant?"

She'd never thought of this. Byron's fame hadn't made her feel jealous as much as defective for not being able to like the guy. "I don't know, Dad. I think I would've been proud."

"Huh. Well, that kind of makes me feel like shit, Hazel. Sorry I wasn't more impressive."

"Come on." Hazel resisted the temptation to add, *Then maybe put your sex doll away during breakfast hours, or cover up her face and cleavage with a birdcage drape at the table.*

"I'm pulling your chain. But I'll be honest; it was hard for me, a little bit, to see you so high up on the hog. That sounds awful, but I'm too old for secrets anymore. You having all that money, it made me feel like I'd only been your dad by accident. Like you'd gone and left us for your true people."

She knew what he meant, actually; she'd found it hard to bring any piece of her old life with her into her new one, and vice versa now that she'd returned. The Hub was like a portal that immediately shut behind her so no aspects of her previous self could follow.

"Well, you're officially my dad again. I wouldn't have a roof over my head if it weren't for you."

"That makes me nervous for different reasons, but okay. Let's have a moment." He held his arms up limply and rotely, as though readying to be lifted into a bath by a caregiver, but Hazel understood to go in for a hug. Her whole life, he'd always seemed afraid to deliver too much pressure, which made the end result feel half-hearted, like he was worried she might be about to throw up on him. But this one was more extended than she remembered his hugs being in the past, and that balanced out its featherweight grip and almost made it seem like her father wanted the embrace. It was an improvement—if he'd been practicing on Diane, it was helping.

"Diane's staying home with me, I assume?"

"Correct. She and I haven't been out on the town. Not sure that's in the cards for the future either. Man, would the bus driver love to get a look at her plumbing though."

Her plumbing? Hazel felt excited about taking a peek when he left. Was looking unethical? Like a form of snooping since Diane wasn't hers? "Do you mind taking her to the bedroom and tucking her in, Haze? I should go wait out front. These appointments are a whole-day production. When I get back I'll probably be ready to drink some gravy and hit the hay." Hazel hoped he was using "gravy" as a euphemism for alcohol. She glanced at the contents of the open pantry. Unfortunately, he seemed to mean actual gravy.

"Sure, Dad. Have a good one." There was the sound of her father whistling over the Rascal's electric motor as he wheeled toward the door, then silence.

Now that they were actually alone together, Hazel felt too shy to look between the doll's legs, particularly if Byron did have surveillance in the house and was watching. No—she'd be professional, like a nurse's assistant.

"Hello, Diane," Hazel offered as she fixed the doll's face. "Guess I'm going to put you down for a nap now."

First she tried a "bride-across-the-threshold" carry, but the doll weighed more than Hazel expected. It felt a little mean, but because the doll was so top-heavy, Hazel had to tip her forward and hold her by the waist, then drag her toward the bedroom. If she gave it the right context, it actually wasn't hard to think of Diane as human: Diane was a friend who'd had way too much to drink, and now Hazel was helping her to her room. Once she got Diane situated beneath the blankets, her head atop the pillow, Hazel could also think of Diane as a long-term coma patient, except without the sadness—it didn't have to be tragic that Diane would never wake up since she'd never been awake.

Even the comical portal of Diane's open mouth began to seem okay now that Hazel had gotten used to it. It was just an exaggerated expression. Diane was really surprised, that's all. Making a face like she couldn't believe what she was hearing.

Hazel remembered a fund-raiser she and Byron had attended where she was in the bar line next to a woman wearing a pair of Gogol concept shoes—they were wedges whose platforms digitally displayed her weight and BMI on the left foot, and the number of steps she'd taken that day alongside the number of calories she'd hypothetically burned on the right; whenever her weight decreased more than a tenth of a pound, the shoes would start flashing and emit celebratory bursts of pink LED light for twenty seconds. The woman had asked the bartender for another glass of a very specific wine, and when the bartender told her they were out of it, she'd made a face not unlike Diane's current expression.

Finally the woman's shoes had started blinking, which broke her out of the trance; she looked down at them, reading the numbers, then shot the bartender a different horrible look. "Apparently," she said, "disappointment is great for my metabolism. So I suppose I should actually thank you for ruining my night." Hazel had watched her blink off into the distance, then wanted to try to cheer up the bartender. "Jeez," she'd said to him, "what's her problem?" But he wasn't rattled. "What did she say?" he asked. "I didn't hear her. I was staring at her chest."

Hazel had nodded and fielded a question to him. "If women could either be exactly like they are now, or you could turn us all into giant breasts, every single one of us becoming just a giant breast and nipple that doesn't talk or think or eat, we just roll everywhere and leave a silicone slug trail in our wake, which would you prefer?" The bartender's eyes had started scanning the room for an answer, as though he might see a woman standing against the wall next to a giant breast, therefore having a convenient visual guide to help him compare and make his decision. "Where does the slug trail come from?" he'd asked. "What's lubricating it? Is there still a down-there?"

Since the bartender was occupied in thought, Hazel had grabbed a liquor bottle and begun making herself a drink while she spoke. "Well," Hazel said, "let me elaborate. Say there's a port the size of a standard vacuum cleaner tube on the side of the breast. That way the breasts can stop at silicone stations, which are just like gas stations basically, and get pumped up with more silicone. The bottom of the breast is porous, allowing microdroplets of the silicone to ooze out throughout the day and make a greasy path for us to slide across. It's all the mobility we have."

"So this port though. That's, like, where men can put it in?"

Hazel had taken a small sip of liquor and tried not to cough. "Of course," she finally responded. "Without arms or legs it would be hard for us to stop you." He'd clapped his hands together. "Brilliant. Done. Let's make it happen."

Now, looking at Diane's mouth, Hazel thought of this port. She had an urge to see what the doll's mouth felt like inside. While the opening was wide, when Hazel squinted one eye and tried to see down it, the interior looked snug. Which she guessed was what people were paying for.

To ease her guilt about violating the doll's mouth with her hand, Hazel decided to pretend Diane might be choking on something. "This has nothing to do with sex!" Hazel began, in a series of verbal assurances that were as much for herself as for the possible Byron-cam. "I'm just making sure you don't have anything lodged in your throat after breakfast. No precaution is too great for your safety, Di." The mouth accommodated Hazel's first four fingers, but getting her thumb inside took some convincing. Finally her hand was in ("Say AHHH, Diane! I feel like a dentist!" Hazel joked), and then her forearm.

For whatever reason, her limb being engulfed felt soothing. It was like her hand was being held in an advanced way. A nontechnological way? As if Diane had placed Hazel's hand not inside her throat but on her abdomen, and then bent over, folding herself around Hazel's fingers and wrist and elbow, the most committed handshake ever. It felt almost intimate, until Hazel pushed a little farther and realized she was feeling the back of Diane's head from the inside.

Then the sensation of Diane's rubber lips squeezing tightly around her forearm got uncomfortable. Hazel thought about the automatic blood pressure cuffs at the pharmacy in her childhood, how she used the machine every time she went, but every time was certain, at least for a moment, that the machine had finally gone haywire—had constricted far too firmly and wasn't going to loosen fast enough for her limb to maintain its necessary blood flow.

Then she thought about the giant snakes she'd seen on the nature channel whose jaws unhinge to make way for whole pigs and other large meals. What if Hazel woke up in the middle of the night on the porch feeling like her legs were bound, but when she lifted the covers, what did she see beneath them but *Diane*? Who had slithered into the bed and was in the process of ingesting Hazel whole, legs first? Diane, who would be able to turn real and come to life as long as she ate a living woman once a month to sustain her? Though Hazel hoped her father wouldn't sacrifice her for the sake of giving his love doll sentience, she couldn't say for sure. Hazel imagined him entering the room in the final moments of her consumption, Diane's lips having crossed the Rubicon of Hazel's collarbone so that only her head remained unswallowed, to say good-bye and apologize. *Sorry, kiddo. The gal's gotta eat.* Maybe he'd pat Hazel on the forehead, the same way he used to at bedtime when she was a little girl, before giving her one last reassurance: "Don't worry; I'll make sure you've fully liquefied inside her before Diane and I get intimate. You don't want paternal moans of inter-course to be the sound track to your death, or for Diane to be in motion so the stomach-acid bath of your final demise is violently sloshing around as you suffocate. No, you're entering the undertow of calm waters now. We'll take it easy while she digests. Just close your eyes and pretend you're out camping underneath the stars, getting zipped up inside a warm, full-body sleeping bag that stings a little and wasn't constructed from a sufficiently breathable fabric."

It was this thought that made Hazel begin to actively recoil.

Then she had a worse thought, triggered by childhood Halloween party games where she'd had to reach into bowls and jars she couldn't see the inside of to feel things that mimicked the texture of certain organs—how often did her father clean Diane? Were her fingers beginning to get sweaty inside the constricted space, or had they stumbled onto moisture?

She forcibly pulled back, so hard that Diane's upper body lifted upright in a startling manner; Hazel screamed, thinking for a second that Diane had come to life and was attacking her.

But Hazel was controlling Diane's movements. They were still connected. Hazel stood and Diane lurched forward, hanging like an oversize ventriloquist's dummy that had been improperly placed upon its operator.

Hazel's arm was stuck. The bedside clock read 11:10 AM. If Byron was sending a surprise for her at noon, the timing was not convenient.

8

JASPER WOKE FROM A DEEP SLEEP JUST IN TIME TO CATCH THE nightly eleven o'clock local news, which he was featured on.

"It was like a pietà," an elderly woman told the camera. She held out her arms in a reenactment of Jasper emerging from the water. "Just like one. If Mary were Jesus and Jesus were a dolphin. This guy was a dead ringer for Jesus!" In the background an intoxicated tourist eating an ice-cream cone yelled, "*I am on the TV!*"

Jasper cursed. Though given the circumstances, he knew he had a lot to be grateful for. No one had followed him back to his old motel room after that afternoon's incident (if you wanted to slip past a horde of people, setting down a living bottlenose dolphin was apparently a pretty good distraction). Despite his legs shaking from exertion, he'd managed to sprint off the moment he'd placed the creature on the sand; everyone had gathered around it and assumed Jasper was sprinting off to get help.

Just one stoner-voiced bystander had called out; his concern seemed heartfelt but not flaring with altruism. "Hey, man!" he'd said. "You need a lift to the, I guess, ocean creature clinic? I got my beach cruiser; I'll just need a few bucks for gas!"

And all the news outlets were reporting the dolphin in good health—they said it had gotten lost from its pod and might've stranded itself farther down the shore had the "unidentified male being termed 'Dolphin Savior'" not helped out. All the news stations were using this nickname. It seemed he'd become an Internet sensation in the past few hours. A photo of him holding the dolphin with the words NO BIG DEAL superimposed at the bottom was now a widely circulating meme; a posted five-second video clip of him holding the dolphin and saying this phrase already had millions of views.

He hadn't been identified yet, but people wanted to know his name. He looked good in the photo with his wet shorts clinging to his body. "He's a bit sexy!" one news anchor exclaimed, a woman with a British accent that delighted Jasper. A less-hot female commentator gave a more elaborate compliment: "Maybe I'll put on a dolphin costume and hit the beach this weekend. Undercover investigative journalism, right? Will the Dolphin Savior appear like Batman if I pretend to be in trouble in the water?" The woman's blond cohost was on board with this idea. "Right, pretend to stop breathing! See if he'll do dolphin CPR and give you mouth to mouth!" The camera panned to a smirking male producer wearing a headset mic. "All right, you two," he said. "I'm going to stop this before the blowhole jokes start!"

What in the exact hell was wrong with every person on earth? Jasper wondered. It was a riddle he knew he'd never solve, so he decided to get some more rest. Tomorrow's incognito relocation would mean a busy day.

THE NEXT MORNING JASPER LIFTED THE SLEEVE OF THE HOTEL BATH-robe to trace his fingers along the raised scabs of the dolphin bite. He needed to be sure to wear sunscreen over the next several months to minimize scarring. The needle-nose teeth had sunk in so deeply that hard tissue formation was inevitable; there would be a series of tiny firm beads beneath the skin. The flaw would be visual and textural.

Jasper sighed. A bad mood was coming on. At least he was alive? But he thought of all the wrist-snap exercises he completed so diligently each week. He had such nice flexor muscles. And now this.

It was still fresh. It would probably fade. He was not his father, and his arm was not his father's ugly spider-bite leg. But beauty was security, Jasper knew that much. His father repeatedly fell in love with beautiful women who left. They had power because men desired them. This had been an epiphany for Jasper in his late teens—that he should start working out and investing in his own appearance too. He'd figure out how to live in a way that guaranteed he'd always be the one to leave and not vice versa.

Jasper started the coffee and as an afterthought opened his door to grab the paper. He read the headline and dropped the paper, then bent over and grabbed it and shut the door to his room as quickly as he could.

"Curious Nation Seeks Identity of Dolphin Savior." Jasper looked to see which local paper he was holding, but it was national.

Syndicated. Coast to coast, people were waking up to Jasper's photo and asking themselves if they'd ever seen or known anyone who looked like him. His anonymous code had been breached.

This was a red alert that required immediate action. It meant his hair had to go.

"I can do this," he whispered, though he didn't quite believe it. He'd heard a story about a man who'd had to amputate his own stuck limb to get to safety. The autoamputee had distracted himself with inspirational thoughts of family. Jasper no longer considered himself to have a family. If his father was still alive, they wouldn't recognize each other; Jasper was scrawny and seventeen when he left the house and he'd never looked back. What did he find inspirational? Money, sex, flattery. All of which his hair had helped him get in abundance. Shaving it was somehow going to feel like wounding his penis. He couldn't explain it but it just would. It was going to hurt all over. He'd likely have phantom pains afterward too, still feel it whipping around when he drove his convertible.

He let paranoia motivate him as he turned on the shaver: If he didn't act fast there'd be a knock on his door at any moment, some crackerjack journalist whose unfulfilling childhood gave him a need for relentless success. Probably a whole crew of them. They'd likely already found and interviewed Moley E. and were en route to his hotel. He needed to have convincingly altered his appearance by the time they found him. The hair would be enough to raise a little doubt and let him escape while they rechecked their facts.

His goatee was easier to part with—he trimmed that frequently, sometimes incredibly short. It felt nice to have more of his face shine through. Perhaps cutting his hair wasn't going to limit his pickup numbers at all; it was just going to shift their demographic. Over the next year's regrowth period, he'd exclusively target women who preferred their men clean-cut. He could invent a military background.

When he finished, Jasper got a wadded-up paper fast-food bag out of the trash and scooped all the hair inside, then put the bag next to his suitcase. He didn't know what his eventual plans for it would be, but he did want to bury it or cremate it or something. He'd once conned a woman, Lila, whose twin sister had died of cancer when they were teenagers. Her parents had gotten the cremains of her dead sister put into a diamond ring. Had Lila been forced to pawn the sister's cremains diamond for cash after he'd taken her money? He'd feel bad about that, but he doubted it had happened. What sort of negotiation process with the pawnbroker would that be: *Also, this ring has dead-person ashes in it.* But maybe that happened all the time; maybe lots of people were walking around wearing diamonds they'd bought at pawnshops that were secretly cremains diamonds. Jasper decided he wouldn't mind a man ring with the cremains of his hair in it. Maybe it would kind of preserve its power, Samson-style. He thought of all the wins he'd had with that hair, all the women he'd taken money from. His hair's length was like a ruler by which he could measure his progress as a con artist. He couldn't get rid of it. Saving it and bringing it with him would make him feel less sad. He could pretend he was going to go to a clinic where it could be reattached someday.

Things were going to be fine. He still had a tiny knot of unwelcome feelings at the base of his spine, but maybe that would be there for a while, until all this Dolphin Savior business in the media died down. Stepping into the shower to remedy the sadness with a quick orgasm before he got on the road wouldn't hurt. Then he'd be on his way.

Jasper's usual masturbation routine involved a visit to a mental room he'd named the Trophy Museum. There were a few items there that had nothing to do with his conquests—favorite porn clips, teenage hookups, images of asses and breasts and abdomens he'd seen on the beach and admired but whose owners were broke university students or full-time underearners or average workers in debt. These formed the collage of the room's wallpaper, but the furniture was certainly the women he'd both slept with and gotten money from; it was the combination that made their memory so attractive. Sometimes he wished he could call and tell them this—*I still think about you all the time when I jerk off. I'll think about you when I jerk off until the day I die.* Sore feelings would keep the women from being touched by this, but wasn't it a little nice how he continued to sexually worship them? Wasn't it evidence that he wasn't as terrible a person as they probably felt him to be? They likely assumed that, having gotten their money, he'd never give them a second thought. But leaving them, especially with their funds, was an assurance that Jasper would remember them forever. He'd never forget one of his victories.

Touching himself now in the hotel shower, though, none of these visual images came forth.

What happened instead felt like a TV broadcast getting pirated. The programming of his usual channel had been replaced with mental footage of the dolphin. A picture of shimmering wet gray skin filled his mind; it looked smoother than any shaved thigh. He had a sort of urge to run his lips across it.

Jasper stopped, cracked his knuckles, and tried to start again. He told himself to choose a very specific target to focus on. Why not his latest triumph, Moley E., so fresh in his mind and maybe even a little hotter for being so pissed about the whole 401k thing? He'd gotten her good. He thought about the way she used to squat on top of him and move her hips in a slow circle while she tilted her head back and moaned; when this happened Jasper liked to gaze at her various torso moles and draw constellations in his mind between them—he'd find a series that could be connected to form a giant triangle (left shoulder, right underarm, the flattish and broad one below her navel), then would try finding outline points for increasingly complex shapes as she began her long journey to orgasm. Moley E. took forever, and of course not bringing the cons to orgasm was out of the question; even rushing the cons to orgasm was out of the question. This was all right though; he was good at entertaining himself: if he counted the small reddish birthmark between her breasts and adopted a relaxed interpretation of symmetry, a dodecahedron was possible. Recalling the tense, pleasurable build in his groin that swelled deeper and drew taut as she'd ride him, as he'd craft geometries focused around her left breast so that its nipple would be his hypothetical ejaculatory bull's-eye— this was always a sure thing to help him finish.

But lust was failing to surge in. He couldn't force even a light drizzle of ache for that image. Jasper tried moving his hand frantically, tried moving it slowly, tried taking his hand off completely and drumming his fingers on the shower's tile for a few seconds to let his penis reset. No sexual love at all for Moley E. astride him. Instead, when he reached down and grabbed himself, the moment his fingers applied pressure, what filled Jasper's ears was the sound of the dolphin's chatter. This noise overwhelmed him with the needy warmth an amorous feminine moan usually delivered, brought the same quaver as Moley E.'s grinding hips.

It felt so good that it was hard to take his hands away, despite the disturbing audio. His body felt a need for it that frightened him. Regulation of his lust, particularly his orgasm's pacing and timing, was the bedrock of his sense of stability in life. Nothing else was fixed or certain or completely in his control, but he was master and commander of that arena. His livelihood depended on it.

Now, though, he felt helpless: all he wanted was to let the surge of pleasure overtake him, hear that sound, see flashes of the dolphin's body being slicked over with foaming ocean waves. He held his cock and stood very still. He worried that if he moved his hand at all, even to let go, he'd orgasm. Then he had to stop worrying about that because it was happening no matter what he did. He could hear his disturbed groans, equal parts ecstasy and terror, echo inside the shower.

He opened his eyes. Jasper felt something drip down from the vaulted ceiling and land on his newly bare scalp, and even though he knew it was his own semen, he had the sensation of having just been shat upon by a bird.

Jasper exited the shower, made a provisional throne of pillows on the bed, and ordered an erotic pay-per-view movie. He'd had a wacky orgasm but would now set it right with a normal one. A visual aid would help him overcome a case of cross-species sexual jitters.

He forwarded to the hard-core action scene and let it play for about five minutes before abandoning various forced-denial and positive-thinking rationalizations to panic.

It wasn't that he didn't understand the movie to be arousing—he did. It just wasn't triggering any sensation. The steamy HD girl-on-girl sequence that evolved into an energetic threesome might as well have been grainy parking lot surveillance footage.

His swollen penis was languidly stretched out upon his thigh. He was no longer hard, but the size and shape of his erection remained, like an inflated thing slowly losing air. Its look was one of overfed repose. There was something very post-Thanksgiving-meal digestion about it.

When he closed his eyes, which was how he usually got to the Trophy Museum, what he saw now on the back of his lids was the glistening opening of the dolphin's blowhole.

This was uncool. But this silly new fetish could probably be resolved, instantly, by having sex with a woman. He had time for only a quick hookup, someone casual who wasn't going to don postcoital love goggles. The last thing he needed was someone studying his appearance and realizing, despite his newly shorn locks, that she'd just found the Dolphin Savior. What he needed was a professional—a sexual equal in terms of general attractiveness and the ability to pretend that they themselves were incredibly turned on. He grabbed the phone book and dialed an escort service.

"Beautiful Girls?" a man answered. "Beautiful Girls?" His intonation made the man sound like a talking bird—Jasper pictured a parrot in a tiny bucket hat on the other line, dangling from the receiver by its claw-foot. A woman would be dispatched to him within the hour.

Hanging up the phone, Jasper told himself not to panic. He'd had a brutal encounter with a dolphin and had gotten the sexual wind knocked out of him; he shouldn't make this a bigger deal than it was. He needed to think of his libido as a scared mouse, curled up into a ball in the corner. It needed pampering and warm, desirable flesh to coax it back out.

He turned on the TV to take his mind off things while he waited. But the newscaster was interviewing a series of long-haired, bearded men who'd come forward claiming to be Jasper, the Dolphin Savior caught on tape rescuing the creature on the beach. He realized he'd been so preoccupied with his sexual woes that he'd managed to forget about the plausibly far more pressing worry: being found and killed by one of the women he'd wronged.

Some of the men did bear a passing resemblance to him, prior to his extreme grooming session that morning. Several did not. The man being questioned by the news anchor was perhaps two decades Jasper's senior. He was missing a lot of teeth.

"What about the tattoos on your arm?" the news anchor asked him. The screen went to a close-up shot of one of the many cellphone photos of Jasper holding the dolphin, then zoomed in on his upper torso. "In this picture the Dolphin Savior doesn't have any tattoos," the voice-over said.

"These are brand new," the man responded. "I got them this morning. I heal quickly and always have. I take an echinacea supplement." The camera panned to a close-up of his faded tattoo, a scribbly outline of a naked woman wrapped around a giant marijuana leaf.

Jasper turned off the television. Despite the room's cranked AC, he was sweating. He pulled the desk chair up to the now-empty minifridge, opened the door, and placed his head inside. The goose bumps that formed on his scalp felt painful.

CALLA WAS THE REAL DEAL.

She had a long black braid that hung down to her waist and swung across her butt like a pendulum when she walked. Normally he loved long hair, but he found himself appreciating the fact that it was out of the way.

Why? he worried. Because dolphins don't have hair?

Her naturally curvaceous breasts had been enhanced with silicone, which added a reassuring density and made the implants feel dough-encased. But her ass was the obvious standout: yielding, spongy flesh rested atop the structure of musculature; something about it was reminiscent of wedding-cake tiers. Normally, Jasper knew this would make him feel horny in a way that was indistinguishable from being hungry. But his appreciation for her body wasn't puppeteering his lust. A vital string between his brain and his crotch had been cut.

He ran the palms of his hands over the hard tips of her nipples, one of his favorite moves, then frowned at her breasts. They felt as confusing to him as malfunctioning knobs on a kitchen sink: he'd turned them every which way, but no water would come out. "Oh my god," he muttered to himself. How could this be happening? Why wasn't he getting hard? "Would you turn around one more time?"

She obliged, swaying just enough to engage all the right parts of her body in movement, bending over, facing back up to look at him suggestively. He saw her fingers reach up toward her braid to undo it but he stopped her. "Actually, your hair's great like that. If you could leave it like that? Thank you." Yes, he was in awe of her physique. It looked remarkable. But what he really wanted to do was open up the screen door and hear the ocean. "Let me go in the shower for a minute," he said. "I'll be right back."

He turned on the water and closed his eyes, letting it pour down over his face—this action brought an immediate surge of relaxation. He leaned forward so that his entire head was beneath the water, took a deep inhale, and began a count of ten to wait before exhaling.

Then he heard Calla shriek.

Were the cops here? A news station? Moley E.?

He ran into the bedroom wet and naked to find Calla brandishing a pink Gogol Taser gun in his direction.

"Oh!" Jasper exclaimed. Maybe she'd figured out he was the Dolphin Savior and was about to blackmail him? He nearly groaned with sadness at this thought because even imagining being blackmailed by a beautiful woman, a woman whose ass was authentically worthy of anything that the material world might piece together as an offering, did not turn him on anymore in the slightest. Whatever had happened yesterday in the water had ruined him. "What's with the Taser?" he finally asked. He sounded annoyed but couldn't help it. He almost wanted her to shoot him so the pain could momentarily give him something else to focus on.

But maybe if she shot him in the groin with the Taser he might be stunned back to normalcy . . . an electroshock therapy sort of cure. He reached down and gathered his genitals in his hands.

"I swear to god," Calla screamed. "Move again and I will fucking do it!"

That's fine, he wanted to say; *I don't think I'll ever be able to have sex with a human being again, and that's how I make my living. You're in a unique position to understand this, given your career, although there are many differences. The fact that you came to my room armed tells me that your job is not as enjoyable as mine. There really isn't anything I don't love about what I do. Sometimes the guilt can creep up to a level that's annoying, but honestly even the guilt is great for my ego because if I weren't so good at what I do, there wouldn't be any reason to feel guilty. Do you get what I'm saying? My life has broken somehow; a dolphin was involved and then I had to shave my hair just to keep from being hunted down by past cons due to everyone having cell phones and devices with freaking cameras. I have lost my reason for being. Pretty sure. So accept my apology for not losing further marbles over this new threat of yours that could not possibly take anything away from me that I care about.*

Except cash! Jasper realized.

"Are you robbing me?" he asked. "Because I don't have any more money than what I paid you when you arrived. I'll open the safe for you right now so you can see." He had a lot more money, but it was not in the safe.

"I found your sick trophy bag, you freak," she yelled. She kicked over the opened paper hamburger take-out bag Jasper's shorn hair was in.

"Oh that," Jasper said. How best to explain the situation? *One wouldn't just toss a severed kidney into the trash!* he wanted to argue. Spilling out of the hamburger bag, his hair looked like it could start twitching to life any second. If he discarded it, he'd always think of it out there in the world—in a landfill, moving around in a low octopus crawl, disoriented but determined to find him. He could foresee a rainy future night at the house of a new con: the two of them seated on a leather sofa, enjoying a bottle of wine by candlelight, just about to go in for a kiss after he'd professed his love. Then a flash of lightning hits and the woman looks toward the window and screams: a mass of hair has crawled up the glass of the windowpane and is hanging suspended from either side by two tendriled locks. When she runs to the kitchen to call 911, he opens the door, understanding that his former coif has returned. Except in his enthusiasm he'd forget that it had been replaced: his hair has grown back. And when the old hair, which crawled through hellish layers of garbage and overcame innumerable odds to remount Jasper's scalp and reign again, looks up in the rain and sees the new hair, it would not be fair to blame it for screeching wildly, leaping up at Jasper, and latching onto his face in an attempt to rip the new hair away. It wouldn't realize its wet torso was cloaking Jasper's nose and mouth as it waged war upon his present scalp, wouldn't feel Jasper fall down to the ground. When it finally rendered Jasper bald (the new hair, olive-oil soft, wouldn't stand a chance against sinewy locks whose muscles had been forged creeping across gravel alleyways in the search for its former host), when it finally slithered back atop Jasper's head, it might feel such relief to be home at last that it wouldn't realize it had killed Jasper until it found itself buried alive.

That mustn't be allowed to happen. Jasper had always been interested in science fiction—not the books, of course, but films—and the ways it intersected with the supernatural. He wasn't ultimately sure about what he believed in terms of ghosts and aliens or even God, but here was the thing: why give something rife for haunting an opening? That's what throwing the hair away would do. The corpse of his former mane would have to be purified with fire, its soul cleanly released into the hereafter, its ashes poured into his next bottle of shampoo except for the small reserve he'd have put into a diamond, or a gemstone. He could find a pawned class ring from a prestigious college and have it applied to that.

Probably no effective way to explain this to Calla, though.

Wait, why was she moving toward the bag? Was she going to take it with her?

"Leave that alone!" Jasper cried; he reached toward it and Calla defensively tossed the bag off into the corner. Jasper chased after it, picking it up and drawing it close to his chest. Then his hands were compacting around the paper bag; they were squeezing it far tighter than his bag of hair should be squeezed. Jasper felt his back arch around a central locus of pain, felt himself begin to shake. The pain in the middle of his back was eating its way through his body;

he looked down at his chest expecting to see the protruding tip of a javelin of some sort, but he knew he had not been impaled. Just Tasered.

"This concludes our erotic session," Calla shouted. "I'm way not into cops, but I will cheer when they catch you. I'm sure they've given you some title that makes you think you're hot shit, the Sunshine Scalper or something. Well, believe me, you are not on your game."

"It's *my* hair," he finally managed to mutter.

"No. That ain't man hair," Calla said.

Gender bias aside, the compliment pleased Jasper. He was able to smile for a microsecond before another stabbing jolt made him howl.

9

HAZEL BEGGED AND SCREAMED FOR DIANE TO LET GO OF HER ARM, as though the doll were a hairless, giant-breasted attack dog; Hazel pulled her off the bed and began kicking her, then started knocking Diane's head against the wall before trying a few other actions that illogically supposed Diane capable of feeling pain or losing consciousness. Hazel then attempted to break the doll's head open on the nightstand like a piggy bank, but Diane's exterior proved to be almost indestructible. This made Hazel realize Diane's makers had designed her to be able to withstand incredible beatings, which made Hazel sad for humanity. *And what does that say about* you, *humanity*, Hazel thought, *that a grown woman whose arm is stuck down the throat of her elderly father's love doll feels sorry for you?* It was not a spirited advertisement for mankind.

Next, in a sort of conjoined-twin crawl, Hazel dragged Diane out of the bedroom and headed in the direction of the bath, stopping in the hallway for a moment to sit and have a break and look at the family portraits lining the walls. "That was my aunt Lena," Hazel said to Diane, pointing with her free hand, even though Diane's head was not facing in the picture's direction. Aunt Lena was dead, and Diane wasn't alive or sentient so it wasn't the most utilitarian introduction, but Hazel was sick of everything needing to have a *function*. Function was the only thing Byron cared about. His first question to everyone, always: "What do you *do*?" by which he meant, *What can you do for me?* Hazel wanted to make a real effort from now on for her words, actions, and existence to be as pointless as possible. From this day forward, she vowed to be a living middle finger of inanity raised in the direction of either Byron or his grave.

But of course she was going to die before Byron did, whether he took her out or not. Technology was on his side, as were any/all powerful forces of evil in the universe, whether real or metaphorical.

"Aunt Lena had the longest braid I'd ever seen," Hazel told Diane, grunting and dragging her a few more inches down the hallway. The doll's fingers made a musical xylophonic sound when they moved over the top of the heating grate on the floor. "Uncoiled, her braid probably would've hung down past her feet like a tail. As a kid I wished my hair was as long as hers so I could do that—tuck it into the back of my pants, then cut a hole in between the rear pockets of all my jeans, and pull the braid out of it so it hung there like I was part horse. Only a small part, since it would just be the tail and nothing else on me horse." Hazel gave a final lengthy tug and at last she and Diane reached the bathroom entrance where the hallway's carpet transformed to tile. Hazel felt breathless; she lay down next to Diane with her cheek on the floor so the heat could transfer out of her face against the cool linoleum.

It wasn't a position void of intimacy there on the ground with Diane. Hazel's face was so close to the doll's that even in the relative dark she could see the tiny raised buttons beneath Diane's hair where a wig snapped onto the scalp. Being on the floor of her septuagenarian bachelor father's personal washroom, Hazel also noticed upsetting body hairs strewn about her field of vision. Nothing was worse for one's emotional comfort than scrupulous observance, Hazel reminded herself. So instead of indulging in the sensory information around her, Hazel gazed deeply into Diane's nearest eye. She tried to think of Diane as less sex and more doll, to make the percentage more 20/80 than 50/50. Though there were things Hazel would've liked to change about Diane's functionality in that moment, such as equipping Diane with an "autoregurgitate" button so her arm could be readily extracted from the doll's throat, Hazel certainly could not critique Diane's listening abilities.

"Aunt Lena never took advantage of my horse-jeans idea," Hazel continued. "What she did instead was wear the braid pinned up into a domed mound on the top of her head. This was her hairstyle from when she was sixteen or so until emphysema killed her in her sixties. She smelled like smoke all the time. I tried one of her scarves on once and it smelled so smoky that I had this image of her braid-dome being filled with emergency rations of cigarettes, like her own sort of camel-hump storage unit to fall back on if resources ever grew scarce."

Hazel sat upright and looked over at the tub, which was outfitted with large silver handles and a bench seat for her father's safety. Her idea was to try submerging Diane's head in hot water to see if it made the doll's rubber throat any stretchier. Hazel still had to foist Diane up, over and into the tub, so instead of wasting her strength standing them both up again to turn on the light, she grabbed Diane's long right leg with her free hand and operated it like an extension wand, finally thonging the light switch between the doll's big and second toes.

Getting Diane inside the tub was a less dainty production. For whatever reason Hazel had an absurd paranoia that water was going to make the doll freak out, so she tried to talk in the soothing, even tone a professional animal groomer might use with a stray cat. "This will feel great," Hazel encouraged, "to take a nice, relaxing bath." She heaved the doll inside then climbed in after her and powered on the faucet. But watching the water rise over the doll's nose and mouth gave Hazel an unsettling homicidey feeing, so she grabbed some shower gel. Maybe bubbles would make the scene more festive. "Smell that, Diane?" Hazel asked. "Freesia!" The bath products had probably been her mother's, kept but unused in the years since her death.

It seemed like the closer Hazel's father came to his own expiration date, the more he granted everything around him an endless life span. Yesterday she'd found a box of cereal in his pantry from Smather's grocery. "So?" he'd questioned. "That store closed over a decade ago, Dad," she'd said. "The chain went bankrupt." "Well, has the box been opened?" he asked. It hadn't, so Hazel knew that was the end of the conversation. "I actually don't even think I like that kind of cereal," he'd added. "When I die, that's all yours."

AS HAZEL WAITED FOR THE TUB TO FILL, SHE THOUGHT ABOUT A story Aunt Lena had told her, an ancient punishment for murder. If you killed someone, the decomposing corpse would be strapped to your body so infection from its rotting matter would eventually spread to you and take your life as well. The foreboding tale had always stuck with Hazel. But she'd never felt that the way Aunt Lena tried to make the metaphor relevant to Hazel's own childhood made any sense. "Killing them would kill you, in other words," Aunt Lena liked to stress as a follow-up, "so be sure to keep your room clean! So just say no to drugs!"

Hazel then tried pulling at her still-stuck arm and was reminded of an unusual fishing practice she'd heard about called "noodling." The fisherman would stick his bare arm into underwater holes to lure catfish, and the fish would bite down on his arm and could then be wrenched from the water. But if the catfish was large enough, it sometimes could drag the person under for long enough to drown them, or it could retreat into an alcove where the person's limb would get stuck and they couldn't surface for air.

And that reminded Hazel of being a kid and getting caught with her hand and arm literally inside the cookie jar, because if her mother saw her she'd yell, "FREEZE!" and Hazel would have to turn into a guilt-statue of her crime and stand there feeling the cookies on the tips of her fingers, even perhaps picking one up then dropping it then picking another up and dropping it as her mother lectured on. "Hazel!" she'd scream. "Why are you hell-bent on hitchhiking the malnutrition highway? Do you know what broccoli is like to your body? It is like a hundred-dollar bill. When you eat it, you are paying yourself with health. Do you know what a cookie is like? It is Monopoly money! You're giving your body fraudulent currency. Your teeth are going to try to go down to the vitamin and mineral store to buy some calcium, and you know what the checkout clerk is going to have to say? 'I'm sorry, Hazel's body, but you don't have sufficient funds to pay for this because Hazel is a blockhead sugar addict who disobeys her brilliant parents.' And your body is going to start crying and maybe even begging.

'Please take pity on us,' it will say. 'If we don't get calcium right now, our teeth will fall out and then everyone at school will make fun of us and we will never have a boyfriend or get a job or be loved.' And the clerk will just have to shrug and say, 'I have no idea why a young lady would behave so stupidly as to eat cookies before a nourishing dinner, thereby ruining her appetite and forfeiting all the nutrients she so desperately needs to grow into a respectable adult instead of a toothless mutant, but if that was her decision then she deserves whatever comes to her.'" And the whole time her mother spoke, Hazel would be scraping as many chocolate and cookie particles under her fingernails as possible so that when the sermon finally ended and she was sent to her room until dinner, she could eat the sugary crumbs and feel like the mission hadn't been a complete wash.

The water had almost reached a good soaking height. She decided to pretend that Diane's head wasn't actually underwater; instead Diane was a civilian who'd gotten trapped inside a storm drain and everything *except* her head was under, and she was very scared and it was Hazel's job to reassure her and help her be patient while they tried to get her out. Hazel reached down and patted Diane's head, then grimaced: the doll's hair was liquifying into a slimy paste. Should she have taken Diane's wig off before bringing her into the water? Hazel gave Diane's limbs a quick feel then cleared her throat. "You know, Diane? Things change but things also stay the same." By which she meant that even if Diane's hair didn't make it, the rest of her body seemed to be holding up just fine.

Applied to herself, the saying had a different sort of meaning. Here she was, back in her parents' house, her hand sort of caught in a cookie jar. "But luckily," Hazel said, "your throat is large enough that it's not like a little kid could get his hand stuck inside. Not unless he was a really big little kid. I only had a problem because I'm an adult. I don't see you as being a hazard to children, Diane. That's another thing you've got going for you."

It was just then, just as Hazel was reaching out her free arm to turn off the water, that the super-white-flash fireworks started up in her brain. Hazel couldn't see a thing except a series of glowing sparks shooting off behind her eyes.

She leaned forward in the bathtub and vomited, then vomited again. But that didn't stop the sparks from coming.

MINUTES LATER WHEN HAZEL REGAINED CONSCIOUSNESS, THE BATH-tub was overflowing and the water had started to turn cold. She realized later that she should've shut the faucet off at this point— that would've stopped the noise and the gushing and probably given her more time to think, but her first thought was SAVE DIANE.

Hazel had a burst of adrenaline. She'd heard about this—how in times of crisis, petite mothers in sweater sets get the ability to lift a station wagon off a child's pinned leg. But she'd never experienced it personally until now. Hazel cried out Diane's name and pulled upward so forcefully that Diane was launched from the bathtub. But when the doll hit the ground, it pulled Hazel's arm with her in an unplanned way. Then all Hazel felt was pain.

Emotional pain Hazel was a true soldier at. She was the equivalent of a wounded Civil War cadet who whistled folk tunes during a battlefield amputation while the bone saw did its thing. Physical pain Hazel had far less experience with. The shoulder dislocation really hurt.

At this point, the running bathtub water in the background no longer even registered. Hazel lay down on the floor next to Di and they sat there together, shipwrecked. Diane's face was completely occluded by her gummy wig, which had a matted golden retriever texture now, and Hazel felt the shame of this too because if Diane's face looked like the backside of a giant dog, it meant Hazel's arm appeared to be coming out of said dog's backside.

What had just happened to her, before the tub filled up and her shoulder got ripped out? It made little sense. In recall, the incident felt a little bit like being in a movie theater, watching a screen.

The movie theater Hazel frequented in college played a concession-stand commercial that made her panicked instead of hungry. Its premise was a roller-coaster ride in outer space on a track made out of filmstrips. Giant snacks hovered in the air as the virtual ride zipped forward: it passed an enormous box of popcorn, massive hot dogs, a soda whose straw rotated in a whirlpool motion.

Hazel remembered the dream from her blackout as being a little like that commercial, except instead of passing by junk food, she'd found herself passing by supersize images of Byron's face. Then the ride had turned into a terrible funhouse, and Byron's head had swelled even larger and his mouth opened wide as she'd tumbled down his throat.

Then she'd smelled spaghetti. Byron had a tincture of this artificial odor on his desk, for sniffing when he ate his meals, which were flavorless nutritional shakes (the shakes were weird enough, but Hazel also couldn't understand how the only food smell he used was spaghetti. "Don't you want to smell something else, for variety?" she used to ask him. "A cinnamon roll? A bucket of chicken?" He'd blink once, twice, then shake his head no.). Aside from these shakes he really didn't eat, preferring to get weekly transdermal supplements via pneumatic injection guns. Eating grossed him out; he felt it was antiquated and menial. He'd wanted to get a port implanted in his abdomen where he could deliver daily sustenance to his stomach via a gel or blended material, some texture just bulky enough that his digestive organs wouldn't atrophy, but he'd decided against it since eating is such a metaphorical act across all cultures. Byron worried that it might affect his business dealings if others, particularly foreign partners from European countries that didn't romanticize efficiency, found out he did not participate in calorie swallowing and traditional digestion.

Maybe she'd had an allergic reaction to some chemical compound in the rubber of Diane's throat?

Her arm hurt badly and her brain was acting strange. Hazel pried open the cupboard beneath the bathroom sink with her foot, hoping to have the good fortune of finding a decades-old bottle of aspirin. Her father had never been big on pills. Whenever she felt ill growing up, no matter what the symptoms, his solution was always to go lie down in bed with a wet washcloth over one's eyes. *It won't make you any worse*, he'd say.

Instead she found the full inventory of a small pharmacy. The stockpile seemed to have been assembled based on an opiate addict's Make-A-Wish fever dream. Hazel curled her foot into a shovel shape and started moving the prescription containers out of the cupboard and onto the watery floor, where they spun and bobbed and eventually floated over to her. "Look!" she said aloud to Diane. "A message in a bottle!"

The first one that landed in Hazel's hand was Percocet. She took a mouthful, scooped up some water from the floor to wash them down with, then sat back against the outside of the bathtub and panted. "I'd share," she eye-roll-joked to Diane, "but your mouth is already full."

When Hazel woke up again, it was to her father's terry-cloth slipper standing next to her face. His slipper was absorbing a lot of water. Hazel was grateful for the rubberized four-prong antiskid bottom of her father's cane.

"Let me guess," he said, his voice thundering down and echoing within the bathroom. From her angle on the ground, with his gray beard and wrathful eyes and bathrobe and cane, her father looked like an angry Moses holding an orthopedic staff. The sea had parted and she'd somehow survived the flood, but now he was going to scold her to death.

"You found my stash of drugs, got loopy and wanted someone to talk to, went to find a sympathetic ear in Diane then got the spins and puked on her. So you tried to bring her in here and wash her off but you were so high things got out of hand. Am I in the ballpark? Why your arm is stuck between her lips I do not know. That's where you've stumped the detective. My working theory is that whatever you took began to kick in after the water started running, and maybe you thought Diane's open mouth was a flotation ring you needed to shove your wrist inside. But I'm open to correction. Enlighten me, please, Hazel. Give me something to focus on besides my obvious failures as a parent."

"My arm's dislocated," Hazel yelled. She wasn't saying this to her father, specifically; she didn't expect him to care or help, but felt it possible to get the attention of a neighbor who'd hear her cries and phone for a medic. Given the frequency of ambulances visiting the Shady Place retirement mobile home community, it didn't seem too far-fetched that one might coincidentally be on its way. Or if a Byron-cam was in the house, she was covered. For once she missed the meddling assistance of her engagement ring. "My arm!" Hazel repeated.

"How strange that my upstanding daughter should have an

issue with her angel wing. Yes, I noticed that, believe it or not. Age has dulled my perception, but an arm extended out an extra foot or so will still raise my eyebrows. Tony's on his way. Leon's kid, a chiropractor. Leon owes me a solid. I filled a badger that moved in beneath his ornamental lawn windmill full of buckshot. However, also at my request, Tony won't be here for a few hours, for two reasons. The first is that I want you to feel more pain. The second is that I'd like you to clean the throw-up off yourself and remove your hand from my pretend old lady's throat before we have guests. If it's not too much trouble."

"It's stuck."

"Not for long." He reached into his bathrobe pocket and took out a spray can of WD-40, then used the bottom of his cane to move the globby wig up and back from Diane's face. "Good night for now, sweet girl," he said to Diane. Then he popped her faceplate off, slid it forward on Hazel's arm like an oversize bangle, and went to work trying to free Hazel's arm. Diane's internal back-of-mouth sleeve had the product name, size, and copyright info tattooed on its bottom in stretched lettering: THROATGINA™ extra small. Had her father opted for the Throatgina medium or even a regular small, Hazel thought, perhaps they wouldn't be in this predicament, but she kept her viewpoint of shared blame quiet.

Luckily the Throatgina's end pouch zipped open. Her father squirted a liberal amount of industrial lubricant inside and attempted to pull downward, but that just yanked Hazel's arm.

"It's not budging," he said. When he slid the bottom up like a sleeve to reveal Hazel's fingers, he coughed—Hazel looked down to see they had grown purple with asphyxiation. "Hell," he said. "We'll have to cut it off. Her throat, not your hand. You're fully reimbursing my replacement purchase."

It made Hazel feel better to know they sold replacement Throatginas. She wasn't the world's first Throatgina wrecker.

But instead of feeling relief when he cut the throat off, her arm started hurting worse—the extreme pressure had been anesthetizing it somehow. "Hold your shirt in the front," he said. "Wow, is it soiled! I'll cut it off so you don't have to move your arm. Then you'll need to dunk yourself in the tub a few times. When all the mess is off you, just wrap yourself in a towel and go wait on the couch. It won't hurt to show a little skin in front of Tony. He's a straight shooter. I like that kid. He's married, but being his mistress would be an upgrade from your last husband in terms of the personality factor I think. If he hits on you in any way, reciprocate immediately. Full force. I'll mention to him that you're newly single and don't have strong opinions. Maybe he's looking for something fun on the side." Her father then took a towel off the shelf and placed it over the top of Diane's open head cavity to preserve her dignity.

"Let me explain," Hazel started. Per usual, the truth would not suffice. "I'd just put Diane into bed and was bent over her, pulling up the covers, when I thought I heard something fall down her throat."

Her father's eyebrows rose with skepticism but Hazel soldiered on. "I figured maybe it was an earring . . . so I reached inside to check and it felt like my fingertips brushed up against something, but they pushed it down farther. So I reached in more . . ."

Hazel bent forward to pantomime, forgetting he'd just cut her shirt open in the back. It fell to the floor, waterlogged, at which point she and her father were both surprised to see an avalanche of prescription pill bottles spill forward. She'd apparently shoved several of them into each cup of her brassiere before losing consciousness—once she felt the pills' euphoria, she must've been struck with the urge to stockpile. Suddenly curious, Hazel tried to surreptitiously shift her weight from one butt cheek to the other, and lo and behold, she'd stashed some in her underwear too.

Now probably wasn't the time to float theories about her ex-husband having placed a microchip in her brain.

"Clean yourself up nice for Tony," her father said, his voice shaking a little. He put his arm around Diane; they were a unified team now, just like he'd been with her mother. Even though Diane was naked, with a towel over her head, there was something solemn about the mood she was radiating, something very *look what you've done to your father*-ish.

TONY WORE NOVELTY SCRUBS PRINTED WITH A FLESH DESIGN OF A muscled bodybuilder in a Speedo. Hazel's father wanted to know where he could purchase an identical pair.

"My female clients love 'em," Tony said and smiled.

"She fell in the bathtub," her father began to explain, offering up a handy excuse for both Hazel's injury and her attire, but Tony was ready to get down to business. He cracked his knuckles, and then his neck.

"This will only take a second. Just breathe in and I'm gonna count to three, then breathe out. One. Two."

On "two" Hazel felt a searing jolt of pain and noticed her eyes rolling skyward, then woke to a view of Tony's nostrils, a tiny flash-light moving back and forth across her pupils.

"There you are. Good as new. If you feel any complications, go right to the ER and tell them you popped it back in yourself. Technically you should get a follow-up X-ray. If you're the sort to make a mountain out of a molehill." With that, Tony turned to leave. Hazel's father jumped onto his Rascal, sidesaddle, like a trick rider, and motored after him, but wheeled back a few moments later looking forlorn. "You're not his type, he told me. I'm guessing by that he means you're too old. Don't worry, we'll think of something. Listen, Hazel—"

Her arm was sore but she could wiggle her fingers. She had to do the thing she'd sworn not to do, call Byron and forfeit a battle to win the war. The blackout in the bathtub was definitely a trick he'd pulled, though she wasn't sure how he'd done it or even what had transpired. She needed to get to the bottom of it. "Hold that thought, Dad," she said.

How he'd pulled off getting her to hallucinate that way she wasn't sure, but Hazel felt confident Byron just wanted her to *think* he'd put a chip into her brain. First she ran to the bathroom and did a full head and face exam for scars. She didn't see any. Maybe he'd sent some nanobot into her father's house that had deployed an aerosol hallucinogen. Maybe he'd lowered a powerful electro-magnet down over her head through the bathroom light fixture. Who knows how he did it? His goal was likely for her to feel scared enough to go talk to him about it, enough to agree to get in a car and return to The Hub. He probably figured that once he got her back on his turf he could either woo or frighten her into staying. What she had to do was make Byron see that no matter how im-pressive the technological magic tricks he was pranking her with were, they were useless: Hazel wouldn't be changing her mind.

She went out to the safe and entered their anniversary date and tried not to be impressed by the way it opened, several pieces rising and clicking, moving into place like shifting puzzle parts against the quiet pops and hisses of microhydraulics.

The phone inside the safe was already ringing. She answered.

"It won't work, Byron. Whatever bad-taste trick you just pulled didn't leave me riddled with fear, and it certainly didn't make me want to talk to you."

There was a click, a brief pause. Of course he hadn't been waiting on the other end of the phone. Now that she'd picked up, he was being hailed.

"Hazel," he finally said. "So nice to hear from you. Thank you for answering my call."

10

Hazel scoffed. "Is that what you want me to think happened? That you downloaded information from my brain? I'll admit, you made me wonder. I even checked for a scar. But there is no chip, is there? There's just you wanting to make me believe something. Let's part ways and call it a day."

"I never thought I'd see you in a bathtub with a sex doll. Admit it, Hazel: after all this time we can still surprise each other."

She felt a trapdoor of despair open wide at the bottom of her stomach, her insides slipping from their normal shelves and falling into one central pileup below her navel. No, Hazel tried to convince herself, Byron was lying. But lies could help her figure out the truth. The bathroom didn't have windows, but he'd seen inside.

"You put cameras in my father's house?"

"Your mind is the camera, Hazel."

"Bullshit."

"I understand your skepticism. Ask me about anything you've seen, thought, touched, or smelled in the past twenty-four hours. Even your drunk memories. Actually, I might know more about them than you do. How much of last night do you remember?"

Her having gotten drunk was an easy guess. What else was she going to do after leaving her husband? "You sound like a bad psychic," she told him. "You want me to give you information you can read into and guess from. The more I tell you, the more you'll incredibly seem to know. It's not going to work."

"Hazel." Then he sighed, and when he sighed Hazel really started to lose it, because he sighed when he got bored. He found it dull when people were resisting something he knew they would eventually accept. The interim, when he had to repeat himself over and over until the other person's view finally did flip and change, was annoying tedium.

"Hay-zel," he said. This "affectionate" pronunciation of her name drove her nuts. As though it near-rhymed with "gazelle." "After all our time together," he continued. "After everything you know about me. You're doubting me when I tell you I've done this?" When Hazel didn't answer, he drew in a sharp breath. "Fine," he said. "Let's do it your way. A cold reading."

"Great," she answered. Hazel thought about hanging up the phone but was curious, despite understanding that her life was absolutely over. Because if Byron didn't have all the information he claimed, he wouldn't dare push it. *The way you avoid losing*, Byron always said, *is by removing any possibility of loss.*

There was a chip in her brain. Byron had downloaded everything she'd done and thought for the past twenty-four hours.

"This will only be embarrassing for you, you know." The tone of his voice lowered now, directed itself a little bit aside, as though he were trying to do her a favor. "You're sure you want to rehash this?"

Hazel swallowed. Her mouth kept growing watery. "Did anything bother you?" she asked. "Or did you find it all hysterical?"

She sat down in the grass now, to keep things from getting too spinny. She probably needed to eat. The painkillers were wearing off. Hazel started pulling up one blade of grass after another, like the lawn was a type of rote punishment: if she ripped up every blade of grass in the backyard, she'd be allowed to wake up and this would all be a bad dream.

"Hazel, come now. Of course the entire timeline of events troubled me. You're my beloved wife. No, it's not easy to see you trying to play teenager. I'm sure it's not easy for your father, either. He clearly wants his space."

In the past, whenever Byron showed Hazel one of his new inventions and she tried to find a flaw in it, he always had a bulletproof answer for everything. He loved that game and he never wanted her to stop playing it with him. The trick to keeping her playing along, and she realized now that Byron had counted on this, was a delusional sense of hope on her behalf—she'd kept trying to beat him because she'd thought that one day maybe she could. It was gambling-addict thinking. *This time will be different; it will make up for all the others.*

Now she herself was his newest invention, but Hazel was done playing. Trying to poke holes in his victory would only result in heartbreak for her.

"Why be up-front about it?" she asked. "Why tell me what you did?"

Hazel swore she could hear his smile through the phone. The scales of his lips sliding across one another.

"I tell my wife everything."

"You didn't tell me you were putting a chip in my brain."

"Okay. I tell my wife everything eventually."

"So I'll just have it taken out." There was a long silence—had she heard Byron just nearly laugh?

"I don't recommend that."

Now she was the one letting out the impatient sigh. "What, will it kill me if it's taken out? What if I'd died having it put in, Byron?"

"Hay-zel. Your life means everything to me. That's why I still want to be there for every moment of it, even though you'd rather not spend it together. The implantation procedure is very safe. Like you said yourself, no scars. I won't bore you, but it's been there for a while. I hoped I wouldn't ever have to turn it on, but then you left and I just missed you so much."

"What about the extraction procedure?"

"You won't be needing that. But I do have to warn you—if you showed up at a hospital spouting some nonsense about a brain implant, you'd appear insane. Like much of our best technology, this is truly ahead of its time. It won't show up on any scan the doctors do."

"Will its performance be affected if I shoot myself in the head?"

"*Your* performance will be affected. You don't want to kill yourself, Hazel. It would make my stock rise. Sympathy buying. It's a real phenomenon."

"So I'll just go somewhere the download won't work. Live in a mountaintop cave in Tibet."

"Ha. Your prototype doesn't have an active GPS because those are detectable. Instead, each download gives us your exact coordinates. You'd have a twenty-four-hour lead, so I suppose we could have a fun chase if you wanted to, but you couldn't outrun us every single day. You wouldn't have the resources."

A wayward ant from the lawn found its way onto Hazel's leg and began crawling across. She looked down and pondered squishing it, then realized this was the closest she'd ever come to understanding what it would feel like to trade places with Byron. She was an ant on his leg. Worse, he'd be delighted after tomorrow's download when he found out she'd had that thought, and delighted by her horror of realizing he was going to know about it.

Every time she went to the bathroom, Hazel realized, Byron would now see whatever she saw. Was she supposed to not look after wiping? No. Screw that. She'd look even longer.

"And what if I come home?" Hazel was curious about the reward Byron would offer. But going home was out of the question. *THERE IS NO FUCKING WAY, BYRON!* Hazel thought very emphatically, since thinking something to Byron was now more or less the same as saying it to him twenty-four hours into the future.

"Then we could proceed with the meld and I'd be the happiest man on earth. I'm probably already the happiest man on earth, of course, but with my wife at my side, I'll be happier than the second-happiest guy by an even greater margin."

Hazel paused. "With the meld, would the downloads stop?"

"It would be a real-time stream of information from your brain to mine. Not a once-a-day push. You wouldn't feel it the way you do now when an entire day's data gets sent."

"I wouldn't get to see your thoughts though, I assume?" Nothing with Byron ever worked both ways.

"Well, no. I deal with very sensitive information, after all. Here's the thing, Hazel. You have important proprietary technology inside you. I cannot convey the time and financial resources that went into getting this operational. Operational inside you, in particular, calibrated to your physiology. We have years of data and research on you. It's too great a risk for my company to have such an asset loose in the world, and too great a waste not to use it. I don't know what might happen if you fail to cooperate. Imagine the competition finding out and abducting you." Byron made a wincing noise. "We can't risk that."

The line went quiet for a moment. "Byron?" Hazel asked.

"I invested in you." His voice lowered with anger. "Your noncompliance will set us back years. Not just in terms of research. Think of the public rollout, Hazel. You're my documented wife of a decade. That's an established social fact. People are going to be leery of melding technology. They trust love and romance, though. If we promote it as part of our marital narrative—us wanting to take our closeness and relationship to a whole new level—it will be intimate instead of invasive. I could divorce and go start a new relationship, but people wouldn't trust it as much with someone I'd just married."

Hazel looked up and saw her father scoot past the window, return from the opposite direction a few moments later, then scoot past again. He was circling the couch, his scooter version of pacing. He was upset. "You know, I need to go clean up the bathroom. Let me think on all this. Will I always throw up during the downloads?"

"I'm not sure. Let me ask. Fiffany?" Hazel blushed; she'd once again wrongly assumed Byron was alone. "Fiffany says statistical probability favors you building up a tolerance."

"How thoughtful of statistical probability, to shine so kindly upon me. Take care, Byron. Always a pleasure."

Hazel dropped the phone on the lawn and headed inside. She needed to smooth things over with her father.

"DAD," HAZEL BEGAN. HE WHIPPED THE SCOOTER AROUND AND PUT IT in PARK.

He was readying to give a speech.

"This doesn't even have to do with what happened today. I'm still not clear about what that was. I don't think I care to be. But I promise this is unrelated."

"Okay. What is it?" Hazel was trying to decide whether or not to tell him about the chip. What would be the point though? There was nothing he could do.

"I need to rent out the back-porch room where you're staying. I'm happy to rent it to you if you can cough up the cash. If you can't, I'm not kicking you out. I want to be clear on that. You can sleep in the reclined La-Z-Boy, or the carport is completely empty now. Except the renter will probably have a car, so maybe the recliner is the better option."

"Rent?" Hazel asked. She knew giving payment in return for lodging wasn't an unusual custom. She'd just been hoping to play the whole "daughter" card until she figured out how to disappear, if she could survive long enough to do so. But disappearing didn't seem to be possible, now. "Do you need money, or is this more a thing of principle?"

For the first time in her life, Hazel understood the importance of having principles and holding them sacred: Don't marry someone evil for money; don't place futuristic mind-sharing technology inside others without their consent, etc. Byron had cured her of her ethical apathy. Maybe telling her father that would make him proud. It seemed worth a try. "Dad, I admit that I lived the past thirtyish years of my life sans integrity. I mean I didn't, like, kill anybody. Not that I feel I deserve a medal for that or anything. Actually I think it's easier to get medals *for* killing people, right? Isn't that crazy?"

"I need money, Hazel. Charging your adult daughter a few hundred a month might take the sting of failure out of the arrangement for some people, but I'm not prone to sugarcoating. You took a shot at adulthood, you blew it, you're regrouping for round two. Me imposing a residential tax on you doesn't make you more successful or independent. I simply need cash."

This confession was frustrating. For years she'd been trying to lavish Byron's money and luxury gifts on her father but he'd never accept a dime. *Your husband's geek currency is not welcome here*, he'd insist. *Quit trying to force the stink of affluence upon me.*

"Dad, if you'd called me days ago, I could've given you anything you wanted!"

He nodded. "An irony not lost upon me. But things can change in a few days, and they have."

"What changed?"

"It's personal." He fidgeted with the pocket of his robe. "I don't expect you to understand, but I need another doll. There, I said it. It's not up for discussion."

She looked toward the darkened hallway where faceless, Throatginaless Diane still lay in the bathroom. Hazel's chest squeezed with guilt: she had synthetic blood on her hands. "I killed her? Diane can't be . . . salvaged?"

"Huh? No, Diane's fine. I mean I need a second doll. I want two."

"Oh." Hazel couldn't help but think how much this was going to amuse Byron. Should she tell her father he was under observation so he'd filter things, or did it not really matter? He was actually hard to embarrass on most accounts. Only Hazel's deficiencies seemed to rattle him.

It was easiest, per usual, to just agree. "Of course, two dolls. A twin thing, kind of? Sister wives? I see."

She didn't, though. Every day, Hazel was learning there were new feelings to be had. Very advanced, complicated feelings that couldn't be conveyed through language or physical expression or any form of art.

"You can think I'm being greedy. That's fine. I don't have to answer to you or anyone else."

"I don't think that." Through Byron, Hazel had been exposed to people who had limitless funds to throw at their insatiable desires, both sexual and non. So much so that her old definitions of greed had become obsolete. Her new definition prioritized others getting hurt, and this meant that moving into her father's house when she didn't know what violent things Byron was going to do or try (and staying, now that she knew her brain was a recording device) were very, very greedy acts. Worse, she was going to continue being greedy in this way a little while longer. She couldn't help it. She had no idea where else to stay while she gathered the necessary resources to travel, but this new information made the problem a lot different. She wasn't going to be able to hide from Byron and begin anew. Wherever she went, whatever she did, he'd know.

Byron had made it impossible for her to leave him. The fact that she was no longer physically in his house didn't matter.

"How much rent do you need a month, Dad?" For the moment,

Hazel decided to pretend things were as easy as going out and finding a job, that her husband wouldn't absolutely have her abducted at whatever place of employment she chose once he tired of waiting for her to come to him.

"Five hundred. That'll be a decent monthly payment on my second lady."

"Okay then." Hazel didn't see how she was going to make this happen, but she wanted to feign confidence. "I'll get right to work becoming gainfully employed." She gave her father a cheerful smile, and he smiled back, but he looked tired, or maybe just really disappointed. "I'll go hit the pavement right now and see what I can find."

Which meant she'd go to the bar and pretend to be hitting the pavement.

"Hazel," he said. His voice was quiet with discouraged resignation. "You're wearing a towel." She watched him motor the Rascal into the dark path of the hallway, then disappear.

HAZEL RETURNED TO THE SPOTTED ROSE TO FIND BLACK SMOKE pouring from the front door and emergency personnel wandering in and out. Her heart began racing—had Byron done something to the place? But there was no crime-scene tape across the entrance, and she watched a civilian walk into the flood of dark smog, then another; when neither reemerged after a few minutes, she decided to try going in herself.

Getting on all fours was the only way to manage. The smoke did seem to thin around a foot or so from the ground, so she trench-crawled in the direction of the bar. When her head bumped into the bottom of an empty stool, Hazel felt her way up it and took a seat.

"What's your poison?" the bartender asked. Hazel opened her eyes but couldn't see anything so she closed them again.

"Whatever's strong," Hazel said. "The air's a little thick today."

"Grease fire in the kitchen," a man next to her replied. She recognized the voice.

"Liver?"

"Hello there." A hand from behind the bar grabbed Hazel's fingertips, guided them down to the drink in front of her and placed them firmly around it.

It was nice to hear someone familiar. "How have you been?" Hazel cleared her throat. "So I need to start networking a little, as they say. Do you have the phone number of anyone who might be looking to hire some help?"

"I don't have a phone," Liver answered.

Hazel felt her pulse speed up.

"No phone? Of any kind?" Her voice was nearly cracking with excitement. "So how do people get ahold of you? Your family? Your friends?"

"I've succumbed to neither affliction," he answered.

"What about women?" she asked, admittedly changing her voice to be a little flirtatious. Hazel decided she'd misjudged him. Anyone getting through life without a phone had skills she wanted to acquire. Rare capabilities that attracted the New Hazel.

"I just meet women in this bar. Mainly they use me to help them reach bottom. I'm like a brick they grab onto midair. Sleeping with me helps them admit their lives have become unmanageable. They realize they want and deserve something more, and then their recovery process can begin. I get laid in the meantime. Win-win."

"Do you have a phone at your job?"

"No."

She chugged the rest of her drink and wiped her mouth on her arm. "Do you have a job?"

"Yep." She didn't know whether it was the alcohol or the lack of oxygen, but Hazel was beginning to feel very drowsy. She started to rest her head on the bar, but fingers found the back of her shirt and pulled upward. "Wouldn't fall asleep in here if I were you," Liver said.

"Yeah. Probably smart. So what do you do?" As soon as she asked, an involuntary yawn overtook her. It caused Hazel to inhale a bit too much smoke. She began coughing and continued to do so for about ten minutes.

"Let's continue the conversation elsewhere," Liver suggested. Hazel dismounted the stool and crawled toward the dim crack of light she could see. It was hard to crawl and cough at the same time but she managed. When she made it out to the sidewalk, Hazel collapsed in the sunlight, breathing in deep, rapid breaths of clear oxygen.

She looked up to see Liver walking out of the billowing soot. It seemed like he was exiting a time machine that had gone up in a blaze. His clothes were made entirely of leather: hat, vest, pants, boots. He was also wearing a necklace of assorted animal teeth.

"Shall we?" he asked.

SUBSEQUENT CLUES CONFIRMED THAT LIVER WOULD INDEED BE A good mentor for shirking technology, like how all the windows were broken out of his truck. He was a "maverick."

When they turned off the main road onto a long drive with a

sizable ranch house, Hazel began to question whether Liver was as nontraditional as she'd assumed. But they passed the house and continued quite a ways into a wooded area until he drove the pickup into the base of a large tree to park it. A few leaves fell through where the truck's windshield should've been and landed on Hazel's lap. "We walk the rest of the way," he explained. Then he took a long rifle out from under the driver's seat.

"This is still a date, right?" He wasn't secretly an eccentric acquaintance of Byron's who was now about to hunt her for sport?

"If that's what you're into," he said.

She wanted to tell him everything: that her worst fears had come true, that her husband had managed to place a surveillance device into her mind, the whole story. But she didn't want to seem crazy. This was shitty because the truth was crazy, not her. There had been a tagline of a TV show, *The truth is out there*, that Hazel had initially misinterpreted and felt comforted by. *That is for sure!* she'd thought, the truth was the most far-out thing possible. Hazel had always felt this—when she learned about periods and sex, when she learned about death, when she learned about the impossible living conditions of the other planets in the solar system and the manufacturing of processed meats. Almost always, the truth was way more bizarre and gross than she would've imagined. Then one night she commented on this to a friend and was told, *No, dumbass, the show is saying that the truth will be discovered. Like how aliens are real and the U.S. government knows it.*

Hazel did not want Liver to discover her truth. But she did want advice. "So if someone were hypothetically able to read your mind, what would you do about it?"

"If someone got inside my head," Liver answered, "they'd voluntarily show themselves right back out. I guarantee you."

Eventually they came to his shelter, which looked like a storage shed. Inside there was a wooden pallet on the ground covered with a few animal skins, various repurposed containers filled with water, some two-by-four shelving holding dry goods. Most impressive was Liver's stockpile of weapons. "Feel free to take your clothes off," he said. "You won't offend anyone." He removed his hat, then his vest. The trunk of his body was a museum of scars. "If you want, we can wrap ourselves up in mosquito netting while we have sex. Avoid bites."

Hazel pointed to his torso. "Did you have an invasive surgery?" It was hard to tell what injuries the scars might be from, or whether or not they were from the same occasion. It was hardly fair that Byron could insert a mind-recording device inside her without a mark. Her father's appendectomy scar looked like an accidental chain-saw bisection, for example.

"I guess you could say that." He took a jar of moonshine out from under the wooden pallet, poured some into an empty aluminum can, and extended it to Hazel. The liquid inside looked sheeny and a little prismatic, like tears mixed with gasoline.

"What else could you say?"

Liver shrugged. "Beware of motherfuckers."

He seemed to sense her hesitation in escalating the intimacy. "Wanna wait till it gets dark?" he asked. She nodded and he held up the moonshine jar in agreement. "Nighttime is the right time."

"You said you had a job?" Hazel mentioned. She didn't mean it to sound as accusatory as it did; she just wondered. A little selfishly, she supposed. Whatever career Liver had wasn't cramping his style. Maybe it was something she could get in on one day, if she ever did get away from Byron.

"I'm a gravesitter," he said. "I visit graves for people when they go out of town, or when they start having sex again after being widowed and feel guilty. The landscapers at cemeteries arrange the gigs for me. I show up, go to the graves they tell me to, and sit for however long the people paid for, then they take a finder's cut and give me the rest."

"Do you talk to the graves?" Hazel went over to the pallet and lay down, choosing to breathe in through her mouth. The animal skin covering had a good memory for odor. Liver stayed seated on the end of the pallet, sipping his liquor.

"No. I could charge more and do stuff like that. Singing, reading poetry. People always want me to sing 'Happy Birthday.' It's a visitation, not a dinner show—that's what I have the landscapers say. If I start agreeing to extras, it will open a whole can of worms."

Hazel thought about what she might say to bond with Liver. It had been such a long time since she'd tried to get emotionally closer to someone instead of farther away. She didn't want to fake interest, which was her usual habit. Conversation with Byron had always been easy because he always wanted to talk about himself, and if she listened then it seemed like they were communicating.

Looking around the ceiling, Hazel noted a number of spider colonies. It had been a good while since she'd been around insects or nature in general.

"Did you mention a net?" she asked cheerfully. Liver reached under the bed and shook it out, then brought it down atop the two of them. "Thanks," she smiled. "You know, if I were hiring you to gravesit someone for me, I think I'd like the fact that you don't talk. I mean, if I believed that they could hear us. I'd worry you'd start talking and they'd be all, 'Hey! Where is Hazel? Who is this speaking? May I ask who is speaking, please?' And sure, you could explain the situation, but they might feel unsettled. If it's nonverbal, and they're just like, *Someone's here*, then they can imagine it's whoever they want it to be. Plus it's kind of more spiritual without talking. Like you're a monk or someone who's taken a vow of silence."

"Talk's overrated," he said. Which maybe was a hint, but he'd have to compromise if the night was going to turn out as planned.

"I need to chat with you more to feel comfortable."

"I figured." He extended his fuller jar toward her empty jar, proffering a refill, but Hazel had to decline. The earlier shot hadn't set well. It felt like she'd swallowed a small, sharp-clawed lizard that was scratching around in her belly trying to find an exit.

"What's the worst thing you've ever done?" she asked. Since Liver wasn't one for small talk, Hazel supposed they could get straight to soul-searching. "I was married, I technically am still married? To a really bad man. So you're not going to scare me. Here's the thing: all of his crimes are done, like, remotely. Through technology and interfaces and scientists. He doesn't leave his desk. But your hands! They're dirty and calloused. And looking around your shed, I see you've killed a lot of animals then undressed them for meat and parts. Your lean frame holds a great amount of scrappy muscle. I'm guessing you're somewhat versed in hand-to-hand combat."

Suddenly it occurred to Hazel that Byron would hear and report anything Liver confessed. Poor Liver would exit his shack to have a pee and be greeted by a SWAT team.

"Actually, never mind," Hazel corrected herself. "That's the thing with me: don't tell me anything you don't want the whole world to know. Not because I personally can't keep a secret. It's more my brain. Long story."

They sat in silence for a while, the light in the shed becoming darker, Liver occasionally making burps that smelled like butane.

Hazel thought about all the different reasons people have sex that don't necessarily have anything to do with physical pleasure. There were reproduction, money, influence, apology, revenge. She wasn't turned on, but she did want to sleep with Liver. For one, it would scandalize and upset Byron. For two, Liver was hugely different from Byron, and nothing seemed more appealing to Hazel than commingling with Byron's opposite. For three, Hazel hoped she might absorb some of his self-reliance. If there was one person in the world who could make someone better at chopping things down with an ax just by having sex with him, this was the guy.

"I think I'm ready," she said.

It wasn't horrible, and that was an improvement from the last sex Hazel had experienced with Byron ("instead of telling me what you like, let me monitor your arousal levels via digital-pulse readout").

Liver had a lot of smells that seemed automotive in nature, so being on her back beneath him, Hazel thought about the flat rolling carts mechanics lie down on to slide beneath cars, and the sex became a little fun the way it might be fun to roll out from below a vehicle and then roll back under again, and again. The texture of his scars was fun to touch as well, like different land features on a raised-relief globe. His body was a new world, and it was possible for Hazel to be alone there: no satellites orbited its atmosphere, no fiber-optic cables ran beneath its soil. It didn't leave her mind that soon Byron would be seeing them together through his crystal ball of data, but for the next few hours what she'd done was truly her secret, and she relished it.

AFTERWARD, WITH HER BODY DRAPED ACROSS LIVER, HAZEL REMEM-
bered one college summer when she and her friend Becca had gone
to an outdoor music festival. They'd stayed up all night taking
Ecstasy then slept the morning away in her parents' station wagon,
parked in front of a supermarket. It was a Saturday so the shopping
plaza was busy, and occasionally they'd wake for a moment to see
young kids peering in at them through the windows, sometimes
knocking on them or distorting their lips on the glass like catfish—
she and Becca were too out of it to even care. They were just a se-
dated exhibit at the human zoo: Collegiate Recreational Drug Users,
and they'd let the gawkers come and go with no concern. One adult
male did knock and yell to ask if they were okay, *Y'all aren't dead,*
right? I saw you in here at the beginning of my shift eight hours ago.
Wiggle a toe for me so I don't have nightmares about your corpses baking
in this hot car all day? but when the two of them opened their eyes
his smile made it clear that he was hitting on them so her friend
Becca put her foot up on the window and right over his face. She
had impressively big feet, and because the festival was outdoors
and they'd been walking around barefoot, her toes were feral looking and caked with mud, and when she lifted her foot back off the
window the man had gone.

They were hot and sticky and nothing seemed real. They'd gotten terribly lost driving home from the festival and had stumbled
on a sad alligator zoo where a shirtless man wrestled an alligator in
a cage every hour on the hour, and they decided to stay and watch
because their hangover was making surreal things seem normal and
normal things, like traffic and driving on the highway, feel incom-
prehensible and scary.

The wrestler and the reptile had a type of intimacy. When he
got to where he was lying on top of it, his belly against its back

and his hands wrapped around its jaw, it was clear he was actually whispering to it. In that moment part of Hazel had wished, in a way, to be that poor alligator, in a different context, despite not finding the man attractive. She wanted to be held and whispered to with the weight of another person pressed down across the length of her body.

Sex with Liver was like this. There was a sense of getting to be closer to a wild creature than most people ever get to be, of the danger being reduced for a moment because the creature was restrained. Not by physical force but by booze and sex. Though because of all the scars, Liver's skin did feel a little reptilian, a little like something a designer purse might be made from. His left nipple was basically missing. There was an indentation that Hazel's fingers naturally went toward and swept inside, and the absence there lowered them just a few centimeters closer to his beating heart.

"Is there any part of your story you could tell me that's legal?" Hazel whispered. "Things that couldn't be held against you in a court of law? Your childhood, maybe."

"I began courting delinquency from an early age," Liver said.

"Are your parents still alive?"

"I don't know," he said. Of course a Gogol ID search could solve the mystery right away.

"You don't care to know," Hazel clarified.

"Sure don't."

Hazel squeezed him a little tighter, not out of pity but out of gratitude. Here was someone who didn't want Byron's data.

11

THE NEXT MORNING HAZEL WOKE WITH AN IDEA. SHE HAD NO CLUE what time it was and neither did Liver—hopefully it wasn't too late. She needed to get home before the next download at noon.

"Would you be able to come to my house and lift something?"

"Is it a body?" Liver asked. He was eyeing a shovel in the shed's corner and clearly wanted to bring the right tools for the job.

Hazel realized that Byron's intervention meant she'd always have to care, at least once a day, about a schedule. Did she have hours until she'd have to withstand the download seizure, or only minutes or even seconds? "If I start shaking and then puke or pass out or both, just wait it out," she told Liver.

"Well yeah," he said.

There wasn't a functioning clock in his pickup, but they passed a pharmacy marquee that advertised both the 11:32 AM time as well as a low-price special on some cannibalistic-sounding vitamins called HAIR, SKIN & NAILS GUMMIES. With luck they'd make it back to her father's house just in time.

"It's complicated," Hazel explained as they pulled into the driveway, "but something's about to happen to my body that I'm going to try to prevent. I need to grab a device from the backyard. You may or may not see my father on a scooter, with or without something that looks like a female mannequin. Pay him no mind. What I need you to do is get the huge wooden box in the living room that's shaped like a coffin and carry it back to the porch."

He lifted a flask from between the truck's seat cushions and shook it to make sure it was full. "Okay," he said. "I've got all the necessary equipment."

In the house, Dad and Diane were playing a card game in the kitchen's breakfast nook. "Hi, Dad; I'll be busy for the next few minutes," she yelled to him. "A friend is coming in to bring Diane's box out to the porch. Don't judge him based on appearance. He poses no danger."

She then ran outside and grabbed the Sleep Helmet Byron had included in the safe. She doubted he'd have included it if wearing it during the downloads could prevent them, but it was worth a shot. After all, why twelve noon instead of twelve midnight? Maybe sleep wasn't as conducive to ripping out her memories. She wanted to attempt every roadblock she could muster.

"Rummy," Hazel heard her father saying to Diane. "You win again!"

She didn't want to be alone when the download came, but she also didn't want Liver to see it. When he brought the box out, she said, "I need to put on this helmet and climb into the box for a few minutes. I'm not sure exactly what's going to happen. You might want to wait in another room."

Liver took a long drag from his cigarette. "You're gonna shut the lid?" She was clearly not the first woman he'd assisted into a wooden box.

"Yes. Could you give me a hand with that?"

Hazel put on the helmet, climbed inside, and lay back. "Let me poke a few airholes," she heard Liver say. "For your health!"

The helmet blocked out all light, but she heard a series of terrifying stabs delivered in near-mechanical succession, and then it was quiet. Hazel pressed the activation button to start the helmet's beta-wave sequence. It was pleasurable, frighteningly easy the way her mind cleared. She knew the visual that always came into her head during the Sleep Helmet's induction wouldn't sound that serene to others: she pictured a zookeeper cleaning the cement floor of a cage, working a large push broom across soapy ground, the ambient rasp of its polymer bristles moving farther and farther away from the center of the room to the periphery. Off went her worries. The bubbly sheen of industrial disinfectant became her consciousness, liquid and thin. Growing thinner still. Spreading into nothing.

WHEN THE IMAGES OF BYRON CAME, IT FELT LIKE THEY WERE HITTING her between the eyes with a paintball gun. One after the other: Byron accepting an award. Byron delivering a speech. Byron standing amid a group of children in a rural African village. They all sped toward her at an incredible velocity, like billboards she was being flung up against. Her head continued to feel hammered upon even after the images stopped.

It took Hazel a moment to realize this was because she was inside a box wearing a helmet and she kept trying to sit up without opening its lid.

The download had not been thwarted. Hazel pushed the visor release so the helmet's eyepiece turned transparent, then pressed against the coffin's lid and climbed out. She was shaking but didn't see any vomit. After using the crate to help herself stand, she teetered into the living room.

Her father and Liver were having a beer. "Are you ex-military?" her father asked. He was looking at Liver with squinted eyes, trying to get a read on him.

"I'm not big on government," Liver answered. Her father looked over and saw her in the helmet—she'd lifted the visor but had forgotten to take it off.

"You kids off to ride some go-carts?" he asked.

Hazel went to the kitchen to grab a garbage bag. It would take time to find work, so she figured she might as well sell the electronics Byron had left for her. And the safe. Hazel dropped the helmet inside and slung the bag over her shoulder.

"I'm going to go scare up some rent money for you, Pops. Liver, what do you have going on?"

He stood. "Need to head up to the cemetery for a bit." With that, he reached out and took Hazel's arm by the wrist, turning it a little in the light, examining it. For a moment she worried that he was about to pull a bowie knife out of the back of his vest and sever her hand in a single pass—perhaps he was under the mistaken impression that she'd stolen a keepsake from his shedhouse, a lottery scratch-off ticket that one of the giant spiders had in fact taken and woven into its web.

Instead he moved his fingers down and gave hers a squeeze, then offered up a wink she would've written off as a nervous twitch if it hadn't been timed just so with his grip of her fist. "I'll be at the bar later," he said, then he held her gaze for a moment and left.

Hazel's father produced a small cough. "Are you courting that fellow? Why wasn't he wearing a shirt?"

"Do you have a wagon or a wheelbarrow or something I could use to get some electronics down the road to the Gogol resale store?"

Her father scootered over to the breakfast nook and climbed in next to Diane. "You can take the Rascal. Make wide turns and don't attempt any hills."

HAZEL BAGGED UP ALL THE SMALLER ELECTRONICS AND SET THEM on her lap, then placed the safe in the Rascal's front basket. It was slow going with all the additional weight, but she supposed she wasn't in a rush.

A few blocks from the store, the cell phone started ringing. She pressed DECLINE the first few times, but when the calls persisted, a far-fetched sense of hope lit up inside her. Maybe Byron was so disgusted by her physical union with Liver that he was now willing to cut her loose. It would be delightful to hear his voice crack with revulsion.

"Yes, Byron?"

"We've got to talk. I have some upsetting news."

Two children on bicycles zipped past, pointing and laughing at the large garbage sack on her lap. One threw his chocolate milk shake at the scooter; the plastic lid came off the cup and left an unsettling trail of brown splatter. Hazel worried onlookers would think it was human waste. She honked the Rascal's horn in protest, but that only seemed to enhance their joy.

"I think I'm caught up," Hazel said. "You put a chip in my brain that sends you a daily report of all my thoughts and activities. The download will put me into an inconvenient state of paralysis and shock each afternoon. Both are troubling developments for me, but they don't warrant a phone call."

"It's your father," Byron said. "He's not being honest with you."

Hazel stopped the scooter. Okay, so probably her dad really, really wanted her out of his house. The renter thing did seem weird after he'd so recently voiced a desire for privacy. Was there some humiliating eviction plan in motion that Byron had caught wind of? Was her father planning to bring in a ringer, one of his Shady Place pals who'd fry offensive-smelling fish and walk around in large cotton briefs while spewing misogynistic comments until Hazel chose to leave so her father didn't have to kick her out and seem heartless?

"The renter? What's going on? What do you know?" Hazel didn't want to ask how he knew it.

"It's about your fa-ther, Hay-zel. We have the Sleep Helmet X7 to thank for this information, by the way. I know your hope was to try to disrupt the download, but you may have inadvertently saved your father's life by putting it on."

A woman walking her dog made a large show of having to step off the sidewalk to move around the scooter. Hazel tried to motor off onto the grass a little bit but the wheels didn't like it. The last thing she needed to do was get stuck. "Sorry," Hazel called out to the woman. "I had to take this phone call."

"I'm sure it's *real important*," the woman yelled back.

"I'm not even the enemy!" Hazel shouted. At times like these, it was shamefully easy to understand Byron's contempt for the general public. Hazel knew relativity could be difficult: that woman would probably be in debt to Gogol for electronics purchases and technology usage until she met her death, but someone taking up three squares of sidewalk with a scooter was her perceived grievance with the world.

"Hazel?" Byron questioned. "Don't engage hostile strangers. Ours is a violent society and you've lived behind protected walls for some time. We need to get you back home to us in one piece."

"What's this about my father?"

"Where are you? Can I send a car? This news should really come in person."

Hazel laughed. Byron did nearly all his meetings virtually.

"Hazel, I'm serious. I have upsetting facts to relay."

"Just get on with it." Whatever Byron was about to tell her was to his advantage—Byron didn't say things that weren't—so Hazel was skeptical. It wasn't above Byron to lie about her father to try to get his hooks in deeper. She also couldn't discount outright the chance that Byron had gotten to her dad. Perhaps the bathtub thing with Di had pushed him over the edge. It wouldn't be difficult for Byron to convince her father that Hazel having free will wasn't in her own best interest and she needed to be returned to him. Her dad probably half-believed that anyway. Now that her father had a sudden interest in purchasing artificial women, he could likely be bought off.

"As you know, the helmet does physical diagnostics. You need to start physical therapy on your shoulder. I also want to add that your nutrient intake since you left the compound has been abysmal. I'll have a drone drop some Vitapax into your father's backyard. Please eat them."

"Why don't you mail them?"

"I don't use government services, Hazel. The government uses my services."

"Liver doesn't use government services either. You two have so much in common."

"Incorrect. I did check into him, for your protection. Disability, Medicaid. He has outstanding warrants in a few states for failure to pay the fines on unlicensed firearms. I hope you two weren't planning on taking any romantic getaways out of the area." It pleased Hazel that Byron wasn't able to keep the hostility out of his voice.

"No need," she said. "We can have sex just fine right where we are."

"Hazel." Byron cleared his throat. "I'd actually recommend wearing the helmet whenever you're thinking of coupling with a new paramour. I understand it if you feel the need to have affairs as part of some grievance against me that you're getting out of your system. Very well. But the helmet also gives readings of others within a five-hundred-foot radius. It's not a bad idea to scan ahead of time for STDs. Of course, those in the incubation period might not show up, so you'll *always* want to use protection."

"Is Liver clean?"

"I certainly wouldn't use that term. He doesn't have any operative venereal infections, no. But it is not pretty under the hood. Your new boyfriend wouldn't qualify as an organ donor."

"Okay. So what did my father's scan show?" Hazel could feel her emotions putting their boxing gloves up, bracing. Whatever Byron was about to say was probably a lie, or a half-truth—a warping of the complete picture.

"It's widespread cancer, Hazel. He doesn't have long."

Hazel scoffed because she had to. Her father dying of cancer when her mother had died of cancer? What were the odds? "He just went to the doctor yesterday. Maybe they did something, gave him something that set off a faulty reading. He'd have all kinds of symptoms if that were true," she added. "He'd know, or the doctors would pick up some abnormality in his tests. He's always getting tests."

Hazel thought about this statement. Why had he gone to the doctor, anyway?

"I'm sure he is," Byron said. His tone was gentler now, unchallenging. He wasn't afraid of losing, which meant there was no chance that he could. The humid air suddenly seemed wavy, nauseatingly so, like what she was breathing in was also sloshing around inside her.

"You mean he knows? I think he'd tell me if he was dying." Hazel realized this wasn't true even as she said it though. The worse her father felt, the more he downplayed any pain. He'd always been this way. The morning prior to a stress test his doctor had ordered when Hazel was in high school, her father had mowed the lawn and subsequently had a micro heart attack followed by a same-day surgery; for a week the mower sat in the middle of the yard at the end of an unfinished strip until one of her father's OCD neighbors had come over and finished it because he couldn't stand looking at it anymore. He and her mother had fought about this for weeks. *Why the fuck were you mowing the lawn with chest pains!* she'd screamed. *That would've been death by idiocy, Herbert! Death is not some pansy baby. You cannot pee down the neck of Death's shirt and expect it to look the other way. If you are flagrantly too dumb to live, it will come to collect.* But her father hadn't been fazed. *Well, if you weren't yelling at me about almost dying you'd be yelling at me about how bad the lawn looks!*

"Oh, Hazel," Byron said. "He definitely knows. The helmet's not designed for medical scanning to be its primary function, so I don't have results with the specificity of, say, a HealthSweep imager. And I'm not a doctor. But I've talked to several today on your father's behalf, and they all concur: based on the information we do have, he's already undergone a variety of chemotherapy and radiation treatments. It looks like he stopped everything except pain management medication a few months ago. Were it legal to do so, I may have also double-checked electronic hospital records to confirm this. I wouldn't be breaking this news to you unless I could speak with certainty."

"So he never told me about having cancer or having cancer treatments, and then he made the decision to die and neglected to share that with me as well?" Hazel had to say it out loud to acknowledge that it was real. Bring the words into the world and examine them.

Why hadn't she asked him about the hundreds of pills beneath the sink? Why hadn't the urgency of sex doll number one and sex doll number two triggered more of a warning signal to her? Why hadn't she thought it stranger that he was willing to spend the rest of his life without a car? Hazel supposed she'd stopped trying to understand her father's logic so long ago that it had become a habit. She didn't question what he wanted anymore, and this made her not question why he wanted it either.

"I understand this information has the potential to feel very hurtful to you," Byron said, the bright horizon of a coming sales pitch already beginning to put a lilt in his words. "And while I believe it's your right to know this, if all it was going to do was cause you pain, I wouldn't meddle. But your father probably made his decision based on the care and treatment options that were presented as being available to him, which, given his financial situation, are minimal. We'll have to do more tests of course, but I can give him access to cutting-edge treatments not available to the general public. There's definitely hope."

So there it was, Hazel thought, his angle. He was using her father's health to blackmail her.

It didn't sting though. She waited for it to—maybe later it would. But in the moment all she felt was a twisted sort of gratitude. She wanted to get help for her father, and she wanted Byron to win on a technicality instead of on a feat that was entirely his own, if he had to win. He was pretty smart, so he probably did.

She had her consolation prizes. She could return with her head held high after having enjoyed a good time: She'd slept with an outlaw! She'd only used a phone twice in several days! If she didn't take Byron up on the offer, no part of her life that came afterward would feel victorious—she'd always remember how she valued her freedom over her father's life, and that it had been a lame, neutered freedom anyway because Byron could still see and hear everything she did. He'd know the guilt and regret that she felt, and that alone would be a victory for him.

But her sitting at his side in silent protest, with him knowing the reason she'd come home was a sense of paternal fidelity? That didn't seem like a total victory for Byron. It felt closer to breaking even. Probably as close to it as she could ever hope to get with him.

"So you'll want me to move back to The Hub. Right?"

"That would make the most sense. If we're together then your father is my family and I'd do anything possible to help him."

"I see. But the father of your estranged wife whose brain you microchipped . . ." Hazel knew she shouldn't push it. She should give in without protest, recite a canned statement of thanks about how much she appreciated his willingness to help.

"Now you're describing a situation where it sounds like I'm unwanted," he said. "And that elderly man, in that case, I would not feel duty bound to assist, no."

"I'll come back home, Byron. Let me go talk to him. I'll call you tonight?"

"Until then."

Hazel started to turn back around, but stopped. She was crying, but the reasons behind the tears seemed like the wrong ones—she was sad about her father, yes, but she was also thinking about all the petty, weird things about living at The Hub that she hated, like how the purified air in their house smelled like pencil lead.

She turned the Rascal's lever full throttle and decided to complete the mission before heading back to her father's. She could still get the experience of pawning Byron's goods. It could be a memory for her to cherish in her older years when she was sitting in a Gogol edema-reducing Masostimulation Recliner.

There were two young children outside the store, facing each other and standing about three feet apart. Each held a water gun, and each was using it to soak the crotch of the other's pants.

"Are you two the owners of this fine establishment?" Hazel asked. "Could one of you please open the door for me?"

"Are you handi-crapped?" the farther one yelled. The nearer one did agree to hold the door for her; in exchange for his humanity he was rewarded with the other heartily soaking the anal area of his shorts while his back was turned.

"Quit giving me butt water," he protested.

Hazel scooted inside to the nearest associate. She pulled the beach towel off the Rascal's basket to reveal the safe and handed over the plastic bag of goods. The clerk let out a long whistle. "You've got some top-of-the-line stuff here." His eyes did a once-over on her DROPOUT sweatpants. "Is it stolen?"

"They were gifts." The boys' parents were on the other side of the store, their faces adult versions of their sons'. The couple was looking at sound systems. "I want something where, like, if a house is getting shot up on TV, it sounds like *my* house is getting shot up," the father explained.

Byron always focused on the ways that nature was unpredictable, but often it wasn't. In Byron's world, deviation, mutation, and evolution were all negatives; anything unexpected was unwanted. With technology too—this is what he felt, how his brain worked— even happy tech accidents, ones with results that were ultimately beneficial, still implied that the programmers had failed to make an adequate prediction. Having a product respond in a way it wasn't asked to hinted toward powerlessness.

This was part of why Byron would never abide her leaving him.

"Gifts, wow. Assuming the serial numbers don't come back hot, you can trade this up for some really primo product. What can I interest you in? You might have enough here for a virtual-reality pod. We don't get those in here often but I've got one in the back today. Seriously exquisite. Have you ever tried it? You lie down like you're in a tanning bed, except when the door closes over you all your simulated dreams come true. No UV rays either."

"No thanks. I just want money."

The clerk gave Hazel a confused frown. "But what for? Any electronic device you'd spend it on we can get you here. If we don't have it in stock, we'll order it."

"I need it to pay legal fees," Hazel lied. "I'm kind of in a hurry. Can we just do this and be done?"

"Ah. Are you familiar with our strategist software? A lot of people use it as a mid-range option for legal defense. You give it the details of your case, and it searches a comprehensive database of similar cases where the defendant achieved a desirable outcome. Then it generates a report on how to make their arguments work for you. It's cheaper than a traditional attorney, so you can get a public defender and use the printouts. Or if there's something specific on which you keep encountering problems with the law, perhaps I could interest you in one of our antidetect products?"

He held a scanner to the first item she was selling and let out a giddy yell. "Man!" he exclaimed. "You said these were gifts? Does the person who gave them to you, like, work for Gogol? Pretty high up I mean? These are *embargoed*. That is so cool."

Hazel removed her hands from the Rascal's controls; she could feel a hot wash of anger beginning to move through her and didn't want to be tempted to drive through the storefront's glass window. "You mean he made it so I can't even sell them?"

"No, we can totally buy them—in fact, they're worth a lot more than they would be otherwise. Embargoed stuff is, like, customized. Either it has features on it that the general models don't . . . features that haven't been released yet? Or it has information that might be sensitive. If it's embargoed, then when it's returned to Gogol, we get, like, three times as much money because they don't want it circulating on the street."

Hazel shuddered to think what surveillance "enhancements" had been made to the gifts Byron had given her. The safe of tech goodies was an egg-shaped Trojan horse.

She emerged from the store with a brick of cash she stowed inside the band of her sweatpants. She didn't know what treatments Gogol was going to give her father. But she was picturing the following Thanksgiving at The Hub's expansive stainless-steel dining table: her father bald, Diane without a wig, Hazel with a shaved head, all three of them in chemo-treatment solidarity, and Byron in front of a screen at the other end of the table doing remote work on a million things as he ate and they all ignored him.

Maybe it wouldn't be so bad.

12

JASPER HAD NEVER BEEN WITHOUT A PREPARED GETAWAY BAG, JUST in case a con or a loved-one-of-a-con became homicidally obsessed once things went sour. It included the stolen driver's license and social security card of a man named Larry Winkler. He didn't look like Jasper but had the baldness and the whiteness, so it was more or less believable that Larry had just gotten really in shape. After the Taser incident with Calla, Jasper had followed the coast northward for a few states then used these IDs to secure a custodial position at the Oceanarium, which owned five dolphins. One of whom, the one who somehow seemed up for the most fun, was Bella.

He'd been at this job for over a year, and was planning a jail-break. He and Bella were going to share a life. It was just a matter of time.

There was the interspecies thing, and she'd need to stay in water, but he was convinced the courtship could be emotionally profitable for both of them. He wasn't sure whether or not actual sex would happen—he wanted it to, but didn't need for it to. That would depend on her, was what he decided was ethical. If she tried things like the dolphin in the ocean that day had, he'd let it happen, and even if that meant drowning, it would probably still be great for him. Any dolphin did it for him, but he'd felt a sort of relief when he'd begun to fixate on Bella and the narrative of their future relationship started playing in his mind. He knew the sexual affinity that had overtaken him was bizarre, so he supposed he appreciated how the context of a monogamous life partnership made him feel less deviant. With Bella, at least he could pretend the affliction was specific: he loved *her*.

The truth was that every dolphin now aroused him to a medically improbable degree. Doing cons, he'd made a living for over a decade by getting turned on—having sex in which each performance was good enough to convince the other party they were soul mates. But he'd never felt anything like this. He couldn't trust his body at work; beneath his uniform he wore constrictive briefs that were designed to be worn to dance clubs. They helped conceal erections, and Jasper further layered these with a plastic liner. It wasn't comfortable.

But it was temporary. He had a plan.

Paying cash, he'd bought a large, nondescript station wagon and removed all the backseats. Bella's height and weight measurements were posted in the informational section by her tank, and going by them, he'd bought an elongated tailgating cooler made for roughly sixty to eighty partygoers from a local fraternity's annual yard sale. It wasn't ideal transport; she wouldn't have room to swim, but she'd be submerged until he could get her back to the studio apartment's bathtub, and then they'd have a honeymoon night together before leaving for the country rental. This was in the middle of nowhere, with a screened-in pool and a very hands-off landlord he'd already met once in person to give a deposit and a year's rent up front, also in cash. He'd worn a prosthetic nose and chin that didn't pass for real, but the landlord didn't ask. Jasper had gotten the man's number off a pawnshop flyer. Its fine print suggested that people hiding out from significant tax collection, an amount they did not intend to pay in their lifetime, might enjoy this rental. It wouldn't be permanent—maybe, for the rest of his life, no residence would. But he was already used to this pattern. They could stay there until he found the next suitable temporary home, then repeat.

But, God. The waiting was getting to him. The Oceanarium was a double-edged sword for Jasper. It was where he got the most stimulation, but it was also where he was reminded of all the stimulation he could hypothetically be getting and wasn't, yet. He knew he'd do something insane if he didn't get to touch Bella soon. And if the game plan in order to not go crazy was stealing a dolphin, Jasper supposed the crazy option would be pretty dark.

"Winkler!" Tiny called. Jasper had gotten better about responding to his alias, but it still took him a moment. His boss Tiny was a middle-aged hippie, but because of his height and size and penchant for macabre medieval costume jewelry, he always looked ready to terrorize or kill. His frame stretched T-shirts in a way that made short sleeves disappear; on Tiny the Oceanarium-issued V-neck looked like a cutoff. Tiny's shoes perhaps were the scariest thing about him; he wore only Birkenstock sandals, but custodial employees of the park had a closed-toe shoe rule to abide by, so Tiny had gotten a kind of metal sandal cage custom made. Sometimes during school class visits Tiny gave talks about the importance of maintenance and cleaning at the Oceanarium.

After his speech, when he opened things up to the kids for questions, the first two were always along the lines of "Are you a giant or some other close-to-but-not-quite-human variant?" (*No really, the kids would beg, you can tell us, we will keep your secret*), and "Why do you have to wear those scary shoes?" They assumed the footwear was part of some court-enforced punishment Tiny was serving, and they hoped this sentence hadn't been imposed on him for life.

"Is there any way you could work late this Saturday, buddy?" Tiny's eyebrows' unchecked overgrowth cast a shadow that made him look like he was scowling even at his happiest. As he focused his eyes on Jasper and his hand went into his pocket, any bystander would guess Tiny was about to produce a switchblade, but his fingers uncurled to reveal a fistful of sunflower seeds. Tiny's wide, flat teeth were always crunching something.

Working late meant there was an after-hours event that required cleanup; sometimes it took until morning. If the soiree was in the park's main convention hall, Jasper could potentially have a lot of quiet time near Bella's tank until the party ended. But if it was a performance in the auditorium, the shift would be a slice of torture; the dolphins would be moved into their nighttime tank after the show. He'd be cleaning up in front of an empty pool of expectant water that would lap in the wind and force him to look up just in case the impossible had happened and Bella had escaped from her holding tank to come greet him.

"I probably can—what's going on?" He'd do it no matter what of course; Jasper wanted Tiny to feel like he owed him in case any favors were needed down the line. Plus work was a useful distraction. Jasper's studio apartment was the equivalent of an oversize video booth at a seedy porn store, except the props were more *National Geographic* than *Penthouse*.

"That clown Dolphin Savior is having a concert in the amphitheater. They're choreographing some special dolphin performance to go along with it."

Jasper felt a voodoo harpoon stab through his heart. Special performance?

It was enough that Bella had to parade her wares daily in front of ungrateful families, the children stuffing their faces with orange corn puffs and blue slushies, overlooking the great beauty before them or finding it underwhelming. Half the brats in the crowd were playing on some sort of Gogol device during the show, screaming murder if a drop of water got on the screen despite the various splash warnings plastered all over the amphitheater walls. One of Jasper's jobs was to empty the amphitheater comment box each night (it got emptied straight into the garbage), and occasionally he'd read them and feel a molten rage: *Put funny hats or costumes on the fishes.* Fishes! *Make dolphins jump higher or come down through the stands on a zip-line thing.*

This was the gratitude Bella received for her performative slavery. And now she was being forced to learn another routine for a concert?

He knew some guy had come forward as the Dolphin Savior, as *him*, Jasper, pretending he was the man who'd rescued the dolphin in the now-famous beach video. The guy was a struggling musician, but after saying he rescued the dolphin and writing a song about the incident, he was topping the charts.

Jasper hadn't been able to make himself listen to the song yet. And he'd been busy setting things up for his new interim life. At the end of the day he was just grateful that no one was looking for him. "What style of music is it?" He tried to seem disinterested but felt his voice shake a little.

"I can't believe you haven't heard of this guy; he's everywhere. Have you been living under a rock?" Tiny began pulling up a video online.

No, Jasper thought, just inside the claustrophobic bubble of a vulgar sexual interspecies obsession. "I don't get out much," he summarized.

"I guess not. I know you've heard the song, though. They play it in the park at least fifteen times a day."

Ah—pop music. Even sadder. Jasper started to head toward his personal locker, where he kept a tube of numbing cream he'd once used to delay ejaculation with cons. Now, due to the constrictive shorts he had to wear, he used it to dull the aching throb of his chafed genitals. He tried not to let the balloon of melancholy inside him well up large enough to pinch his organs and make breathing difficult.

Yes, he had fallen. Yes, his life had become very, very different. But he was working toward a better day. Mourning the loss of his human playboy era was useless. The glories of his former self were now the currency of an overthrown country. He'd tried everything.

"Remember how the Internet went crazy when this guy rescued a distressed dolphin last May?"

Jasper snapped out of his mournful thoughts and swallowed. When he turned his head, he was horrified to find Tiny staring straight at him, expressionless, his face unmoving except for the hairs across his Cro-Magnon brow, which danced to life for a second each time the breeze from the oscillating desk fan hit them. Jasper felt like he'd been placed into a vacuum chamber, as if all the air in his lungs was being sucked out and breathing in was impossible. Was Tiny messing with him—did Tiny know? Jasper wanted to choose his next words carefully. But all that came out of his mouth was a dry, squeakish "Not really."

"What? It was like the story of the summer! This guy carried a lost dolphin that needed help to shore then just ran away and disappeared, like he didn't want the fame and stuff. So this national search was on and tons of people were coming forward saying they were him. Different women were on every TV channel saying they knew the guy and he'd dated them and taken their money and all this stuff, but it was never the same guy, always different names and similar looks but not quite." Here Jasper couldn't help but feel a little pleased. Maybe all this time he'd been safer than he thought—he looked too much like himself to actually be himself, apparently. "Anyway, finally the guy comes forward—says he got a concussion on the day of the accident that gave him temporary amnesia. It took him a while to remember what had happened. But when he did, he wrote a song about the experience. He hadn't planned to share it with anyone . . . he'd been trying to make it as a singer/songwriter for years but sometimes wrote personal things that didn't go into his repertoire, and this was one of them."

Jasper wanted to scream. Why couldn't he have been born gullible? Why were his shoulders a custom-fitted resting place for the burden of cynical reality? Where others saw an inspirational story, he correctly saw bullshit. Why couldn't everyone realize what a con this was?

On the computer screen, the music video began with a song titled "Saving You Saved Me." A CGI dolphin was lying asleep in a hospital bed with gauze across its head and several IVs coming out of its left flipper; the camera panned out to reveal the dolphin in the operating theater of a large hospital, with surgical staff moving around its bed. The opening bars of music played and Jasper recognized them as a tune he'd often heard playing over the loudspeakers in the Oceanarium food court; he'd never listened to the lyrics, though, or imagined that any top 40 song had to do with dolphins. Especially not from an artist pretending to be him.

In the video, the Dolphin Savior entered wearing surgical gear, except the top of his scrubs was more like an open vest that he was bare-chested beneath, and oiled. He began singing a dramatic ballad as he put on a headlamp and approached the bed, holding out his hand to receive a scalpel.

"He's not going to put on gloves first?" Jasper asked. Offscreen, a fan was blowing DS's hair back off his shoulders in a way that made it easy to imagine what he'd look like riding a very fast horse.

Dolphin Savior then cut a long slit down the chest of the dolphin, and when he opened it, a glowing heart made of red crystal was inside. He reached in, removed it, and held it up to the light— there, in the center of the heart, was an image of him holding the dolphin in his arms.

"For Christ's sake!" Jasper exclaimed. He felt his face bloom red with malice as the song reached the chorus. The singer and the dolphin were flying through white clouds together, riding a gigantic life preserver magic carpet–style.

This guy, this Dolphin Savior, used Jasper's dolphin rescue to springboard his singing career into a hit song, and now he was going to have Bella learn a *special performance* for his concert? They were probably going to let him don a wet suit and enter the water with her, do the photo opportunity from the aquatic-show routine where a member of the audience comes up and a dolphin is signaled to put its nose against the person's cheek while the camera flashes.

"Yeah, the whole thing is so cheeseball," Tiny said. "Guess it was too much to ask for a video that hey, I don't know, addresses the environmental destruction that's threatening the dolphin's natural habitat or something."

Sure, Tiny, Jasper thought. *No topic makes a song climb the charts faster than environmental destruction.* He appreciated Tiny at least not fawning over the music, but why couldn't people see that it was all artifice? Dolphin Savior hadn't rescued anything except his failed career. He probably didn't have an overwhelming appreciation for dolphins as a species. Yet there he was, getting to have a design team bring Jasper's wildest fantasies to life.

When the video continued on to the next verse, the dolphin was sticking its head and dorsal fin out of the third-story window of a burning building; Dolphin Savior showed up in fire pants, boots, red suspenders, and a hat but nothing else, and climbed a ladder to do a rescue. The song's conclusion had him provide a moral redemption for the dolphin rather than a physical one: the dolphin was seen at a casino craps table making bet after bet and losing everything, then it passed out in an alleyway with an empty syringe sticking out of its pectoral fin. Until Dolphin Savior came along and handed the dolphin a Bible (at this offering, the dolphin just opened its eyes and looked at DS with gratitude; the video cut to a new scene before it showed the creature attempting to accept a book but not having any arms to do so); in the final shot DS and the dolphin were seated together in the front pew of a church dressed in their Sunday best.

"So wait, is this video about Dolphin Savior being an attractive guy people want to have sex with? Or about him spreading the word of God?"

"Well, he's a physically attractive Jesus figure. That's like his whole thing." *That was sort of my whole thing!* Jasper wanted to scream. "His fans call themselves melon heads. Melon, like the forehead of a dolphin? And he calls them his 'followers'—it's all got this religious twist. In my opinion it's becoming a cult. People are giving up their jobs to follow this guy along the coast to all his concerts. Their whole thing is finding stuff to save. Which, I mean, noble goal and all, especially if you're well-organized and well-funded and addressing true community needs. But it seems like they're all on recreational drugs and just scrounging for things to save—saving garbage by hoarding it in their vehicles? Saving bugs by capturing flies and mosquitos and stuff in jars and releasing them out in the country where people will be less likely to kill them? Saving time by not bathing?"

"I'd better get to work," Jasper said. He needed to figure out the remaining obstacles in his plot to rescue Bella immediately, before the weekend and Dolphin Savior's show, before that fraud ever got to lay eyes upon his woman.

All this news made Jasper feel better about his condition though. He'd been seeing his new sexual affliction as a social handicap, but in reality it was a gift. People were idiots. Opting out of the human race to live with another species on the periphery of society was probably the best thing he could do.

This belief was affirmed for him as he walked past the Dolf and Fina exhibit. They were Gogol robots built to look like dolphins; their vocal software could "hear" and respond to questions about aquatic biology. They were capable of fielding them in over fifty languages. The weird part to Jasper was that the Oceanarium put bathing suits on these dolphin robots. Dolf was in a pair of trunks, while Fina wore a bandeau bikini. Jasper sometimes worried that the swimwear might ignite his own affliction in others. Seeing that had to be confusing for hormonal teenagers, he thought. Hormonal anyone. Really mixed messages.

As if on cue, he watched a male adolescent leave his group of friends, approach the female robo-dolphin, and yell, "Take off your top!"

JASPER BEGAN FILLING HIS APARTMENT'S BATHTUB, THE SITE THAT would become his and Bella's first-ever watery nuptial bed by nightfall. It was the final item on his preparation checklist, and the most satisfying, a reward he'd saved for the end of a long morning of groundwork. The filled cooler was in the back of the station wagon (he tried not to think about how, since he'd removed the anterior two rows of seating and placed the enormous cooler in lengthwise, the inside of the car now looked a lot like a hearse). He'd be wheeling Bella from the pool to the parking lot inside a transporter sling used to lift dolphins out of the water for medical procedures; it was kept in the park's veterinary center, which he had custodial keys to in the office. He planned to place a large tarp over the top of the sling on the way to the car and avoid security cameras when possible. When impossible, it would hopefully just look like he was wheeling out trash or defunct equipment—he'd be in his Oceanarium uniform, after all.

The plan required him waiting until the end of his shift, which had been made slightly easier by Tiny calling in with car trouble. Jasper hadn't been sure about the best tactic to take with Tiny. He'd debated dropping a piece of false information to throw the cops on the wrong trail the next day when the dolphin was found missing—hint to Tiny how much he found himself thinking about taking a trip to Mexico. Or he could go the flattery route: tell Tiny what a great boss he was, ask him if he'd ever done something bad. Say how terrible he feels for the dolphins in captivity and that lately he'd been thinking how sometimes the right thing to do was one that few people would understand. Maybe then Tiny would have his back for a little bit once the investigation started.

But now the time for setup was over. A large amount of the custodial work was done in the morning, so security would assume any tasks he'd neglected that evening were going to be done the next day—he just had to hide out before and during their final sweep-through at closing. The night security guard only did two regularly timed perfunctory walk-throughs. He would not stop to count the dolphins.

AT CLOSING JASPER APPROACHED ONE OF THE PARK'S OVERSIZE SEA-cow–shaped trash cans, removed its heavy lid, and climbed inside. All the tops of the waste bins were painted to look like the heads of manatees. To dispose of waste, visitors pushed against a black circular flap that appeared to be the creature's open mouth. (What exactly was this teaching children? Jasper wondered. Why were they being encouraged to force-feed garbage to an endangered species?)

The inside of the can smelled worse than he'd hoped; he hadn't counted on disposable diapers or the contents of sweepers. Some errant reward sardines from the show had apparently found their way to the park grounds—birds often stole them—and they'd been baking for several hours. Jasper switched to mouth breathing. This was for Bella, he reminded himself.

He'd essentially climbed into a manatee-shaped solar tin oven. Five minutes into the wait he was already drenched in sweat, nauseous, mildly dizzy. This worried him—he'd need his full reserves of strength to get Bella into the cooler in his car. But he could hydrate at one of the sinks in the medical center.

Jasper had bought a watch with an alarm in case he happened to fall asleep in the container—of course he now realized this was impossible, but losing consciousness due to heatstroke was not. He hoped that if he passed out, a persistent Casio beep would be enough to nudge him back into reality, and that he'd have enough fumes left in his tank to lift his wilted body from the can.

The whole experience was anxiety producing. There was a sudden motion near his shoulder that he thought was a pigeon or a rat, or perhaps a hybrid pigeon/rat species indigenous only to that particular trash bin. It turned out to be a chili-stained hot dog riding the hydraulic lift of a crumpled soda can. There were several times when his eyes started crossing and inner-barrel stains in the metal appeared to be taking on the shape of a two-inch cockroach. But once he was dehydrated enough for a reel of daydream footage to thread itself and begin spinning through his brain, things got much better.

When the watch finally beeped, he was imagining himself asleep and bobbing on an inflatable raft in the outdoor pool at his rental house, his hair magically grown back to its previous length, Bella waking him up by pushing the thick lock that had fallen across his cheek and eyes back with her cold wet nose, and why not, giving his nipple a playful nudge before she swam away, inviting him into the water to join her.

IN THE TWILIGHT HOURS, THE AQUATIC MAMMAL-CENTRIC EQUIPMENT inside the Oceanarium's medical center made Jasper feel like a human slave escapee running through the main village hospital in a *Planet of the Apes*–style world ruled by dolphins instead of primates—on the walls, the anatomical diagram posters were of dolphins, not people; instead of examination tables there were recessed bathtub-like rectangles in the ground with drains and overhead faucets.

Jasper had never been into BDSM. He had little tolerance for physical discomfort on the masochistic side, and the sadistic side went against all his con instincts: he derived power from treating people far better than he felt they deserved, with an amount of care and tenderness that made them assume he liked or even loved them way more than he did. But he supposed in this parallel universe, if he'd just escaped from the Homo sapiens' holding tank and was trying to hide from his dolphin pursuers, there would be delicious suspense in waiting for them to find him, and probably even in the way they tortured him when they discovered him.

He finally found the sling, tucked back into an alcove instead of in its usual spot. He good-naturedly wagged a finger at it, like it was a relative with Alzheimer's who'd inadvertently wandered off, then began to gather the rest of the necessary items.

The sling collapsed for transport and storage into a shape that looked like a folded ironing board with wheels. He wrapped the top of it with a sheet, disguising its metal frame and bright blue fabric holster, then he wrapped himself, covering each arm and leg with a separate sheet so he'd still have full range of motion— complete mummification except for his eyes and nose, which would be facedown anyway. What he figured would be best in terms of the cameras was to make one quick motion at a time, followed by a minute of complete stillness, each motion taking no longer than a blink. He cracked the outer door just enough to slide the sling's frame out sideways, wheels to the wall, then counted to sixty and as quickly as he could turned it over flat onto the ground. After another minute, he moved through the door and stood flat against the building itself, feeling his stomach leap as he heard the cracked door close. He was back outside in a land of surveillance now.

A minute later was the squat down. A minute after that he was lying flat upon the ground completely. Then the finale: kicking off from the medical center's door, he rolled the frame surfer-style beyond the entrance video camera's line of sight, then finally stood up in order to de-sheet himself and reassemble the sling in the shadows. He barely registered the rest of the journey pushing the sling along the tree line to the auditorium: suddenly he was in the holding-tank room. The dolphins were asleep and silent in the water.

The image was almost more than he could stand—his beloved's vulnerable, dreaming face.

Jasper had befriended the daytime security guard in order to get as much info as possible. He'd brought him coffee, listened to him retell the jokes he'd heard that week from his fellow bowling leaguers ("What did one butt cheek say to the other? Together we can stop this shit!"), fraternally grabbed the guy's shoulder as he leaned forward and laughed and got good long looks at the security camera's range for each control-panel screen. The holding tank had a blind spot thanks to remodeling. A new section of the tank whose extended lip was out of sight on the security camera was where he'd draw the dolphins over to him with sardines and place the sling on Bella while they were distracted in a feeding frenzy. He had no idea if this would go smoothly or be an arduous process; he just needed to get her inside the sleeve—once she was out of the water, his car wasn't more than a three-minute run away, though her four-hundred-pound frame wouldn't be easy to push. The sling included a muzzle, which he hated to use (he wondered if he could simply continue feeding her for the duration of the trip to the car in order to keep her quiet?), but until they were safely back at his apartment, discretion was essential. There he'd lined the walls of the bathroom with sound-capturing foam and invested in a number of Gogol noise machines, whose ambient static would hopefully drown out any cries of confusion or alarm.

But his plan hadn't taken into account the beauty of her sleeping form. In repose, Bella's eye seemed shut in an act of pleasure, the mild curve of her nose a gracious smile she was making as a lover worked upon her. Jasper's arousal was throbbing and immediate, which he'd expected, but its persistence was what threw him for a loop—his body failed to understand, the dolphins bobbing there like permissive apples, why it couldn't be satisfied when the additional time this would take was inconsequential. Jasper attempted to ignore it. He went to the cooler, filled up large buckets of treat fish and placed them down on the sling's rolling platform. But walking was difficult. Was it silly to try to enact his plan when he was so handicapped by attraction, particularly when the cure was such a simple and obvious one?

Yes, he thought, in an ideal world he and Bella would be getting out as quickly as possible. But why not take a quick minute to relieve himself? With the dolphins this proximal, without any sort of glass between them, it would be as quick as a sneeze. Jasper climbed the tank's steps for a better look (which he nearly had to do on all fours; his entire lower torso had effectively shut down), and found that the decision seemed to have been made for him—a dolphin (not Bella, Sven—in Sven's biographical wall in the halls of the auditorium, his personality was described as "pensive") was sleeping just below the tank's lip like a docked submarine.

In the months after his mother's abandonment, there was a brief time when Jasper's father had attempted a salve of religion. They went to church frequently, and now Jasper remembered the parable of the ill man who'd touched Jesus's cloak as he passed by and had been instantly healed thanks to faith. Here, with Sven, Jasper realized all he'd have to do to be cured was touch the tip of himself against Sven's blubber.

"Are you kidding me?"

The voice was coming from nowhere and everywhere all at once—it had to be God.

He'd creeped out God. At no point in his deceptive philandering had he appalled God enough to make an appearance. But apparently, Jasper thought, he had finally crossed the line.

Then he realized the lights had come on. For a moment his brain had to reboot, like a copy machine warming up; all he could think of or see was the shock of brightness. But when the realization hit him, it was very bad news. Oh dear. It was Tiny.

On anyone else, Tiny's tie-dyed shirt would've been a signal of pacifism, but stretched across his broad chest, particularly with his current facial expression, it made him look like a bad man with supernatural powers. The twisting red pattern didn't seem to be a shirt at all so much as muscles forming a central wormhole in the middle of his stomach. Jasper almost expected balls of fire to shoot from it.

Tiny was gripping a long wooden flute like a police nightstick. "I understand people can resent the creatures they're employed to care for," he said. He stepped closer, repeatedly striking the flute against the palm of his hand in controlled slaps. "And that's okay. All feelings are valid. But actions are different. All actions are not okay, and you have trespassed into a very not-okay place. You aren't the first of my workers to act out. Once a guy drew a swastika on the forehead of the ceramic beluga in the marine gardens. But urinating into the blowhole of a dolphin is not just a pubescent stunt. That's a form of torture. Do you know what that would feel like to one of these innocent creatures who arguably already lives a pretty sad, imprisoned life? It would feel like waterboarding. And I mean, as far as I'm aware, even when our own government resorts to horrific and illegal acts of barbarism like this, they use water rather than their own urine. To my knowledge. So if you think about it, that makes you more depraved than the U.S. government. I get how harsh that statement must feel, but I have to tell you, from one living organism to another, I think you need a wake-up call. The Oceanarium has a psychologist on retainer. If you agree to see him—"

Jasper stood up and Tiny's eyes bulged wide. He stopped talking. Jasper looked down and saw his unbuttoned pants had fallen to the ground. His physical excitement was visible. "I love dolphins," Jasper managed to say.

"I'm going to ask you to put your pants back on," Tiny said. His voice was filled with caution and a little fear—he seemed to doubt Jasper would oblige. "Security knows I'm here," Tiny continued. "It was altruistic concern for *your safety* that brought me up here tonight, man. You forgot to kill the lights and lock the door in the maintenance office—I mean that's what I figured had happened when they did their check and found it open and lit up, but since you don't have a cell phone I worried I should make sure, just in case, that you hadn't knocked your head and passed out cold in the chum tank or something. Yeah, I happened to walk in on a situation you wish I had not walked in on; we've got some common ground there for sure, but *good intentions* were what brought me here tonight. You do not want the karma of hurting someone who was operating in your best interests, right? What I just saw indicates to me that you've got challenges in your life already; crosses are being borne. You don't need things getting more effed up for you. And I think I can say, because it's objective and I am indeed humble, that karma is sort of my copilot. Karma is that loyal dog that would sleep on top of my grave each night should I die. I think it would really sink its teeth into the flesh of anyone who did me wrong, especially if I myself were unable to seek justice on my own behalf, because I was, say, dead."

"I'm not a violent person," Jasper said. Tiny's eyes glanced down at Jasper's bare crotch again, just for a second. Jasper wished he didn't have so many sores and abrasions from the chafing rubber pants.

"You're not going to harm me?" Tiny asked. "In any way? Bad-touch categories included? Any touch at all from you right now would be a bad touch, to clarify."

Jasper began putting his pants back on. It was easier to take another man's word at face value when he was wearing pants. "Of course I'm not going to harm you."

"Okay, good," Tiny said. "So let's move forward. You're definitely fired. I'll just tell everyone I caught you stealing cleaning supplies—this is for my sake, not yours; I don't want to have to rehash this. But if you do something insane like put me down as a reference for another job, I will not blink twice before I tell them I caught you trying to have conjugal relations with a dolphin."

"I wasn't going to do that," Jasper said quietly. "I was just going to touch it to the side of a dolphin."

"I'm going to have to burn sage here," Tiny said. "Everywhere you patrolled actually. I am going to really have to smoke it out."

ON THE DRIVE BACK TO HIS STUDIO, JASPER FOUND HIMSELF CAREEN-
ing in and out of lanes as he wept. His modified station wagon now
ferried a sizable cooler that did not feel empty at all but filled with
Jasper's dead dreams.

He wanted to drive the car straight onto the beach and into
the ocean but knew that would result in an anticlimactic shutdown
of the vehicle before its back tires even got wet; he'd also receive a
hefty fine from beach patrol, who would ask him for identification,
and given his current luck, the license would probably come back
as being stolen. He'd probably been about to get fired for fraud
anyway.

Tonight really had been his one chance. He'd blown it.

Pulling up at his shit-hole apartment only emphasized this.
He'd told himself that living in misery was going to be such a fleet-
ing means to an end. He remembered reading an interview with the
CEO of Gogol, the company that made all the phones and gadgets
and other stuff that everyone was hooked on in their daily lives. The
one whose professional-grade microcameras were responsible for
all the photos and videos of Jasper holding a dolphin on the beach.
In the start-up days, the CEO said he'd just moved into an office
space and worked on the floor in the corner—hadn't even bought
furniture!—because he was so driven that creature comforts were
the least of his concerns. Jasper had told himself this was what he
was doing too; he'd had tunnel vision because nothing mattered
but getting Bella.

Now it was time to go inside and make a decision. Would he
drive to the paid-for house with the pool that represented all the
planned joy he wasn't ever going to have? Would he go to another
city, where he still wouldn't be able to sleep with women and therefore couldn't make decent money, especially if he wanted to work

under an alias? His real name wasn't safe; exes he'd conned whose parents or relatives had deep pockets probably also had private detectives who'd figured out his identity and were salivating, in wait for him to reappear.

Stepping indoors, he saw the outline of his blow-up mattress in the efficiency's corner. It was covered with various plushy-dolphin stuffed animals he'd brought home from the Oceanarium gift shop and used in shameful ways. He'd been meaning to take them to the Laundromat but worried about someone seeing him washing a load of dolphin stuffed animals and making a call to the police based on a general hunch of something's-weird-ness.

The apartment's walls were haphazardly decorated with ripped-out print images he'd found, mainly in children's activity books. One was a connect-the-dots illustration of a dolphin that he'd hung up right above his pillow. At the time he'd felt it was almost like a cave drawing, a symbolic representation made all the more meaningful by its crudeness: it was the lowest-passing image that could attempt to summarize the greatness of this creature. And in terms of his thoughts and feelings toward interspecies romance, he was a bit Paleolithic in a first-responder, early-on-the-scene type of way—sure, most people who heard about his plan would want to discuss reasons why he should *not* attempt to seize a dolphin from corporate ownership and pursue domestic cohabitation with the mammal, but the first guy who discovered fire probably had a lot of naysayers too. That's how Jasper had felt these past few months— like a chosen pioneer. After all, he hadn't asked for this attraction. He hadn't been born with it. It had struck him, seemingly literally; dolphin cupid had hit him with cone-tooth-shaped arrows and he hadn't lusted for a human being since.

But it was clear to Jasper now that natural selection had not called out his name. The roster had been posted. He hadn't made the team.

He walked into the bathroom and looked at the tub he'd pre-filled for Bella that morning.

That was the closest he was going to get to Bella now—the bathwater he'd intended for her to be in.

Tiny had ruined Jasper's shot at not becoming a Shakespearean tragedy. Maybe, Jasper thought, he should just embrace it. If the dolphin that attacked him on the beach had wanted Jasper to meet his end in a watery grave, well, it was about to get its wish.

He'd had a good run. *Jasper, you scoundrel, you've had a good run*—he thought this and looked in the dark bathroom mirror and gave himself a congratulatory wink. He could go live it up first with the cash he had left—the life earnings of all his cons, the nest egg he was going to use to fund his life with Bella. But live it up how? The only things he enjoyed were sex and conning people out of money (by having great sex with them), and he couldn't do the latter anymore, and with the former he couldn't cover any new ground unless he had a live dolphin, and he didn't.

He *could* leave a note identifying himself as the true Dolphin Savior. Who knew if anyone would believe it, but he could try. To add validity to this claim, he could put his stockpiled money in a bank account and leave a list of all the women he'd conned—he'd do his best, anyway, to remember—along with the Dolphin Savior note. Jasper could pretend he was riddled with guilt about what he'd done to the women. He could write that seeing another man being a fraud in public made him realize what a fraud he was himself, and that he wanted his victims to divide up the money in whatever way seemed fair.

But ultimately he didn't have the energy. It was time to move on. Jasper felt the familiar antsy feeling, centered in his gut with twitchy roots moving down into his crotch and thighs, that preceded all of his relocations, except magnified to a degree he understood as being the actual end.

He didn't just need to leave the town or the state this time. He had to go Elsewhere, forever.

JASPER DRAINED THE TUB AND REFILLED IT WITH WARM WATER, climbed inside, and placed a razor on the nightstand. He wanted to do the cutting underwater. It could get all red and cloudy and feel like an attack, which was what had started this nightmare. He'd been attacked and it had left him a different person, and he did not care to go through life being that person. With Bella, with the ability to feel satisfied, he could've done it. He'd been excited to try at least. Though that would not have been a very carefree, easy sort of life to maintain. It might have gone down in flames in a far worse way than this.

And he had won so often, for so long. He'd known it wasn't possible to win forever. Jasper hadn't expected his streak to end this soon, or to end in such a weird way. But since it had, here he was.

Just to make sure he had enough motivation to go through with it—he didn't want to have second thoughts halfway—he grabbed the Gogol tablet he'd permanently borrowed from one of the Oceanarium's educational classrooms and pulled up the Dolphin Savior's hit song.

As the song began playing, an ad popped up in the corner of the screen: a bikinied woman was giving him a seductive wink. Her face reminded him a bit of a former con's—Nele? Christina?

Maybe it was a sign. He clicked on the ad and decided to try one last time to get aroused by a human woman. Life or death.

The bikinied woman leaned forward to speak, her lips hovering just above her cleavage. "Complex, individual problems require customized solutions," she said, shaking her hips a little. "Solutions as unique as the individuals who need them." The sound of hopeful string music began to play.

Jasper lowered the volume. The ad's content wasn't as sexy as he'd hoped. But her body was great—that's what he needed to focus on.

"We work one-on-one with people whose wishes can't be answered by mainstream technology," the woman continued. He had to stop himself from staring at the water, watching it ripple.

He realized he was hoping a dolphin might appear.

Sighing, Jasper watched as another bikini-clad woman pushed a quadriplegic male amputee several decades her senior down the beach in a wheelchair. Two more women—also bikini clad but wearing safety goggles and unbuttoned white lab coats—were approaching. They were carrying something together, balancing it on their right shoulders. Was it a kayak?

It was not. They stopped and stood it upright in the sand. It looked like the back half of a rigid wet suit. Together, the three women picked the man up and snapped the suit around the back of his body like a cell-phone case.

And just like that, he was standing upright. The man let out a high-pitched whistle and an unmanned Jet Ski came bounding across the water at high speed. It stopped at his feet like a well-trained dog, idling. The man climbed onto the Jet Ski. How old was he, exactly? Eighty-two? The bikini-clad woman who'd been pushing his wheelchair then climbed onto the Jet Ski, and he lowered himself down so she could climb atop his shoulders. The other women joined too, stepping out of their lab coats, tossing their safety goggles to the sand, wrapping around the man in a big sandwich. They Jet-Skied off into the water and somehow even over the motor, even as they receded farther into the distance, the sound of them giggling together was very clear.

"The possibilities of tomorrow can be yours today," the voice-over encouraged. "Come to Biotech Medical and let the future help you. Biotech, a subsidiary of Gogol."

13

HAZEL MOTORED INTO THE HOUSE TO FIND HER FATHER SITTING BE-
tween Diane and his newest doll, also a redhead. "Knock first!" he
yelled.

"You could also lock the door, Dad." Hazel stood and turned
around, surreptitiously taking the brick of cash out of her pants, then
placed it on the coffee table. "Here's some cash. It's about a year's
rent. But I have a better proposal—I'm taking you to Gogol's medical
facilities. I appreciate it that you didn't want to tell me, and if you
want, we don't have to talk about it at all. You can just pack a suitcase
and we'll get into a cab. The whole way there, we can talk about the
weather or baseball or make a ranked, ordered list of the ways I've most
disappointed you. I won't bring up the cancer. I'll come spend each
day there with you too, or if you'd rather be alone that's fine. I'll visit
as much or as little as you'd like. You can call all the shots."

"I know I can call the shots, Hazel. It's my damn life." Looking at him nestled there between Di and the second doll, what struck Hazel was how the dolls' expressions stayed unchanged and bubbly no matter what words were said around them. It was as if they were in a country where they didn't speak much of the language and had misinterpreted the conversation as a lighthearted one, or were willfully trying to keep the party going despite a developing scuffle. Maybe she could talk to Byron about this. Gogol surely could make a sex doll whose face was appropriately responsive to conversational stimuli. Then again, that was probably a terrible idea. Hazel felt a pang of nausea imagining the customers who'd be delighted to have a doll whose face looked worried when yelled at, or a doll who cried.

"I agree; it is your life. So let's go save it."

He slid his glasses down to the end of his nose and squinted, which was what he did when super-perplexed. As a teenager she'd called it his "Chancellor Moleman" expression. He looked like an underground creature who'd had to surface for a practical errand, to file some sort of paperwork on behalf of his species, and was repulsed by everything he saw in the daylight.

"That's why I didn't bring it up, Hazel. I knew you'd want me to go to some crackpot laboratory. I didn't want you to take it personal, kiddo. It's not like if we got along better I'd want to try to live forever. I'm done with treatment."

"What you've tried is basic compared to what's possible. You can't just give up and die."

He smiled, which to Hazel hurt more than anything. She wanted him to yell and tell her it was none of her business, or say that he probably got sick in the first place from worrying about all her bad decisions. He could even tell her she was such a failure that dying would give him some peace. Anything to keep some distance from this gruff man she'd always cared about despite herself.

Distance had always been their agreement. It was how he'd been able to go his way while she went hers. This smile that drew her closer was not something she could protect herself from. "Hazelbear," he said. She felt ill. When had he last used that name? "Too much of anything is torture. I've seen the movie. I know how it ends and I don't need to sit through it again. I'd hoped you'd be moving along about the time the going gets rough. I don't know how much longer that will be, but I wanted to spare you. How'd you find out?"

Hazel considered lying: she wanted him to believe she'd figured it out by herself, through her very own cleverness.

"Byron. This Sleep Helmet I wore. It diagnoses illnesses in those around you."

He made the Chancellor Mole face again. "Do you see what I mean? It's my time. The world that made sense to me has retired."

"Don't end your life over a stupid helmet invention." Hazel wanted a reason for his giving up that she could accept, and she hadn't heard it yet. "Is it because of Mom? What you saw when she did the treatments?"

"It's because I'm done. And I want to spend the short time I've got left in my own home surrounded by beautiful women. Or replicas of them. Whatever. I've never been picky."

"Okay," Hazel said. She let out a long exhale. Despite what this meant for his health, she had to work not to smile. She felt so relieved that she didn't have to go back to The Hub. "Well, I'm here for you. I'll be here with you till the end."

Her father shook his head. "I appreciate that, Hazel. I don't think it's wise though. You always have a hard time staying out of trouble, but the stench of crisis on you now is at an all-time high."

"Dad, don't die alone." *Also, don't kick me out*, she thought.

"Hazel." He took Di's left hand and the other doll's right hand. "I won't be alone. That's what the gals are for. Meet Roxy. Also, I think we should all be drinking."

"Are you worried about the gross parts? Don't be. I'm so glad you're not a machine! Bodies breaking down . . . that's what Byron wants to stop, but there's something special about it. 'Special' is the wrong word. Correct? Orderly? Maybe even benevolent? The fact that we end. A body that's in the woods long enough will deteriorate into nothing. We're guests that clean up after ourselves. That's, like, a sign of our goodness in a way? Our cells if not us? I don't want you to feel embarrassed. I'm sure you never thought about me having to change your diaper or something. But to me it's like, you're *real*. You're separate from things that are manufactured."

"Jesus Christ, Hazel. Byron really did a number on you, didn't he?"

He did. Hazel walked over to the mirror on the wall and stared. Looking at herself meant that in several hours she'd be looking at Byron.

It was possible that her father would change his mind when the going got tough. She could keep working on him. But he was stubborn, and for the moment wouldn't budge, so she decided to take the opportunity to tell Byron to go to hell since she'd hopefully be begging for his forgiveness soon, calling to tell him they'd had a change of heart and were ready to be picked up. "Byron," she said aloud, "he doesn't want the help. But thank you for the offer." In the background reflection, Hazel saw her father's eyes go wide.

"Who the hell are you talking to?" Then he smiled and in a half-joking voice asked, "That mirror's not some kind of spy camera, right? Byron hasn't been watching us?"

Hazel could only imagine what living room ménage à trois antics her father and crew had performed.

"Don't worry, Dad. When *you're* alone, you really are alone. At least I think you are. I'm a different story."

"Huh? Hazel, you're not making any damn sense."

"I'm just kidding," she said. "Forget it."

Part of Hazel wanted to go down to the bar to meet Liver, but then she had an image of him gravesitting for her father's own grave and she decided to just take the night off everything. Instead she'd go out back to the porch and sleep in the casket box while her dying father slept in the next room with two women who were never alive.

In the morning she'd try to decide what the hell to do. If it was better, after her father was taken care of, of course, to live out her days inside Byron's spyglass. Or if it was preferable to take herself out and make Byron's screen go black.

It was nighttime, and now that she didn't have to sleep next to Byron she felt a little like masturbating. But then he would see it and know all the embarrassing scenarios she thought of to help her orgasm. He'd hear her come. Her mind thought forward: as she got older and softer and probably more out of shape, he'd see her naked body and its sagging contours, intimate sights meant to be viewed through a loving lens. He'd see them all. And if she one day found a significant other, everyone she met and cared about, actually—he'd see them too.

The only way to not be spied on was to completely not exist.

HAZEL WOKE WITH A BURNING URGE TO WASH HER FATHER'S FEET and trim his toenails, really ceremonially, disciple-style. Maybe she'd been going about this wrong. Maybe instead of pissing Byron off by sleeping with ex-convicts or taking herself out she needed to embrace saintly duties and live a life of self-deprecation. It wouldn't count as much as it should since Byron would know the thoughts she was having, know how miserable she was, know how a martyr's life of restraint was a performance for her. But wouldn't it count for something?

"No." Hazel said this aloud. She looked over at the wide, attentive eye of the plastic flamingo and the word seemed to have come from him, an emphatic voice of agreement. Byron didn't feel compassion, and Byron wasn't her master. It wasn't like she was a caged dog who'd bitten a child and had to prove she was rehabilitated enough to be released. Nothing she'd ever do would cause Byron to say, "I'm freeing you; you've earned it." She couldn't earn it. Byron had to give it and he never would. She had three choices: surrender and return to him, live in surveillanced exile, or die. Which option would be the least horrible, she wasn't sure.

But there would be something of a personal redemption in tending to her father. She'd made the wrong choice in marrying Byron, and in staying with him for so many years. Even if it wouldn't matter to Byron if she did something good, it could matter to her.

The thing was, her father was a grouch. As someone who wasn't dying of cancer, and as a freeloader, Hazel knew she didn't have a right to complain audibly, but wow was he difficult to spend an evening with. Diane and Roxy only complicated things—they were a silent presence, yes, but still a presence, and seemed to make him automatically win every argument—it was three against one.

Tonight they were all watching a movie about a past war. Diane was lying sideways across Hazel's father's lap, posed as though he'd just carried the doll over the hearth of their new home, one arm bent up around his neck, holding on in an almost casual way, Diane's head turned to the TV. As the white flashes of gunshots and violent noise washed over her permasmile, the juxtaposition made it hard for her to not seem sadistic. She grinned through the most gruesome close-up shots of disemboweled soldiers. They each seemed to be a personal enemy; she was delighted to watch them get their comeuppance.

In his bathrobe with a painkiller-induced expression of seren-ity, Hazel's father also seemed appreciative of the violence. Was it a masculinity thing he was going for, watching these films? If so, she didn't understand it. It wasn't like Diane and Roxy were complain-ing about his performance in the bedroom.

Instead of watching the TV, Hazel watched him. He was a new species of being, an About-to-Die, which Hazel hadn't interacted with much. She'd purposely stayed away from her mother during this time; she'd feared what her mother might expect from her. But now she had the reverse problem: Hazel found she expected some-thing from her father, particularly given the fact that he was all she had going at the moment. She wanted an increased profundity in manner, maybe. When were they going to have tearful all-night talks where he spoke of his numerous regrets in parenting her and begged her forgiveness? When was he going to wax poetic about what a cel-ebration her existence, despite her failed marriage and current lack of employment, ignited daily within his heart? When was he going to bequeath her diamonds of wisdom gleaned from a near-full-term life span? Hazel always took a geological approach to epiphany—if she didn't understand something, it was because she was too new at it; she just needed to get more layers of "experience crust" to put weight on the memories and information she did have so the an-swers would squeeze out.

Maybe things would get more important-seeming when he grew more helpless. Perhaps it would take the intimacy of crossed taboos—her washing him, changing him—for her to earn any sort of tenderness or gratitude.

It *had* to feel more worthwhile at some point, because otherwise Byron would win yet another argument. Hazel liked to think that nature must have some wisdom, but Byron felt nature was a series of defects. *People want to think of anything in nature as normal, and anything human made as abnormal. Nature isn't normal*, he'd once said. *Nature is weak. Dying is normal if nature's your reference. Why would I want to subscribe to a system whose best-case scenario is decline speeding up into fatality?*

If Byron saw her tend to her father until his death and saw that the experience was an empty one, wouldn't that be an implied *I told you so*? He'd be more convinced than ever that humanity was a problem to engineer beyond. Hazel wanted her father to affirm that the traditional life cycle held inherent value. The thought that there was a loophole, that soon technology could flatten the circle and make linear vitality go on indefinitely, added a new level of tragedy to every prior death, to Phyllis, to the fact that one of Hazel's formative Christmases had been ruined unnecessarily. And it increased the wrongness about herself that she felt in the pit of her stomach—if she had a hard time enjoying her natural life span and finding adequate worth inside the experience, how could she hope to make it through an eternity?

Byron's internal surveillance added a pressure to achieve happiness that was counterproductive to happiness. Every failure she had, emotionally and otherwise, would be amplified by the fact that Byron had watched it play out.

"Dad? You said the other day that you could die at any moment.

I mean we all could, but you said it's pretty likely for you. Which I think was hyperbole—all the more reason to go to the Gogol facility and just see where things are with the cancer. But, let's say you're right. The end could come in an hour. Why do you want to spend the last moments of your life watching war movies?"

His face was drawn up in a cringed expression; two soldiers on TV were torturing an enemy POW to try to get information. He didn't respond.

Her father and Di's and Roxy's matched stillness seemed like a trick from a horror movie. What if her father had in fact just died, and his departed soul had entered Di's body? What if she had to spend the rest of her life living with her father whose spirit was living inside the body of a highly sexualized female mannequin? Or what if Di was secretly possessed by an evil demon—it had been lying dormant inside her, waiting to be awakened by the repeated sound of automatic weapon discharges, and this movie had made it happen? It seemed that if Hazel reached across Diane to place two fingers on her father's throat to check for a pulse, the doll could spin awake and bite her wrist. Hazel stood over him and slowly began to lean down.

"It's cathartic!" her father finally yelled; Hazel jumped back. With each word, Diane lifted and fell slightly, awash on the rough seas of her father's booming diaphragm. "I'm dying of cancer. What do you want me to watch, cartoon kittens? I'm in the trenches, Hazel. I'm in the rabbit hole about to be shot." He extended an arm to the television. "These are my people. What are you doing, sitting around here anyway? You should be out living. Ideally *making* a living. You might actually be getting my stink of death upon you. Death does have a smell. It stinks. You think you're going to be able to pick up a new man smelling like that?"

Hazel told herself to be fair. She hadn't been able to predict all the bad in life, which meant unpredictable good might unfold too. She wanted to see—*But not for you, Byron!* she made sure to add inside her head—just what would happen with her father. If there really was nothing, if life really held nothing, then maybe her self-controlled exit could have nothing at all to do with Byron, and that would be a sort of vengeance. She'd be running away from something even greater than him, even greater than a person with a godlike comprehension of her daily life. She'd be fleeing the fact that nothing, in either the natural landscape or Byron's world of technology, could remedy her despair.

She'd been so worried about Byron putting out a mercenary hit on her. But what he'd done was one better. He'd more or less convinced her to do it herself.

THAT EVENING, LIVER WAS NOT AT THE SPOTTED ROSE. "HAVE YOU seen him?" Hazel asked the bartender. The woman was stretching the side of her mouth flesh out in front of a mirror, seemingly looking for something on the inside of her cheek.

She shook her head. "I have not. Not all evening, and that has never happened. It isn't unreasonable to think the worst. He's always here, so the fact that he isn't means he's too physically impaired to come. I don't mean too drunk, I mean too broken limbed or dead. I'd say try the ER, but he'd never go on his own."

Hazel swallowed. Byron wouldn't take out such a small fish, would he? "Do you have a car I could borrow?"

Now the woman took both hands out of her mouth and turned around, eyeing Hazel.

"Those are like two different questions," the woman said. "I do have a car."

"I slept with him," Hazel offered.

"What does that have to do with my car?" the woman worried aloud, suspicious.

"Nothing. I just mean my concern for him is real." Hazel paused. "My ex found out that I slept with him and I'd like to check in. But his dwelling situation is not close by. I think I can remember how to get back to it, but I'd need a car."

The woman shrugged and reached for her keys. "It won't go well for you in this car if you get pulled over. And I don't care if you try to steal it. But care will be given by others, and I mean, woman to woman, you don't want that brand of justice on your tail. If you do, that is gross."

"No," Hazel repeated. She decided this word would be her brain's new autoreply in uncomfortable situations, or during times when someone asked her a question and she hadn't really been listening. Social pressure seemed to push her toward the other direction—to want her to nod and agree to everything. Flash a timid smile that could be interpreted however the listener liked. But after her marriage, Hazel found no combination more appalling than the vague with the affirmative. Know the full story; that's when you get wholly on board. That's how you avoid becoming an evil tech genius's science-project wife.

"If you find him please call an ambulance instead of taking him to the hospital in the car," the bartender said. "Cloth interior. I don't have time for that."

To this Hazel said, "Yes."

The car was an older model, the longest size of regular-vehicle car possible. Driving it felt like simultaneously towing and plowing.

There was a thud on the car's roof. When Hazel got out, a large snakeskin boot was standing upright on top of it.

Was it Liver's? She looked up in the tree, the same large tree they'd parked in front of the last time she'd visited Liver's shed, but didn't spot the shoe's mate. She couldn't remember if Liver had worn shoes at all. But if he had? What would make him climb a tree?

Hazel felt herself beginning to run, then sprint. She hadn't done any type of exercise in years—with Byron she always had the urge to be invisible, which to Hazel seemed to correlate with stillness. Don't move; don't be spotted. Blend into the wall.

Liver's shed was completely gone. In its place was a yard sign declaring the area to be the property of Gogol Industries. Tresspassers would be reported. There was a singular camera mounted on a stick, a tiny orb Hazel heard move to focus on her face. It began snapping several pictures. She didn't know whether to run or cry or hold up her middle finger.

She ran.

She had to get back to her father's house; the car she could abandon a few blocks away with the keys inside. It was the least of her worries.

HAZEL WENT STRAIGHT TO HER FATHER'S BACKYARD. SHE WAS SURE there would be another safe there, with a phone inside, just as though she'd never pawned anything at all. It was a game Byron could play forever—she could get rid of the safe every day for the rest of her life, and by morning a new one would be right there waiting.

But it wasn't identical. When the safe clicked and hummed and its nanoparts opened, all the same electronics were there. But Liver's necklace of teeth was draped across them.

Byron's video call was already up on the phone, waiting. His hands were folded in his lap, his eyes directing the circus of monitors. "I saw," Hazel told him. "Did you have Liver arrested or something?" Hazel wanted nothing more than to hurl the device against the side of the house and make Byron's image crack into jagged pieces of glass. "This is over the line. Let him go." She paused. "I'll come back home as soon as I know Liver's okay, even if my father won't agree to treatment. Are you happy? You've successfully negotiated a hostage trade." Being away from The Hub wasn't worth others getting hurt.

"I'm so glad to hear that you're coming back, Hazel. We've all missed you."

"If I know and see that he's okay."

Byron put his lips together and made a "hmhm" sound. "Whom are you referring to?"

Hazel swallowed. "You didn't have him killed, did you?"

Byron's Adam's apple gave a happy bob. She used to look at its Ping-Pong-ball shape and size and think how his tiny heart could actually be housed there instead of in his chest. "Hazel, who? It seems like you're referring to an imaginary friend. Someone of whom there's no trace. You know what happens when you search online for someone imaginary? You don't find anything. *You're* real, and I can prove it by searching for you on the Internet. You're mentioned countless times. You're there in photos, listed as my wife."

Her lower intestines felt like they were filling with very cold yet somehow molten copper. The sensation spread and she had the urge to cut herself down the middle and take out all her organs and bury them. They were screaming inside her like infants who wanted to be swaddled.

"I am having a different reality from the Internet's reality," Hazel said. Her voice was quiet and slow. She felt drugged by sad desperation.

"It's one hypothetical measure of a man, you know," Byron said. "Or of a person, I guess. Not just men. If someone dies and no one knows about it . . . you see my point. This is something you don't have to worry about, Hazel. I saved you from anonymity. But don't be content to stop there. You're an integral part of something really big, something we've been working toward for years. You get to represent millions of dollars of work and groundbreaking research. You're important. I'm offering you a true partnership here. An enormous place in my legacy. It's silly to waste any more time. Come home, and think about bringing your father with you. We can probably save his life."

Stalling would end the conversation more quickly than saying no. "I need some time to mourn Liver," Hazel said. "I'm feeling pretty upset that he never existed."

Byron sighed. "Fine. Spin your wheels a little longer. But please don't test my patience. You can grieve all you want at The Hub. I can even have a black veil waiting for you. Whatever you need, Hazel. I'm a supportive guy."

The call ended and Hazel found herself down in the backyard's grass, crawling toward the porch's sliding-glass door. When she reached it she put her forehead against it and sat there waiting, like a pet who'd been let out to urinate.

Hazel wished her father owned a dog or a cat, some animal who could give her blind comfort. Her parents had never allowed pets. *Living things that don't wear undergarments aren't welcome on my sofa,* her mother used to say. *And dogs can't feel guilt. Not enough guilt, anyway. Not nearly enough to where I'm okay having a relationship with one.*

Hazel began to bang her head against the glass, halfheartedly trying to break it but also not minding the way it hurt or the possibility that she might be able to knock herself unconscious if she kept at it long enough. "You and mom were so aloof and cold," Hazel suddenly yelled. She was yelling through the glass, at her father, even though he wasn't in the room. What she could see in the glass was her reflection, so she was actually yelling at that, which made her yell louder. "Don't you think that has something to do with why I married a monster? Are you aware that my whole life you've winced whenever I came through the door? It's not great for self-esteem. In my brain I was all, *Am I a human? Am I a tumbleweed made of fiberglass insulation? Am I the polio virus?*"

Hazel found she was crying in the really hysterical way that made her face wet and plastery. There were some mucal fireworks as she began to pound on the glass with her fists in addition to her head.

It felt like if she made enough noise, the house would transform into her dream parents' home instead of her father's. The bright suburban décor that filled its rooms would be a convincing argument that it was not inhabited by a dour hermit couple but by two warm parents who weren't too depressed or cynical to attempt home improvement. Hazel often thought of how different her life might be if she'd been raised by people who knew wallpaper could make a difference and proved it. Parents who were enthusiastic and boundlessly accepting and messaged her sayings like "Failure is part of the journey to success." Ones who were politically active in causes of social justice and didn't base their voting decisions on xenophobic rumors they heard from the line cook and sometimes counter waiter at the corner diner who felt Hitler was not a saint but did have a lot of good ideas that should not be thrown out with the

Holocaust bathwater. "I'm grateful for the myriad ways you did not abuse me," Hazel clarified. "I was never starved or kept inside a cage or repeatedly burned with cigarettes. I guess it just sucks how a lot of parents like their children but you didn't like me. It also sucks how even though I didn't really like you, I never stopped wanting you to like me, because you never cared if I liked you or didn't."

Now she was trying as hard as she could to break the glass. "Do you know how when people are really hungry they will be driven to eat the inedible? Grass and soil and the like? That also happens with love. If you want love badly enough, you will start gobbling harmful substitutes like attention and possessions. Do you know what I thought when I first met Byron? 'He doesn't seem to hate me! I can easily work with this!'"

"STOP!" her father yelled, wheeling toward her from the other side. "Jesus and Joseph! What is happening here?" He slid the door open and looked at the blurry smears of knuckle blood Hazel had left. "This is always unlocked. God, look at you. You're having an emotional meltdown? I don't want to get into a discussion of feelings. What I can do is dismiss my expectations regarding the light household tasks it would've been civil of you to have not fallen behind on, particularly given the state of my health and mobility. Come inside and shut the door behind you and don't wash a single dish today."

"You're dying," Hazel said. "And you're refusing medical attention. I get the feeling you aren't going to miss me."

"Oh, Hazel." He raked his nails through the chest hair beneath his bathrobe. "I just want some peace and quiet."

Was he talking about death? About the present moment? Both? "Liver's dead," Hazel near-whispered. "Someone killed him."

"Good grief," her father said. The silence filled with the mechanical sound of him moving the Rascal back a few inches then forth, thinking. "Go to the kitchen and make yourself a drink then join me and the girls in the living room. We're going to watch *Jeopardy!* and pretend for a half hour that things aren't going to hell in every direction. Let's do it while we still can."

She didn't want to feign normalcy, but drinking sounded okay. And from her time growing up and her time being married, Hazel knew that if you were having a moment where you couldn't bring yourself to pretend, sitting quietly was a good enough substitute.

Out of nowhere, Hazel thought of the driver who used to take her between The Hub and her father's house. She'd been fond of him; he had a family. Byron could hurt all those people. Then she scolded herself for having the thought. Since he received all her thoughts, any fear she experienced might as well be a wish.

She'd call him soon. *I will talk to you soon, Byron,* she thought. She'd wait until her father got so weak he couldn't fight being admitted into medical care, and then they'd both go to The Hub together. She didn't want to screw things up for anyone else.

14

HER FATHER HAD BEEN TELLING HER DAILY THAT HE MIGHT HAVE ONLY a few weeks to live, but Hazel factored in some wiggle room: nothing was ever as bad as he made it out to be. Growing up, prior to each summer vacation they'd take in the family sedan, he'd recite a lengthy soliloquy as they packed about how the next week was going to be the worst waste of time and money imaginable: every motel they'd find to stay in would be a rat hole with broken plumbing; every bedsheet would be rife with parasitic infections; every tourist trap would be packed and overpriced and an uncomfortable temperature. "I'm going to walk around all day and get a groin rash, then we'll retire back to the motel and some bug with a heavy abdomen will crawl on my thigh while I sleep and lay her eggs in my open sores." But the vacations and rooms were never that awful. "Boy," he'd exclaim as they headed home. "We really lucked out. We really dodged a bullet."

This time, though, her father had perhaps underestimated. His fever wasn't breaking; he couldn't keep anything down. Hazel kept begging him to go to the medical center with her, but he still had enough strength to forcibly spit on the floor and refuse. "I'm not leaving," he'd stress. "And no one's asking you to stay."

Hazel wished he was, but it was becoming clear his decline would not include emotional delicacy. He'd had her place Diane and Roxy into bed with him. She figured that soon his slips in and out of consciousness would become deeper and farther apart, and then she could call Byron and tell him they were ready.

There were things she ideally wanted to say to her father before medical personnel were present, some a little bitter, but now also didn't seem like a good time to pick a fight. He'd retreated into his cave, and Hazel knew he'd prefer to stay there alone. He wanted to advance toward expiration without giving his embarrassment an audience. At least not a living one.

Since they had no physical needs, Di and Roxy could keep a constant vigil. Maybe lifelike mannequins were the way to go in terms of hospice. They could be tailor-made for this purpose—Diane's full breasts could lactate morphine, for example. Roxy's torso could slide open on command and double as a bedpan chamber.

Hazel found it depressing, or maybe just disappointing, on a personal level, how even though her father was fatally ill, on the whole she was still incapable of appreciating him. She tried watching TV on the bed with the three of them—she placed eye masks on the dolls so it looked like they were resting, peaceful and waxen. It was like instead of dying, her father was turning into a doll too.

But the smell. Death did have an odor. She kept the bedroom window open although she hated the vulnerable feeling that caused. It was illogical; a pane of glass wasn't going to make any difference to Byron. Plus he was already camped out inside her mind. But it felt so much easier for him to get to her when there was just a screen between the inside of the house and the open air. She looked out of it at least twelve times a day, fearful that he'd somehow transported her father's entire house into a warehouse chamber of The Hub without her noticing. It was a slight comfort when she looked into the yard and saw palm trees instead of the wall of a cement bunker.

Hazel decided to go watch TV by herself in the living room instead. She found a sitcom about a horny single mother who ran a secret yoga studio in her living room after her children went to bed each night; the only moves and positions she taught were ones adapted to allow for autocunnilingus, and for two hours other single mothers would come over and guzzle red wine then lie on mats and lick their own crotches to orgasm. The show's sound track featured bursts of soft jazz and the punctuated orchestral swelling of frenzied violins. *Hey*, one woman on the show said. They were panting and heaped together on the mats post-session; their thin legs had intertwined to form a nest of Lycra and spandex twigs. *It's great we can touch ourselves like that. Independence and all. But why don't we ever touch each other? I mean, we're all just here to get off, right? Does it have to be a solitary thing?* The rest of the women giggled in unison. *But then it's not yoga. Then it's an orgy!* Now everyone laughed. *Orgies on a school night would be a little strange,* said a third.

When their sex had begun to wane, Byron installed something for Hazel in the shower, and in the bed. *You seem increasingly uncomfortable with that aspect of our companionship,* he'd told her. *So be it. I've long had efficient and solitary ways to bring myself to orgasm. I'd like to make these available to you as well. Physiologically, daily orgasm is healthful. I have to insist on your continued monogamy for social reasons.*

We could certainly do scans of potential partners and take precautions against disease and pregnancy, but it's the secrecy we can't guarantee, and an affair going public would irrevocably maim our image in the media. We're a deeply happy and deeply private couple. That's who we are. To summarize, I'm encouraging you to touch yourself often and develop an effective self-satiation routine. This will minimize any temptation you might feel in terms of breaching our union. I'll discontinue all physically romantic advances toward you until you ask me to resume. Well, Hazel had thought at the time. *That's that.*

She'd tried out the machines, and they were effective. But too effective? They worked in seconds and made climax feel like a reflex. Afterward she had the feeling of having watched something on fast-forward, the need to go back and see it again on normal speed so she could understand what had just happened. Plus she knew that Byron probably watched surveillance video of her using them. *So when you're pleasuring yourself,* he'd asked her one night, *what do you think about?* Hazel had swallowed, laughed. *There's not really time to think, with those things,* she'd joked, but if she'd answered honestly it would've been something along the lines of how she thought about having sex with everyone she met or saw while Byron was made to watch, in person. It was the in-person part that was critical. It didn't count if he was watching it on a screen. He'd have to stop working entirely and just be there, and have to see both Hazel and whomever she was fucking actually see him being there. He couldn't hide.

But she'd stopped using them because it angered him. Anything healthful she failed to do made him mad, as did her abstinence from cell phones and tech devices.

Hazel blinked. The living room TV screen had just turned a weird sky blue color. One second she'd been watching a woman in capri leggings theatrically lift a glass of wine between her toes, pretzel her body to bring it to her mouth while she held a uttana padasana pose, and drink through a crazy straw. Now, nothing.

Hazel got up to bang the TV on its side, which she remembered her father doing when she was younger. That was something she felt nostalgic about—the good old days when people beat the shit out of technology if it didn't perform. She knew from her father's rants that he agreed with her on this. *These silly phones! People treat them like they're porcelain eggs holding the fetus of the baby Jesus.* Now the concern was on protecting and encasing devices, not giving them repeated blows.

Some of her father's roundhouse fights with their old TV had been epic. He had treated the thing like it was an insane cow that had charged into their living room.

HAZEL, the TV screen suddenly read.

"Oh," Hazel remarked. "Oh shit."

HAZEL, YOU NEED TO PUT ON THE HELMET. THIS IS URGENT. LET US DO A CHECK OF YOUR FATHER'S CONDITION. HE NEEDS TO BE HOSPITALIZED. IT IS NOT HUMANE TO LET HIM SUFFER THIS WAY.

"TV," Hazel remarked. "Tell Byron that my father is dying of cancer. Humane is not, you know, possible. I get that there might be more we can do to mitigate his physical discomfort. But in the global sense, which I think is what my father has chosen to tether himself to, in terms of his death, in that his body is painfully breaking down against his will and is going to continue to do so until he is gone and then he will be gone forever and that is all, humane does not apply. Also maybe tell Byron that 'humane' is a funny word for him to use! For example, murdering an eccentric renegade who mainly lived off the land and wasn't doing anything criminal in any of the moments I knew him just because I slept with him? That is not humane. Bring up how his company masterminds futuristic weapons and betrays all individual rights to privacy—both those created by law and those imposed by the insight of biological evolution, like the sanctity of one's own fucking brain!"

IF, the TV continued, YOU ARE FINDING MEANING IN THIS SETUP AND FEEL YOUR CURRENT PURPOSE IS BEING PRESENT FOR YOUR FATHER AS HE VENTURES INTO SOLITARY EXIT, AS SOME OF YOUR RECENT THOUGHTS SEEM TO INDICATE, THEN CONTINUE. BUT ONCE HE DIES, WHAT IS YOUR PURPOSE THEN? WHEN YOUR FATHER IS GONE, COME HOME. YOU CAN ENTER INTO THE NEXT CHAPTER KNOWING YOU SAW HIM OUT OF THE WORLD HONORABLY AND HAVE NO OUTSTANDING PERSONAL RESPONSIBILITIES TO GET IN THE WAY OF YOUR DEVOTION TO THE BIGGEST MEDICAL-TECHNOLOGICAL ACCOMPLISHMENT OF ALL TIME, AND YOU CAN FULLY NETWORK WITH YOUR BELOVED SPOUSE. MAKING HISTORY IS EXCITING! LET'S START TO GET EXCITED. IT'S ALSO A WAY FOR YOUR FATHER'S DEATH TO NOT BE TOO SAD, BECAUSE IT MARKS THE HERALD OF A NEW DAWN FOR NEUROLOGICAL ENHANCEMENT. HIS DEATH WILL BE THE LAST DOMINO, AND ITS FALL WILL BRING AN END TO THE OBSOLETE WORLD OF ISOLATED THOUGHT.

The TV returned to a woman in a pretzeled position, her bunned head moving up and down rhythmically between her thighs. *I don't know about Syrah, as a vintage,* her muffled voice said. *I think it numbs my tongue.*

Do we have it all figured out, or are we lonely? another woman mumbled between dubbed smacking noises.

I'm just trying to make it to Friday without killing myself, a third woman said. This camera angle showed only the woman's back, but her voice implied her mouth was open very wide; she sounded like someone talking to one of those dentists who asks patients questions while he drills. *I'm just licking my way through the week.*

Hazel tried out the position they were all in and failed. She looked up at the cracks on the ceiling and imagined it falling down upon her. She'd made bad choices in life. Irreversible wrong choices.

A low wail came from her father's bedroom. It was not a sound so much as an aural collage of human misery. A fresh one whose glue hadn't dried.

When Hazel was young, her mother had taken her to an art gallery and Hazel had been surprised to find most of the paintings ugly. Early education had taught her that art was supposed to be beautiful—that was its point! *Mom,* Hazel asked, *what's it called when you're looking at something, I mean staring at something, like how we're doing, but not at something pretty? That's the whole reason to stare usually, right? Because something's beautiful. What about when something isn't nice to look at but you're still looking at it and thinking and stuff?* She'd watched her mother's thick brow wrinkle up and push out, which always reminded Hazel of the top of a cardboard milk carton being opened. *When you're looking at something that isn't nice to look at and thinking?* her mother said. *Well, that's called reality, Hazel. That is called L-I-F-E.*

WHEN HAZEL ENTERED HIS BEDROOM, HER FATHER'S MOUTH OPENED like he was going to speak, or play a single note on a wind instrument. "Whoa," Hazel said, realizing what she was seeing. She ran to his side and listened for a final word or noise, some hiss or pop or fizz of a soul leaving the body. Instead his silent lips parted and froze. More than life exiting his body, it looked like death was entering into him between his teeth. "Dad?" Hazel asked.

He'd been wearing only a bathrobe the past few weeks, and between the dolls seemed like an elderly gentleman partier who'd just died of a cocaine overdose. It was a far more festive deathbed than she'd imagined him having. For some reason she'd always pictured an ill-lit room full of beeping machines, a hospital bed, her father yelling at an orderly about the lack of flavor in that day's turkey. Then his face turning bright red mid-rant as he clutched his chest and flatlined. "I guess you went out on top, Pops," Hazel said. "Sort of."

She did, then, begin to start hearing vague digestive noises and gurgles from beneath the covers, the staccato bursts of sound a cooling engine makes when turned off after a long drive.

Hazel walked back into the living room and felt very weird. Sadness wasn't hitting her in those exact terms. It felt more like the acceptance of anticlimax, which was what all major events seemed to be. Nothing ever felt like a big enough deal. Her father had just died and she didn't feel transformed or epiphanic or even especially glum. She tried to get upset about not feeling that upset.

Now what, though? She looked at the clock; it was just after 4 PM. Best-case scenario, she had twenty hours before Byron knew her father was dead. Twenty hours to think about what to do next. She had to go back to The Hub now. Otherwise no one still living whom she might ever think about, even briefly, would be safe.

Except Hazel didn't seem to be thinking. Instead she was turning around to take a focused walk down the hallway to the bathroom. It felt very easy, like she'd practiced it a thousand times. Like she'd done suicide drills to make sure that when the time came she would take her life with record speed. First she used tap water from the bathroom sink to swallow a full bottle of her father's heavy opioids. Then she went to the kitchen and took terrible, profound gulps of the cheap whiskey her father liked to drink. He felt that in social settings, its ethanol reek made other men respect him.

If she died now, maybe there wouldn't be another download. Maybe Byron would never see her father's last moments, or hers. She liked the thought of that: perhaps she was stealing a private death for the two of them. She didn't want to go back to Byron; no matter how glorious the general public might find the "break-through" of their synced brains to be, there wouldn't be any joy or meaning in it for her. And Byron would hound her until she returned to him or died. So that was that.

Hazel climbed into her father's bed, angling herself between him and Di. She took the dolls' eye masks off and put one of them on her father and then one onto herself. Cuddling up to her father's body was awkward, but in a way she was grateful for the opportunity—it wouldn't have been all that possible when he was alive. At least not alive and conscious.

He had wanted to die alone yet not alone, which Hazel understood—other people bring their own wants and needs and sadness into a situation that is already too full of feeling—but loneliness is hard. And now with the three of them she was getting the same thing: people were there with her but also were not, being in a category of either "dead" or "never alive." As the pain-killers began to kick in, she felt a little noble about it all. It was like her father had decided, as captain of their retirement-trailer ship, that it needed to sink and he and all his creations, including

Hazel, should go down with him. She felt like she was following orders, and owning up to her failures—she'd screwed up and it was probably best to just call it. His body was still warm, and the deep echo of Hazel's slowing breaths that she could hear with one of her ears pressed to his chest was relaxing in the way that hearing his heartbeat might've been. There was an acrid sharpness to his smell that insisted everything was expiring: it was okay for her to leave because everything was almost used up, including the oxygen around them.

She hadn't cuddled with anyone in a very long time. Byron sure didn't cuddle. Early on, if he held her after sex, it was more an immobilization than an embrace, like a parent putting his arms around a child before a vaccination shot to ensure stillness. It felt like something bad was going to happen and Byron knew about it but she didn't. Which made perfect sense now.

She thought of Liver. Holding him hadn't exactly been the same as cuddling—it had been pleasant, but he was cold-blooded in a different way from Byron, and rubbery. Their snuggles were more akin to two hard-boiled eggs rubbing up against each other as they pickled together in a jar.

Now, though, Hazel felt flooded with a connective warmth. She knew it was mainly the drugs, about to put her to sleep for the last time, but she felt incredibly *close* to her father, incredibly *loved* by him in a way that she never had before. Maybe the shared genetics in their flesh were swapping nostalgic stories as she twined herself against him. Maybe his brain hadn't been sentimental or capable of giving her a warm good-bye, but his skin and bones were.

It took an incredible amount of effort, but Hazel managed to lift up her head and slip off her eye mask as she spoke, wanting to glimpse her father one last time amidst the new vapors of kinship she was feeling.

But when she took off her eye mask, she realized she'd been spooning with Diane. There was a thin string of saliva hanging between her bottom lip and the doll's collarbone; in Hazel's periphery it glistened and seemed to flicker. Diane's hair had never been the same after the bathtub incident, but one of its patches seemed a fine nest for Hazel to lay her heavy cheek down upon now. It looked like a hologram of a kinder planet's sun. Like a brand-new, safe-to-touch form of fire that was invented as a toy for babies. *Go ahead and feel*, it said. It meant this in every sense of the word. Hazel's eyes closed and she breathed in and felt lucky, because Diane's hair smelled like freesia body wash. Which was not a bad last breath to draw at all.

15

ON ANY OTHER DAY OF HIS ADULT LIFE, THE GOGOL INTAKE PROCESS would've sent Jasper running. He'd compromised his anonymity for the rest of his lifetime just by stepping in the door.

But he'd come to them with nothing to lose, ready to spend what remained of his life savings of cash. For an extra fee, he'd been able to get the earliest available appointment the following day, and had driven all night to get there. It was a long drive, and a disconcerting one—multiple times Jasper felt he had to be lost. The place was essentially in the middle of a field and guarded like a fort. Upon arrival he was shown to an eerie unmanned vehicle that drove him from the front gate to the actual building.

Procedures were apparently expensive. Prohibitively so for the average person; many times, the operator explained, fund-raising initiatives and charity walks were organized to fund individuals in average income brackets. What sort of solution was he looking for?

Not one that would make people line up in droves to run a 5K.

He assured her it would be financed with his life savings. The appointment operator was hesitant to schedule him when the initial survey revealed he had no physical assets or employment record, but he convinced her he'd be willing to pay the hefty consulting fee upon arrival, and was able to prepay for the procedure in cash.

The building housing the diagnostic wing looked made of steel-colored ice. Its silver entrance doors were impossibly thin, like two giant razor blades. Walking inside, he tried to shake the feeling that he was about to be sliced in half.

A woman inside holding a file folder beckoned him. "Mr. Kesper? Right this way."

No one had called him by his actual last name since high school. Hearing it formed a knot in his throat. But they wouldn't schedule the appointment without exhaustive identification confirmations. He'd had to be himself.

"When I made my appointment," Jasper began, following behind the woman. "They said something about an imagination team I'd meet with today? To brainstorm solutions to my goals?" His throat was going dry. Had he himself been conned? Gogol sure seemed on the up-and-up; their products were everywhere. But maybe it was getting into bed with some medical quackery to keep the shareholders happy. The commercial sure seemed primed to coax desperate millionaires out of their money prior to death.

Maybe he'd just fallen into the trap he'd made his former living from: people are eager to believe in the reality of what they want.

"You're in excellent hands," the woman said. Jasper couldn't see her hands though. She was wearing a tight pair of silver gloves.

THE DIAGNOSTICS TOOK HOURS; IT FELT LIKE AN ENTIRE DAY HAD passed but Jasper had no real sense of time because there weren't clocks anywhere. He kept being ushered inside machines that moved around him or above him; he'd get out of one and be led right inside another. He took a few naps. "Why haven't I gotten hungry yet?" he asked. "Why haven't I had to use the bathroom?"

"We gave you some injections," a woman explained.

"Like shots? I never felt anything."

"You wouldn't feel them," she said. "They're not exactly like shots."

The final scanner required him to lie on his stomach while wearing a helmet that covered his eyes; the machine's two halves were going to enclose him in a chamber, like an embryo growing in an egg. For how long?

He didn't know. Jasper was beginning to worry. He hadn't said *that* much about what he wanted yet. How much did these tests cost? What if when they were finished, he didn't have enough left over for the procedure?

Then it appeared in his brain, unprompted: an image of a dolphin's glistening stomach, the sun glinting off its surface, its wet satin finish relaxed against the bar of gritty sand it was beached upon. He felt himself get aroused, a particularly uncomfortable pressure lying facedown in the confines of the egg.

A montage began to follow, flits of fin and the occasional quick tooth. Desire and the fatigue of the past few days, running on adrenaline and excitement and then adrenaline and heartbreak all seemed to catch up with him at once. Jasper felt the wall of civility he was trying to maintain, flimsy as the fake backing he'd hidden his money behind in his closet, give forth like wet paper; he began to weep. His erection was pushing into the exam table and he was pressing his weight against it now. His tears were building up inside the helmet; he felt himself wanting to draw oxygen at a rate the thick filter of the helmet's face mask might not support—he could asphyxiate; he could possibly drown in the condensation of sweat and grief. He was either about to black out or die or orgasm, or some combination of these three things. He couldn't wait for plea-sure, or erasure. And erasure was pleasure, given the status quo.

JASPER WOKE TO THE PEERING EYES OF SEVERAL SCIENTISTS. A large group of observers stood holding tablets, their fingers moving at blurry speeds of documentation. One older woman in a lab coat was chain-smoking. She was visually shorter than everyone else but felt like the tallest person in the room.

The other scientists were standing behind her as though they were afraid of Jasper. She was the mother duck who would protect them.

"Did I black out?" Jasper asked. The helmet had been removed; he'd been rolled over onto his back.

The scientist exhaled and a concentrated amount of smoke blew out into Jasper's face. "Yes," she said. "Right after you climaxed."

"Oh," he said. The scientists did not seem scandalized or turned on. In his former life, this might've disappointed him. Now all he cared about was advice.

"Can you fix me?"

The short scientist exhaled again. Jasper felt his lungs make a small spasm. "My name is Voda," she said. "Why don't you come to my office. We'll talk." She dropped her cigarette onto the floor and a small robot immediately appeared and ate it.

Voda took out another cigarette, lit it, and turned. The crowd of scientists parted to make a path for her exit, then all turned and followed her. Jasper sat up—he felt woozy.

A medical team disrobed Jasper and began washing him. He found he'd lost any sense of care or shame about his body too. He was now a patient. In less than two minutes he was clean and in a fresh hospital gown. Another woman appeared.

"Mr. Kesper? You can follow me to Voda's office."

He stood and was aware of the air on his buttocks. "Should I get dressed?"

"Voda would like to see you immediately. This way."

In her office, Jasper noted that Voda's skin looked very processed, as if someone had tried to soak it in chemicals and develop it like photographic film. Her expression was relaxed and pensive. It reminded Jasper of the way reptiles in pet stores look when they're lying on those electric rocks. She lit another cigarette. "I think I can help you," she said.

"Great," Jasper said and nodded. Voda shrugged.

"Maybe," she said.

"Why?" he asked. "What's the catch?" He wanted to add, *How old are you?* He really couldn't tell. It seemed like maybe she was very old, but was so unconcerned about the passing of time that it didn't affect her. Her hair was a buoyant nest of tight brown curls whose lushness stood in stark contrast to the condition of her skin; they looked like the edible salad end of a root vegetable.

Now she smiled though. "The same catch as everything. Loads of risk."

Jasper shifted in his chair, trying not to think about his back-opened gown. The brisk temperature in Voda's office made its chrome seat feel refrigerated. He was excited to hear what she was saying but the surgical feel of the facility had activated some castration paranoia in his brain. He didn't like the creeping feeling in the back of his mind that his manhood was being iced down prior to amputation.

"I didn't think doctors smoked," Jasper said. Beneath Voda's desk, a pack of cigarette-butt-eating robots roved around her ankles, in wait like toy dogs. The only thing hanging on the wall was a vintage calendar bearing a photo of a nude man.

"Your case is of particular interest to me for several reasons, Jasper. What you're wanting—and don't worry, our diagnostics are thorough. You were vague on the phone with the consult operator but we've filled in the holes. So to speak."

The way her eyes moved over him seemed like she was checking him out, but maybe it was a science thing. Jasper didn't know what to think. "So you can cure me?" he asked.

"I don't like the term 'cure.' It limits solutions to pure reversal. What's going on in your brain right now would be tricky to undo, because we can't be certain about how or why this happened to you."

"I got attacked by a dolphin that tried to . . . I don't know, mate with me," Jasper blurted out, his voice rising in volume. This was not his fault. Yes, after meeting Tiny especially, a small part of his brain had worried that the entire scenario was some sort of punishment for his years of conning women, maybe even one self-imposed by his own conscience. But he remembered that day on the beach, prior to the attack. He'd been happy, not guilt stricken.

"The thing bit me—" Jasper started.

Voda interrupted. "We can't know causality, Jasper. Maybe there is some bacterial explanation for what happened. Maybe that dolphin had a mutant virus. There's a bacteria that sometimes presents itself in cat feces, for example. It causes mice to be drawn toward cats. Infected mice will actually seek out a cat and present themselves for killing. We could spend decades and millions of dollars chasing down the reason why you're feeling this way, and still not find any concrete answers. What I'm proposing, my solution, is a reconfiguration. We'll work with your current desires instead of against them. Afterward, you'll be able to get aroused and have sex with a human female."

She dropped her cigarette to the floor. Jasper felt his gown pull forward, away from his body for a moment in the instantaneous frenzy of the robot vacuuming that followed.

"You're an awful person, Jasper. 'Awful' isn't a very professional term, but it's an accurate one. I'm sure you're aware you're a narcissist. Did you know you're also a bit of a sociopath? I'd like to show you something."

On the chrome wall to their left, a projection appeared. The images came from a microscopic wand held by another scientist. Jasper noticed she was holding the projection pen between her first and second fingers like a cigarette.

"That's your brain. See the highlighted portions?" Other images tiled across the wall, stacking above and below Jasper's scan. "For comparison, these are the brain scans of other sociopaths, some of them violent serial killers. See the similarities? Though you're not aggressively violent, you have the strong capability of hurting people and feeling no suffering or empathy after doing so."

Fair enough, Jasper thought. What did she want him to say? Oops?

"But that's not why you're here today of course. That's not what you want fixed. You want to be able to have sex with women again. So let's do it."

Jasper nodded. Was he missing something? If he was, did it matter?

"I'm glad you're on board," Voda continued. "What I'm going to say next I don't disclose out of any sense of personal ethics or obligation. I think you're a wretched man. In this world where so many good people unfairly suffer, you might not deserve to live. I'm telling you this because it's easier to not have you confused or attempting to ask questions after the procedure when you might very well be mentally compromised."

"Mentally compromised?" His thrill at the thought of getting his old life back had made him as erect as he could currently get without a dolphin being involved. It was a sensation he'd come to think of as hot-water-bottle penis—warmth and volume only. Jasper uncrossed his legs, pressed his swollen member against the refrigerated seat. "Like, slow?"

"Neural damage and death are both significant possibilities, yes."

Jasper nodded. "I know some people are able to live without sex. Unattractive people and monks or priests or whatever, but I don't get that. It was my whole life. I want to try to get my life back. Do I have enough money for the procedure?"

"Not really. But given the circumstances, I'll cut you a deal. Your brain has a lot more value to me than the cash in those bags." Voda stood and dropped her cigarette. A surgical team entered with a wheelchair and began to help Jasper get into it.

"Um," Jasper said. "We're doing it right now?" A worker approached him, pointed a small gun at his arm, and fired.

"No time like the present, Jasper," Voda called after him as they wheeled him away. "Maybe we'll see you on the other side."

THE BLINDING, OMNIPRESENT LIGHT WORRIED JASPER—IT WASN'T heaven because that was *not* his idea of heaven, his face and eyes feeling trained upon with interrogation-level spotlights. It did correlate pretty tightly with his concept of hell though.

So did the thought of the atmosphere's oxygen being replaced with cigarette smoke.

Jasper coughed and reached up to feel his head for bandages. Was he still on the operating table? He felt strapped down.

A firefly glowed in the distance, came closer, clarified into the ember of Voda's cigarette. Had she been smoking during the surgery? That couldn't be okay? Jasper was pretty sure.

"Truth time," Voda said. Jasper tried to clear his throat. What would he have to confess? Would a microphone be involved? "We're ready to see if it works. To do that, we could have you bring yourself to climax and tell us your initial thoughts—if you think you'd be able to sleep with a woman and duplicate the feelings and visuals you start having, et cetera. We could also bring someone in for you to try it out with, an impartial third party. But I'm interested in your partner's experience as well. Would you be opposed to trying it out right now, with me? It may strike you as irregular, but it's practical. We're both already directly involved."

Voda's hair moved in front of the light for a moment.

"With people watching?" he asked. As if in response, the lights seemed to further brighten and blind him.

"Would you care? I prefer it that way."

Well, Jasper thought. Probably not. What mattered was whether the surgery worked. Had it been surgery? Did he need to recover? "Will you be smoking?"

"I'm willing to do without. You're restrained, and it might be easiest for you to remain so; if it's all right I'll take things from here in terms of the physical exertion. May I begin? Is that okay?"

"Please," Jasper nodded. "I want to try it out. Let's go." He closed his eyes and waited, smelling the air cleared of smoke.

Was a different smell beginning to hit his face now? It seemed the vague promise of saltwater, the mackerel odor of a full treat bucket at the Oceanarium. He let out a gasp when he felt it, unmistakable—a rubbery bottlenose seemed to graze across his thigh.

In his mind, Jasper found himself lying poolside by Bella's tank. She was rising up out of the water, hovering over the top of him and moving closer, so close he could almost feel the cold surface of her skin—she was joining him; it was happening. Jasper felt a wind of relief begin to blow through him in puffs that seemed to correspond to thrusting. When he came it felt like the two of them had rolled into the pool—he had the sense of falling, a large amount of water around him draining somehow. Was someone emptying the tank? His eyes opened just for a moment and he saw a glimpse of Voda, though seemingly far away, or behind a thick lens made of several panes of glass. Her head was thrown back; she was astride him and her body was rising and falling with laughter—she seemed to be orgasming as well?

He closed his eyes again, hoping to get Bella back for a few more seconds, but her aquatic show had just finished. Everyone in the stands was clapping, rising, gathering up their things and readying to leave.

Jasper opened his eyes but the sound of applause didn't fade. It was growing steadily louder. Around him on all sides, the surgical crew was clapping. He was vaguely aware of Voda dismounting him, buttoning up her white coat. "There are several ways in which

I have now earned a cigarette. I'd say it worked, Jasper. I'd say we did it. Would you agree?"

Only now was he aware of feeling winded, of his racing pulse. He could see a medical pit crew coming over to work on him, tugging free various restraints on his numb limbs. "It felt like I was fucking a dolphin," he whispered. The words left his mouth so quietly they seemed unspoken. But Voda heard.

"It did. My team will help you get dressed, show you to a room where we'll have a little reception. Come eat. We'll give you something to help your appetite return."

Jasper began to smile his old smile, the smile that came at the successful end of a good con. A smile from his former self.

It didn't feel the slightest bit familiar, though. Everything about him felt replaced and new.

JASPER WATCHED VODA EAT SEVERAL POUNDS OF SHRIMP BEFORE deciding to stand on the opposite end of the room and eat a lot of shrimp as well. Everyone except Jasper was wearing a lab coat. They'd placed him in a nondescript gray sweat suit.

When the soiree began to break up, Jasper wondered why he wasn't taken with the urge to try to leave—was he free to go?

"Well, well," Voda said, walking over. "It all came together. It's so exciting when something surprises you. Perfection isn't the norm in experimental neurosurgery."

"That was fun," Jasper said. He meant it. Then he realized this was something people said, with sincerity, at the end of actual dates that they had enjoyed. Through the years, with many a con, he'd been forced to watch lots of romantic comedy films where this happened.

Was there something he liked about Voda? They had just slept together, though he didn't feel like they had. The dolphin imagery had been that real. But hypothetically, that could explain whatever sense of fondness he was currently feeling. Couldn't it? His cons always seemed more wrapped up in him after the relationship got sexual, even though he himself had never felt that way.

Was he feeling something?

"It was fun for me too, Jasper. Few of my career wins have had such a pleasurable physical dimension. And you're in pretty good shape."

He nodded, wanting to return the compliment.

"You're a lot more energetic than I expected. Especially for smoking so much."

"I do all right for having had cancer twenty-eight times."

Jasper choked on his shrimp a little. He'd made small talk at plenty of happy hours but had never heard that one. Regaining his composure, he said, "Well, you look great, all things considered."

"Sounds worse than it is. We nip it at the nanophase. The procedure's less invasive than a dental cleaning."

Jasper scratched his head. "That's um . . . an option?"

"Not for many. Say, Jasper, I saw where you're living. Not personally, but I got the idea. I have a big house and I'd like to keep an eye on you for a bit. Do you want to stay with me for a while?"

Jasper found himself nodding. He didn't ever want to see that efficiency again, or any person or part of any of his old lives. Any of them. What would be better than a nice place where he could hide away from the world?

He knew his old self would be freaking out right now. Cohabitation with a strange woman he'd just met! But something about Voda felt familiar. Felt great, actually. He was looking forward to spending more time with her.

16

JASPER'S YEARS OF SWINDLING HAD MADE HIM AN IDEAL HOUSE-
guest: very tidy, overtly accommodating. Not that there was anything
to clean. Everything cleaned itself. His days were spent like the most
Zen security guard ever, strolling the home's vast interior grounds,
stopping to appreciate the koanlike stillness of the machines' various
hums. In any given room, he had no idea where the control boxes
and panels were stored. They were hidden from surface view, tucked
away like sleeping animals.

The only place off-limits to him was Voda's home office. There
were several surveillance cameras in front of it, but the largest was
programmed to detect and follow motion. Jasper liked to do really
slow dance moves in front of it and make its eye follow his limbs
around.

He also still enjoyed looking at his reflection. Almost every surface in Voda's house was reflective; it was like he'd moved into a

house made of mirrors. Which was something he used to daydream about.

His days of relative freedom gave him lots of time to contemplate various ironies. Foremost, Voda was the richest woman he had ever met, let alone slept with. But he couldn't swindle Voda. Somehow she knew everything about him; there didn't seem to be much that she didn't know everything about. But he also didn't have the urge to swindle her.

Not once had he come close to falling in love with any of the women who'd fallen in love with him. And Voda wasn't falling in love. She really liked having sex with him, despite knowing he was visualizing a dolphin. But then she'd go work, or exercise or read or watch something, and how he spent his time didn't seem to matter to her.

Jasper understood that he hadn't gotten his sea legs yet when it came to morality, so when he did finally work up the courage to approach the subject, he did so with caution. "I guess I notice that you don't love me," he said.

She looked up from her book, interested. If she was interested, it meant he was speaking about something related to her work. Knowing this caused Jasper to feel a little awful. It was a new feeling. He seemed to be having foreign sensations all the time now, living and being with Voda. He might liken this one to someone crumpling up a large piece of paper inside his stomach.

"Are you saying you love me?" she asked. "How certain are you?"

"Totally certain," he answered, surprising himself. "I know that I love you. I think about you all the time. I hate being apart from you. I've never had that before, with anyone." His former self would've felt so defeated by the situation. In a twofold way: defeated to have this feeling, and defeated to be honestly admitting it. But it felt good to get it off his chest. And since so many women had loved him, it didn't seem far-fetched to hope the one woman he turned out to love might feel the same.

Except she didn't. "You're young and handsome," Voda said. "But you're right; I don't love you." She exhaled and sat back in her seat. Her posture made it look like the chair was moving forward at a great speed: her legs were spread wide, sticking out of the bottom of her white lab coat; her small feet were extending outward to form a large V. Voda was always in a lab coat, except when they went to bed; then she changed into a nightgown that looked a lot like a lab coat, except instead of buttons the front clasped together with a magnetic strip.

"Do you think you could ever grow to love me?" Jasper felt his voice crack. He sounded like his father. Once that would've devastated him, but now he felt hard-pressed to care.

"Don't worry about me," she told him. "I don't have time for dating. You're in no danger of being replaced."

He'd been good at pretending to love people, and now he decided to try to simply reverse course and pretend he was loved. It wasn't that difficult because Voda liked to be touched. In his previous relationships, he'd cuddled and spooned and massaged and neck-nibbled to give his cons a false sense of security. His body language with them had been genuine in terms of arousal, but the implied affection was a lie. Now he was doing all the same things with Voda, but with her his touch spoke the truth. He'd developed a fondness for everything about her. Even the aged crepe of her skin. He loved running his hand down the length of her sprawled body again and again, like he was brushing the fur of an anesthetized leopard.

Guilt about his previous life was hitting him hard, though. When she wasn't home, he'd begun spending more and more time crying in Voda's atrium, which had a haunting, glazed feel to it. All the plants were faux succulents made of porcelain. She'd had living ones once but said her smoking had killed them all no matter what she'd tried. He was pretty sure she saw everything he did during the day, or could see it if she wanted to, but he did his best to hide these crying spells until he couldn't.

One evening he lost track of time, became so melancholy that he didn't realize the sun had set and he was weeping in the dark. Jasper heard the pack of vaccu-dogs coming down the hallway, smelled Voda's fog of nicotine. When she entered and the lights came on, he was sprawled out on the floor in the center of the room next to a large ceramic fern. "I'm sorry," he sobbed. "Please don't kick me out. I promise I'm not as awful a person as I used to be."

"You're feeling a toxic amount of empathy," Voda said. The cloud of smoke she exhaled fell flat with gravity; instead of hanging atop her head it sank in the air, almost like a dirty car window being rolled down. He looked up to see Voda's forehead wrinkling with worry. "You're going through empathy puberty. It's all coming in at once and overwhelming you. I didn't mean for that to happen. Not to this extent."

Jasper swallowed. "What did you mean to happen?" He suddenly felt guilty that he'd estranged himself from his father, that he'd never contacted his mother after she left.

He had a vague memory of his mother telling him that she didn't sleep through a single night until he was three years old; every few hours she'd keep getting seized with the fear that he'd stopped breathing and go check on him. He thought about this a lot after she left. If that was true, how could she move out when he was still a kid?

But what did he know about her life outside him, really? He'd left his father too. When she left, it had felt like solidarity with his dad for him to refuse his mother's calls and return the mail she sent. He'd been so mad. But even mad this had been hard to do. There was a game he and his father used to play where they would come up with worst-possible-life scenarios for his absentee mother to be living out at that very moment. *Maybe she's dating a circus clown,* his father would say, *and she's severely allergic to the greasepaint he wears and it never fully washes off him, so she's always broken out in terrible rashes. And all they eat is circus food because they sleep in the back of a van that they drive from show to show and don't have a refrigerator to store meat and produce. Plus they get a discount at the circus concession stand, which they need because they're so poor. Seniority wise this guy is the most junior clown and he also gets the least laughs from the audience each night so management keeps paying him less. And for months all he and your mother have eaten are cotton candy and elephant ears. Her teeth are rotting out and she's gaining weight even as she's becoming malnourished. She's gotten so unattractive that the clown has started cheating on her with one of the trapeze artists because he feels that infidelities that take place in midair don't count.* Then his father would look to him for a contribution. *Well, the clown snores,* Jasper would add, and his dad would nod and say, *Nice, but think of something bad about her life related to the circus.* So Jasper would think and say, *Maybe there are cages with lions and tigers that always get set up next to where their van parks at night. Their van gets boxed in by the lion and tiger cages in every town no matter how hard they strategize. And she's so scared of the lions and tigers and hates walking by the cages so much that most of the time instead of getting out of the van to go to the bathroom she pees into one of the concession stand fountain drink cups and then pours it out the van window. Except the smell of fresh human urine makes the lions and tigers go crazy, so they roar and growl all night and she's either wide awake and terrified or asleep and having nightmares to a sound track of wild cats snarling inches away.* And his dad would say, *Good. That's a bad life.*

In hindsight, as an adolescent it was kind of a bad life playing that game with his father. It was kind of a bad life the way they stopped using the word "mom" after Mom left and started using the word "she," and "she" meant "absent mom" until his dad began dating and sometimes marrying a new woman, who got to have a name while she lived in the house but relinquished it upon her exit and became the new "she."

"I meant for you to fall in love with me so you'd live here and I could keep having sex with you," Voda said. "I'm busy and this is a convenient arrangement. I wasn't trying to turn you into a Boy Scout. I thought full-throttle sympathy stimulation on your brain would be like throwing a paper towel into a volcano. But look at you—a full month post-op and you're spewing regret everywhere! You're feeling a level of guilt that's . . . admirable."

What she was saying about his conscience was true. He could feel it growing steadily no matter what he did, as painful and insistent as hunger. "Damn it," Voda added, then she picked up a clay rhododendron and hurled it against the wall. It shattered and the robot vacuums momentarily circled the carnage like buzzards, adjusting their internal settings to the specifications of the spill before zooming forward to eat up the shards. Jasper suddenly had the clearest, most frightening image in his head: his own bisected corpse on the floor, the skin of his chest peeled back like opened curtains, the pack of vacuum robots feasting on the mess of his organs.

"Would they eat a person?" Jasper asked. "Like what if I tripped and fell by accident?"

"If you feel up for intercourse, we can have one last go. Otherwise I think our cohabitation experiment has concluded. There's a guest casita out back you can sleep in for a few days if you'd like, but tomorrow you'll need to leave."

THE WALLS OF THE CASITA'S BEDROOM WERE A PINKISH PLASTER that looked indistinguishable from spread frosting. He found himself briefly fantasizing about fantasizing. In his old life, he'd be imagining that he was waiting inside a giant cake right now—that soon, wearing an edible loincloth, a slice of the wall would be removed via forklift, and he would exit out into a giant reception hall where hundreds of newly divorced women were celebrating the end of their nuptials, ready to use his body to make their dirtiest rebound fantasies come true.

Instead he found his morning erection a tiresome presence; he was too wracked with guilt and sadness to want to think about dolphins or Voda or anything. His new brain seemed to be forcefully devoting him to redemption.

But maybe some part of him had always wanted that? Staring up at the ceiling fan, he thought about something Voda had told him one night. They'd been watching a show called *Definitely Cheating* where suspicious partners brought camera crews home to interrupt their spouses' acts of adultery.

Jasper was shocked to find himself outraged. He was flooded

with an unfamiliar attitude of *How could they?* and mentioned this to Voda. He also found it surprising that every accused partner was, in fact, definitely cheating. Not once did the camera crew burst in to find the other spouse baking a chicken or doing sit-ups or grouting some tile.

Voda had shrugged. "People are obsessed with the concept of free will," she'd said. "But from a neurochemical standpoint I think that's insane. Hormones, genetics, experience—our choices aren't *that* independent. Why is everyone so afraid of letting science help? If a couple wants to guarantee they stay faithful to each other, I could actually do that. It's still too risky an operation to put into common practice, but pretend the procedure is harmless. A lot of people would balk and tell me that renders fidelity meaningless, because free will is what makes it count. But you can't depend on free will. To say to someone else, 'I won't cheat because I decided to make myself incapable of arousal outside our relationship'—isn't that a much deeper commitment?"

Jasper had shifted in his chair. If Voda was a little insane, he told himself, that wasn't a huge problem. As long as she didn't do more operations on *him*. "They couldn't get aroused with someone else? Or they just wouldn't want to?"

"It wouldn't work to make them physically incapable of fulfilling desires they still had. That would breed unhappiness—discord between the mind and the body. It's the *urge* to be unfaithful that gets removed. Why is that bad? They voice a desire for fidelity, so I silence a lesser desire that might get in the way of it. They choose what gets privileged in their brains."

Jasper hadn't desired empathy. But if Voda had "privileged" it for him, didn't that mean it had to have already been there? The tiniest pilot light? It was easier to accept the fate of having to begin doing right by others if it felt like it was actually coming from him. Even a really small part of him that he would've formerly ignored every time.

There was a knock on the door and Jasper fell out of bed in his rush to answer; he half-crawled and half-ran because surely Voda had changed her mind about him leaving. Maybe she'd even performed surgery on herself (could neurosurgeons do that, he wondered, the way tattoo artists could?) and now loved and desired him in the same way that he ached for her—they could be a force of altruism together, an unlikely union devoted to the good of all humanity!

But the woman standing at the door was not at all Voda. She was much taller, and wearing a plastic rabbit mask. "Hello," she said. She held a small device in front of her lips that changed her voice to make it sound like a chipmunk's and was carrying a refrigerated lunch pail. "May I come in?"

"I guess," he said. "This isn't my house."

She entered and took a seat on the sofa. Jasper could tell that if she were to take the mask off, she'd be very attractive. She had that confident movement, that specific ease of being in the world. "You don't know me," she said.

"I'll have to take your word for it," he answered. "What's with the mask?"

"Voda and I are close," she replied. "Colleagues, confidantes. What she did to you is messed up, in my opinion. That's nothing I haven't said to her face, by the way. And now she's making you leave."

"Oh," Jasper said, scratching his leg. "You're like the person who comes with a box and makes sure I get my things from my desk without making a scene. If I worked here and had a desk and possessions, I mean. I don't. Let me grab my car keys and flip-flops."

"No, wait. I have a proposal for you." The rabbit woman opened the cooler and held up a syringe. "Voda told me you're burdened with a swollen conscience. You're driven to be a do-gooder now, right? I know how you can begin. It's very risky. I feel that to adequately repent for past wrongs, to do it in a way that matters, you have to put your life in danger. Do you feel that way?"

"Well," Jasper said. If she wanted him to be on board with whatever she was offering, she could've chosen a dolphin mask instead of a bunny one.

"There's someone who really needs help. The same way Voda played with your brain, they played with hers, only much, much worse. There's a chip in her head." She wiggled the syringe. "This will deactivate it. You'll get to do something heroic."

She pushed the lunch pail toward Jasper. "And I'll give you back all the money you paid for your operation, plus some bonus money. You'll have cash to begin repairing your past crimes. If we're going to help her, we need to hurry, though. Emotionally she's not hanging in so well. Here, have a look."

Jasper opened the file and began sifting through pictures. "You mentioned my life would be at risk? Why do you want to help her?"

"Because what they've done to her is barbaric? What they'll do to you, if it doesn't work or you get caught, is barbaric too. That's true. But you'll be rescuing another person—you'll go, in just one day, from not deserving to live to deserving to live more than a huge majority of other people do. Plus her husband needs to move on. Specifically, with me. Rage leads him to action, so if she can escape from him he'll be irate and open to coupling sooner than if she dies and he feels he has to publicly mourn. But long-term I'm all about moving things to a more humane-ish place. I have a lot of big plans for the future."

Jasper looked down at the photo of the woman, who did indeed look very sad. A specific sort of sad that a shower could possibly improve on one level, at least in terms of its most basic outward expression.

"My parents," Jasper blurted out suddenly. "Can you find out if they're still alive?"

17

THE RABBIT WOMAN WAS GOING TO SEND A NOTE TO HIS MOTHER and father, both of whom, she researched and confirmed, were still living. The messages were cryptic, but he hoped they'd still be nice to receive. Now that he felt bad about his cons and understood what a terrible feeling that was, he worried that his mother and father were wracked with similar regret in terms of their parenting or lack of a relationship with him. He'd never had an adult relationship with his mother to miss, and it had seemed that his father's idea of them spending time together was always for Jasper to listen to his father whine about his most-recent heartbreak. So Jasper didn't long for that either. He didn't want to be close to them, but he also didn't want them to feel sad over him or wish they'd done things differently. The letter said, *For reasons that are complex but not negative, your son is unable to contact you. But he'd like to ask you to think fond thoughts of him out in the world, and know that he loves you and does the same.* It was more true than not? He wanted them to be happy. He loved them in the sense that he cared about their well-being and wished they'd all liked one another more. It felt good to send something that would hopefully be a comfort.

He left Voda a note also, by the door in the casita. *I love you,* it said. *You forced me to but still.*

He loved her and he knew he'd never see her again, which felt agonizing—he realized now that this was how the cons who'd loved him had felt when he left. Only even worse because he had their money.

The high sun was strong and now he was driving down the road not to move to a new city or steal or maim anyone's ability to trust others, but to try to save someone. And if he succeeded, he had duffle bags of money in his car that he'd do his best to return to as many of his past cons as he could find, ringing their doorbells and leaving unmarked packages filled with cash on the porch. He was embarking on a tour of goodwill.

If he made it past this first stop.

The rabbit woman said that from what she'd watched of Hazel's downloads, the trailer's back sliding-glass door was the best entry point if no one answered the front. But it looked like there were several people in the bed inside, a few of them very attractive women. Did he have the right house?

He knocked again, more fervently. Why weren't they waking up? He was wearing a fake parcel delivery service uniform, holding the lunch pail cooler containing the shot. With all the people inside on the bed, it seemed like a setup for a bad adult film.

"Hello?" Jasper slid the glass door open and stepped inside. He felt bad waking people up, but this was pretty important.

"Huh?" Jasper said. Was this a joke?

Two of the people were not people. He touched them just to make sure, but they definitely weren't.

Then there was the father, and he was not alive. If a "Rose for Emily" scenario was in play here, Jasper would've preferred the rabbit woman to have given him a heads-up, but maybe she didn't know. Or maybe something worse had gone on. She hadn't told him a lot about Hazel, but the things she did say were easy to sympathize with: her husband was terrorizing her. Her father hadn't been mentioned much, aside from the fact that Hazel lived with him, and he was allegedly grouchy. She hadn't killed him, had she? Jasper wanted this to be a clean rescue in terms of justice. Any vibes complicating the good-deed aspect of the mission, such as patricide, were pretty unwelcome.

Then Jasper saw the blue tinge to her lips, noted the discarded pill bottle at her feet. The man's corpse looked healthier than Hazel did in terms of color. "She's dead," Jasper said.

Disappointment flooded through him, then anger. Now what? Did his kick start to a life of atonement have to perish alongside her? What was the right thing for him to do if she was already gone? One idea was to take the dolls with him and move her body to the living room couch so her deathbed would have less of an incestuous group-sex feel to it when the paramedics arrived. That would probably count as a good deed.

Then Hazel made a gurgling noise. A small cluster of bubbly foam came out of her mouth. "Yes!" Jasper exclaimed. "Yes! Hazel, help is here!" He began running through the rooms of the house trying to find a Gogol phone or computer to search what the best steps were for an overdose. He could give her the chip-deactivation injection and call the paramedics, but then Byron would get to her in the hospital; he'd be the first person they called once she was identified. The rabbit woman had stressed that if anything went wrong, hospitals were a last resort. It would be no good to save Hazel's life only to have her wake up in Byron's private care and find she wanted to commit suicide even more than before. But probably couldn't, due to round-the-clock surveillance.

A pool of froth was collecting on Hazel's chin. It looked fancy in a way, nearly culinary, like whisked foam. "Warm," he said aloud, only because in movies doctors were always reporting things aloud even if no one was there. If he could only call Voda, or the rabbit woman. "Hazel?" he yelled. "Can you hear me?"

There was a medical action he should be performing. An urgent one. Jasper knew this much. But what it might be he wasn't sure. To buy time, he decided to go ahead and administer the injection, which he'd need to give her whether or not he called an ambulance. He opened the cooler and removed the long syringe, took the protective casing off the needle.

The shot was gigantic, like something used to impregnate a cow. "Better you than me," Jasper mumbled.

Then he heard the click of the rifle.

THE GUN'S BARREL PRESSED INTO THE CENTER OF JASPER'S FORE-head. He'd raised his arms up in a stance of surrender and knew it was the best practice to never look directly at an assailant, but something was up with the guy's chest. It seemed like his ribs were opening. The man wasn't wearing a shirt, but he was wearing something. A vest. But it was also made of skin. Whose skin?

Jasper, he told himself, *you do not want to know whose skin it is.*

He swallowed. "Gogol sent you, huh." His lifted arms were trembling. Part of him wanted to just make a go of it, just leap forward and inject her, but he figured his arm would get shot off before he could push the plunger down.

The man spat something brown onto the carpet, which made Jasper cringe. He'd really prefer to die on a clean carpet. "I am not a Gogol user," the man said.

"You're not here to kill me?" There was more brown spit, which Jasper willed himself not to acknowledge.

"I might be. Depends on what you're doing."

If he told the man the truth and the man was from Gogol, he'd kill him. If he lied and the man was from Gogol, he'd kill him. But if he told the truth and the man wasn't from Gogol, he might have a chance. Jasper pointed his syringe hand at his non-syringe hand. "It will sound pretty wild when I explain it out loud, but I came to give her this." Jasper watched the man's eyes move to the injection needle.

"What is it? I'm not afraid to party."

"Well, this woman, she has a chip in her brain," he began, then paused to gauge whether the man seemed incredulous.

"She mentioned something about that," he responded. "She and I, we've been cavorting."

Jasper's mouth dropped open a little. This he would not have guessed.

"Is she alive?" the man continued. Jasper found himself on the barrel end of the gun once more. "Or are you planning to kill her for that chip?"

"No!" Jasper screamed. When the man had walked into the room and Jasper was sure he was going to die, that was one thing, and then when the man didn't seem to be an assassin and Jasper felt certain he'd live, that was another, but he couldn't deal with going back and forth between them. "I'm here to deactivate it for her so she can escape from her husband. Please, lower the weapon. I got here maybe five minutes ago and found them all on the bed just like this. Her dad's dead and it looks like she overdosed on pills."

"Oh, overdose." The man stepped forward and shoved several fingers down Hazel's throat until more foam came out, then kept at it. Finally half-digested pills began to appear. "She'll live," he said. "You need to find a vein on her for that?"

"No. It's just like . . . you know, the way they'd do a shot at the doctor's. My name's Jasper, by the way."

The man grabbed the syringe from Jasper's hand and sank it into Hazel's arm. "Call me Liver," he said. "You a fed?"

"Me? No, I'm—" Jasper stopped. What was he? "I'm just trying to make up for a lot of bad things."

More foamy puke came out of Hazel's mouth, followed by a belching cough. "Ahoy!" Liver yelled, helping her sit up. "Atta gal. Let's get you upright here." Jasper noticed Liver wasn't overly concerned about disturbing the father's corpse; as he bent over to grab Hazel, his knee was pinning the expired body down by the throat. "Do you have tales from beyond? Did you get to whiff the air in hell? A buddy of mine was in a coma and swears he saw the eternal lake of fire. Said it smells like cinnamon."

"You're alive," Hazel said. Her speech was slowed. It took nearly a minute for her to get both of the words out.

"Yeah. They had it in for me. Blew my shack to bits then torched the thing. I'd seen them coming, though. Snuck out in the meantime. Didn't want you to worry, but I thought it was best to lay low for a few days."

"Dad's dead," Hazel continued.

"Yes," Jasper said. Liver realized he'd been perched atop the man and scooted back, lifting the blanket up over the corpse's face.

Hazel turned and looked at Liver, then turned and looked at Jasper. He cleared his throat. "Hazel, you don't know me but I'm here to stop the downloads. I just gave you an injection that should disable the chip in your brain."

Hazel let out a giggle, then made a sad noise. "Byron is going to kill you," she said.

"Well, we should get moving," Jasper agreed. "The rabbit woman, she's who sent me, said we should disappear before your next download."

Hazel looked down at the blanketed shape of her father's body, put a hand on its chest. "Rabbit woman? But we can't leave Dad here," she said. "Byron's insane. If we leave him, Byron will get his corpse to use as cryogenic blackmail. We've got to take him with us."

Liver turned away from them for a moment and briefly hunched over. Jasper scowled. Was he snorting something? "Fine by me," he said, standing back up and thumbing his nostril. "Not my first rodeo transporting a body. But we should ice him down somehow. It is a sunny day and there are people in society who know the smell of death."

"We've got to take him with us," Hazel repeated. Jasper worried that she'd had some type of chemical concussion, or maybe was going into shock, until she added, "How can we keep him cold?"

"I do have a cooler in my car," Jasper offered. "It's big enough to hold an adult human." Hazel and Liver turned to look at him. "It's, like, dolphin size."

"Sounds like we're good then," Liver said.

"Wait." Hazel grabbed Jasper's arm. "Your car," she said. "How many can it seat?"

18

MORE THAN HER OWN FUTURE—IT WAS EXCITING TO THINK THE downloads might be over, but she doubted it—Hazel found herself thinking about her father's wishes in terms of a funeral. Her mother had asked to be cremated for two reasons: the first, because the cancer drugs had made her look so horrible (*Cremation,* her mother liked to quip near the end, *the best diet ever! Think of the weight I'm about to lose*); the second, because she wanted revenge (*This body has put me through hell. Light it up, Bert*). Her dad probably wanted the regular: a hole in the ground, a wake with visiting hours, and a notice in the paper. It wouldn't be possible. Even if Hazel were able to task someone else with its oversight, or drop the body off at a funeral parlor with a wad of cash, Byron couldn't be counted on not to find it and have it dug up. It had to be destroyed. She wasn't sure how, and she knew it would be a disappointment for her pops, so she'd decided to give him a consolation prize. He could exit pharaoh style: he could take the dolls with him.

But for the moment, it was Liver who was king. They'd tried to arrange Di and Roxy in the back of Jasper's station wagon, surrounding the cooler, but this looked like a suspicious tangle of realistic body parts. It was easier to put aviator sunglasses and baseball caps on the dolls and strap them into the backseat properly. Liver sat between them, one arm around each, a happy grin on his face. "Road trips aren't my thing," he said. "But this is a wonderful morning. Your deceased dad and your near-suicide excluded."

Jasper was all work and no leisure. Hazel noted his clockwise observation schedule of rearview mirror, right-side mirror, left-side mirror, road in front. He was very worried about cops. "Not to pressure you," Jasper stated to Hazel about forty minutes into the drive. It was the first time he'd spoken since they'd left her father's house, when he'd turned down Liver's suggestion that they save themselves all a lot of hassle, douse the home and body with kerosene, and make her father's double-wide a funeral pyre. Hazel had vetoed it due to the flames' likely spread to other trailers, most of whose residents had mobility issues. Jasper's rejection stemmed from a healthy desire to avoid police intervention.

"I just think, on the off chance we get pulled over, that it behooves us to . . . send the body to rest . . . as soon as possible." Jasper's eyes were locked into a cold stare with Liver's in the rearview. "Especially since this guy refuses to wear a shirt." Before they left, Jasper had tried talking Liver into wearing one of Hazel's father's button-up polos and some khaki shorts with tiny lobsters embroidered all over them. Liver declined.

"I know," Hazel said. "I'm just not sure about the best way."

Jasper fidgeted in his seat. "What do you mean? Isn't burying him somewhere unmarked okay? I grabbed a shovel from the garage."

"No, we can't just bury it. The body has to be completely gone by noon tomorrow. Otherwise, if the deactivation didn't work, he'll know right where the body is. And if it does work, Byron will pull out his best tech for a treasure hunt of anything about me he can find, including my father's corpse."

"So what do we do with it?"

At this, one of Liver's jerky-textured fingers rose into the air. "If I may," he began. "I fear we're short the time and equipment to destroy all this man's DNA via fire. You've got to go hotter and longer than you'd think. Even if we were lucky enough to find an empty metal Dumpster, without an oven the burn will take a while, accelerant or no."

Jasper's disbelief now directed itself not at Liver but at Hazel—she could see him giving her a horrified stare, asking her how and why she'd coupled with this man. "Compared to Byron," Hazel said, "Liver is an archangel of virtue." She turned to him. "What do you recommend?"

Liver didn't miss a beat. "Consumption."

Jasper jumped. The car swerved and was reprimanded by the heavy air horn of a bread company's semitruck; Hazel turned to see its oversize slogan written across the truck's body in cursive and felt her stomach lurch as well. GO AHEAD—it instructed—ENJOY A SLICE! Suddenly the air in the car seemed very hot, like she was breathing her own recycled breaths in and out of a plastic bag.

"By animals," Liver clarified. "Birds. Hogs. Gators." Hazel looked back at Liver as he spoke—when had he placed Di's legs across his lap?

"No way," Hazel said. She had ruined her life, and because of her choices, her father's corpse was going to have a messed-up farewell. Sure there were various hostilities between them that would remain eternally unforgiven, but doing whatever she could to make his funeral the least messed up as possible seemed fair. "I don't want to feel like I'm *disposing* of him. It's not like he's someone I killed and I'm trying not to get caught."

Jasper smiled. "So you didn't kill him? That's awesome."

"No. He died. I know we don't have a lot of time, but we should make this as nice as we can. I want to at least." If the injection didn't work, it might be the last thing she got to do.

Liver made some guttural noises. He seemed to be having a private debate in his head.

"I know a place," he said. "But you need to pull over and let me drive." He pointed a finger at Jasper, talking to his reflection via the rearview. "And your squirrely eyes have got to be blindfolded."

"Absolutely not!" Jasper yelled. But then he took another look at Liver and put on the turn signal to exit.

19

JASPER WAS NOT SURE ABOUT CRITTER OR SPLEEN OR WHATEVER the man's name was. Hazel had admitted she'd only known him for a few weeks, alleged they'd met by chance at a bar.

What if it wasn't by chance? What if the guy was working for Gogol?

Jasper wished for the scenario to be closer to what he'd envisioned signing up for in the first place—just him and a de-chipped Hazel, making their escape.

Instead he now found himself blindfolded between two sex mannequins, listening to Liver narrate about some friend of his who owned a manure farm with forty acres of forest behind it. "Essentially a Bermuda triangle of undiscovered evidence. Chippy keeps to himself down on the farm," Liver stressed. "And due to the property's remote location and odor, his privacy is universally respected."

Jasper didn't want to have to trust another person—Liver was already one more than he'd been planning on—and he tried to voice this protest in the politest way possible. "It's just that if he sees me and Hazel and then later gets offered a persuasive bribe, say . . ."

"Chippy won't know you're there," Liver said. "I'm going to stay behind and make sure your tracks are covered. You'll be long gone before Chippy would get wind of it. That's what I'm telling you. It's the place."

THE PLACE, OFF AN OVERGROWN TRAIL INSIDE A SERIES OF DENSE woods, was essentially a parallel universe. Its fauna looked like crude near-replicas of living things. All the plants' evolution seemed to have been dependent on retainer trays they'd been too lax about wearing and their biological design had therefore slipped back a few hundred centuries. The bark of the pine trees was coated with a powdery orange spice. Liver and Jasper somberly carried the cooler with the air of two pallbearers, one on each side, while Hazel carried Liver's rucksack and the shovel.

The tall grass was waxier and more juice-filled than Hazel was used to grass being. It made her feel squeamish, like she was stepping on bugs.

Jasper looked like he was having a breakdown. His eyes were watering; he'd put his shirt over his nose and mouth to provide a thin filter for the smell. "I just don't want to die *out here*," he said again. He'd said it a few times since they'd arrived. "I feel like we should get moving soon. It would be an irony, right, to get found and killed because we stopped to have a funeral."

"Sorry," Hazel said. "I need to." She had a lot of sympathy for

Jasper. It was generous of him to be risking so much for her. In the car he'd talked about a woman he was in love with, a woman he was never going to see again. *It's almost like she died*, he said.

Not being Byron's wife anymore, if the chip deactivation worked, meant the rest of Hazel's life would be as if she'd died too. That would be the perception of everyone. That Hazel was gone, forever.

"I think here will work," Liver said. "Lots of trees and shrub cover. This spot okay?"

Hazel nodded and they set down the cooler; Liver enlisted Jasper to go back to the car with him and get Di and Roxy, and Hazel was left alone with dusk drawing near. She felt exhausted and still a little drugged and sat down on the cooler without thinking for a moment, then remembered its contents and stood back up. She was thirsty and looking at the cooler felt strange. Her brain kept telling her to open the lid, insisting it had to be filled with drinks. Why couldn't that miracle happen—why couldn't she peer inside and find that her father's body had been transformed into rows and rows of frosted beer bottles?

Jasper was heading down the trail with Roxy, carrying her via piggyback to better bear the load. Liver came into view on the path a few minutes later ferrying Di. Hazel hadn't thought to put them into more modest clothing before they'd left the house. Di had on a sequinned tube top and an orange miniskirt; Roxy was wearing a bikini top and spandex underwear that read CELEBRATE across the backside. They placed a doll on either side of the cooler and all gathered in front of it.

"Should we all say a few words?" Liver asked.

"He was dead when I met him," Jasper said.

"I'm sure he didn't mean anything personal by it," Liver answered. A natural moment of silence followed. "I noticed he spoke his mind," Liver said. "That can be a good quality. Well, sometimes."

Hazel thought for a moment. What had she admired most about him? There were a lot of things he managed not to get addicted to, which she thought was impressive if someone lived to old age. He never tried, to her knowledge, to ruin anyone's life on purpose. "Sometimes he made me laugh," she said.

"Should we have the dolls pretend to say something?" Jasper asked. "We could do voices for them." Hazel saw Liver's face start to twitch. "Like they were in love? I know I mentioned that I recently fell in love, for the very first time. Things didn't work out though. Oh well. It sort of feels like being buried alive, actually. In a way. I can't get out from underneath it to think about anything else. Ha! It's like it's pinning me down every moment." He started to cry a little, which Hazel thought was actually good, even though the tears weren't technically for her father. It was a funeral and any tears counted.

Liver placed his hand on Hazel's shoulder. "Do you want some time alone with him?"

She shook her head. If the chip was still working, time alone with him wasn't even possible. "What's the plan for the body?"

"Can Hazel and I have a moment?" Liver turned to Jasper. "Why don't you wait in the car? She'll be down soon."

Jasper nodded eagerly. "I'll have the engine going."

Hazel reached out and gripped Liver's hand. She couldn't tell if he liked this or merely tolerated it. He wasn't big on reciprocal touch, but he didn't pull away either.

Now she felt the urge to weep building up inside her too, followed by a sense of shame that her own tears weren't for her father either. She'd nearly gotten Liver killed once before; she should be the one insisting that he stay far away from her. But seeing him again after she thought he was dead might have been the one thing that happened in her life where the reality of things turned out to be better than she expected. The time she'd spent with him had felt like she was making new memories. Everything besides Liver seemed like nothing more than dealing with her past mistakes.

Liver was squinting toward the sunset. His wrinkled eyelids looked like glossy walnut shells. "Hey now. Let's pack up the tears. You're better off with me not coming. I stick out in certain situations. I'll handle burying your dad." He didn't seem able to take his eyes off the sky. Was he also tearing up a little? It looked like he was reading words off a giant teleprompter in the clouds. "I'm going to nestle some explosives in the cooler with him. If anyone tries to disturb his peace, boom. And I'll sit with the grave for a while. It's what I do. If your brain turns out to be fixed, maybe we'll see each other again sometime."

He kissed her and Hazel felt more tears come. She was sad she'd given up a normal life for a chance at a special one with Byron and it hadn't turned out to be special at all. Before him, back when she'd planned on having a somewhat regular existence, it was probably love that she'd wanted most out of life. She'd really thought love would develop. It didn't.

Love hadn't developed with Liver either, but she had a fondness for him and it felt horrible to let it go.

"Are you going to bury the three of them together?" Hazel asked. "A mass grave?" Watching Roxy's hair flutter in the wind, it seemed strange to put the dolls underground. Even motionless they looked full of vitality and spirit, far more than she or Jasper or Liver did, ready to go let loose on a dance floor or grab front-row seats on a roller coaster. "On second thought, maybe Dad wouldn't want that. He'd probably tell me to make sure they went on and had the time of their lives. Maybe they could stay with you?"

Liver winked. "I'll try to show them a good time then. Hope to see you again," he said. "I don't say that much." He turned and began wheeling the cooler off the path. Hazel started walking in the other direction, straight toward the sun. It felt like it was burning her tears out. When she got to the end of the trail and had to turn to the car, she looked back for one final glimpse. Liver was hoisting one of the dolls up into his arms, carrying her tenderly, as though she had broken her foot. Then he disappeared into the brush.

20

HAZEL WAS FLIPPING THROUGH RADIO STATIONS WHEN JASPER SUD-
denly hit the brakes and twisted the dial to shut the music off.
"Sorry," he said. "I can't take that 'Saving You Saved Me' song. It's a
long story but that music gives me thoughts that bring on strange
feelings."

Now Jasper looked even more motionless than Di and Roxy
had been capable of—he seemed to have been taxidermied in the
blink of an eye. There was something off about his posture—he
was trying to cover up his lap. *Oh,* Hazel realized. It could be a
stress response, maybe. A fear erection? She wanted to give him
the benefit of the doubt. For some reason it seemed more hopeful
than creepy, like a divining rod pointing to a better tomorrow for
both of them.

It was actually difficult not to stare at his lap. He was an attractive man; there was no doubting that. But she didn't know anything

about him and felt overcome by a desire to keep it that way. He was really starting to make her wonder.

And they hadn't discussed what she was going to do or what he was going to do if her noon download happened tomorrow. Did he have a backup strategy? Hers was round two of the pill bottles. She'd brought several with her, an arrangement Jasper might want to get in on.

Hazel put her hand on his arm as it gripped the steering wheel, then took it away. With his obvious arousal, no matter where she put her hands on his body she felt like she was touching his penis.

If the chip hadn't deactivated, this could be her last chance ever to sleep with someone. Though it was probably best not to make Byron want Jasper dead even more than he already would. Bad enough that she'd just considered it.

"Do you think we should split up soon?" she asked. "If the chip's still working, it's better for you if I don't know where you are." She checked her watch—7 PM. Jasper had nearly seventeen hours to get as far away as possible. "If you go now, you could be on the other side of the world by download time."

"Let's get you a little farther away first." He shifted in his seat; he seemed to be trying to get his condition under control. "Where should I drive you?"

Hazel had no idea. "Just away, I guess. If you asked me where I don't want to go I could tell you. I only seem able to wish for things through a process of elimination. It can only be 'I guess I want this because I don't really *really* not want it.' Like I hate pain, for example."

"Well, for money I used to pretend to love people," Jasper said. "So I can't really offer you wisdom about yearning and its ideal state."

Hazel looked out her car window, and considered. "I sort of pretended to love someone for money too. I mean, it wasn't my idea. To date or marry him. But when it fell into my lap, it was hard for me to conceive of a scenario where I turned down a multi-millionaire's marriage proposal." Byron really hadn't seemed horrible at first, just strange. And who wasn't? Though she hadn't tried very hard to look for something horrible. It would've needed to be pretty glaring, though. "Marry me and then don't worry about anything ever; be relatively immune to the vast majority of life's material consequences" was an easy sell. "I really planned on it being a marriage, though. You know how when you learn to ride a bike? How you're being pushed or supported or whatever but then it's all you? I thought I'd train myself to love him. I'd never been in love but it seemed easier than a lot of things people train themselves to do. I don't know, like bodybuilding. Though I've never done that either. But romantic love seemed very 'how hard could it be?'-ish. At the very least I thought I could reach a point of stasis. You know, 'this is good enough; this is void of acute suffering.'" Jasper guided the car onto the freeway, which made Hazel think of cameras, tollbooths, roadblocks. But they could just as easily be trapped and ambushed on a rural dirt road. "You never accidentally fell in love?" she asked. "The pretending never led to something more?"

"No," he said. "I never felt like I was in the risk group for that."

Hazel studied Jasper's face. "What's it like to be so good-looking?"

"I'm just driving, by the way. I have no idea where I'm going."

"That's fine. I just wondered if you've always been really attractive."

Aimless driving was the way she and her friends would hang out without being supervised in high school. They'd circle the same blocks for hours, listening to music and smoking pot and making out and swearing. They drove around for so long they could've left town and gone somewhere interesting and gotten back by curfew, but nothing seemed like it would be more fun. Hazel couldn't decide whether this was an example of contentment or of failure of imagination. Odd, Hazel realized, that those nights were probably the safest she'd ever felt in her life: as the backseat passenger in a car piloted by a stoned teenage driver who maybe only had his learner's permit. But she'd been away from the critical eye of her parents, away from any form of obligation, away from any feelings that weren't numb giggles.

"I was sort of goofy in middle school," Jasper said. "I didn't get hot until later."

Maybe she was hitting on him; she couldn't decide. It did seem dumb not to sleep together if they were both about to die. That sentiment was the most famous joke ever, wasn't it? We're gonna die so let's do this? What was true of her in high school was probably true of her now, and maybe just as sad: if presented with a variety of options and activities, what she'd choose to do, always, was whatever promised the greatest reprieve from loneliness. She could be dead in a few hours, and she couldn't think of anything she wanted to do more than feel less alone.

"I have a sort of brain chip too," Jasper blurted out. "A modification. I should tell you this. It's kind of dishonest not to, and I was a dishonest person for a long time. I'm only attracted to dolphins. So I got a procedure done that lets me feel like I'm sleeping with a dolphin when I sleep with a human. If I close my eyes it's a perfect simulation."

"Oh," Hazel said. She looked at the radio. "That song earlier. You mean that turned you on?"

"It led to thoughts that did," Jasper said. "Anyway, just so you know. I can sleep with women physically but for the mental part of it I go somewhere else."

"I can actually relate to that," Hazel said. "My life has been a failure in terms of human connection." There wasn't anyone she felt she had to see before her life ended, which made her feel sorry for herself. Even more than Byron's oddities and cruelties coming forward, and even more than the shock that an incredible amount of money could make things worse instead of better, more perilous instead of more secure, the biggest surprise for her to come out of marriage was how lonesome it was. Byron worked constantly of course, which she'd been prepared for—it was when the two of them were together and she felt alone, more so than when he wasn't even there, that was dejecting to the point of suffocation. Part of her excitement about marriage, one of its elements that had seemed innate to her, was its supposed guarantee of companionship. "I mean, it's also a failure in all the other usual aspects. But that one's, you know, the real bummer."

"For me too," Jasper said. "I did not make loads of friends."

Hazel started crying, but not in a dramatic way. It was subtle, like sweating while lying out in the sun. She felt she needed to think about things in a metaphorical fashion that would take the existential pressure off, and she decided to visualize a box of damage. She had this box that she was carrying through the world, and it was filled up with all the broken things about her and all the bad and shameful choices she'd ever made, and she had to carry it around until she died, because that was how things worked, but that was all she had to do. Exist while holding her box of damage for as long as she could survive. She could do that, couldn't she? And if she did it mindfully, maybe some absolution for past ways in which she'd failed to be brave or aware was built in.

"I'm sorry about your dad," Jasper said. "Truly. Before, that was something I'd say to be polite, but due to brain adjustments now I really am sorry."

"Thanks," Hazel said. "I loved him as my dad and all. But it was never great being with him. Or my mother. I think it doesn't say nice things about me that I don't have a burning wish for them to come back to life so I can hang out with them again. Or that my husband wants me dead, even though he's evil. I mean, here are three people I was supposed to be really bonded with. My relationships with all of them were a disaster."

Jasper nodded. "I don't speak to my parents. It happens, I think. I mean, I know that it does because it happened to me."

"You don't feel guilty, though? I was always like, *Be more tolerant, Hazel! Be more tolerant!* But I never could be. They annoyed and bored and enraged me, each of them, to the end. When I went to college I felt like I was escaping. And then I had to escape from my marriage. I have no idea how to live in a place I don't want to run away from."

But right now, all they had to focus on was running away. Assuming everything had worked.

21

A FEW VEHICLES BEHIND THEM AT THE STOPLIGHT, THE PASSENGER-side window of a minivan filled with middle-aged women rolled down. A woman with a bad haircut, the sort done at a walk-in chain that advertises with Sunday mailer coupons, leaned out of the vehicle. Jasper winced. He almost wanted to talk to her about her hair, in a kind way. Could that be a new form of charitable service? Had she ever, for example, thought about getting a haircut at a nice salon every other month instead of getting a haircut at a terrible salon every month? Not spending a dollar more and looking better, even during the month of split ends, than she looked with regular but uninspired trims?

He leaned into his rearview mirror to make sure—yes, she was wearing a T-shirt with the face of Dolphin Savior on it. I'VE BEEN SAVED! was written across the shirt's graphic in neon pink cursive lettering. Wow, Jasper thought. How great that that catastrophic event in my life worked out so well for the guy.

After driving all night, Jasper and Hazel pulled into the parking lot of a diner in a small southern town off the interstate. "You should get going," Hazel said. "I'll eat here and sleep there." She pointed to the diner, and then to a run-down efficiency motel across the street. "We should've dumped my dad's body and brought that cooler," she joked. "I could've just napped in that for a while. Provided I didn't accidentally close it so tightly that I suffocated inside."

There were people who paid a lot of money to get inside something and feel suffocated, Jasper knew—one of his cons had been convinced that a birth reenactment ceremony would be the key to unleashing her full sales potential at the auto, home, and life insurance company where she worked. Coming out of the birth canal as an infant, her clavicle had gotten stuck against her mother's pelvis for hours. *I've been stuck ever since*, she'd declared to Jasper. *I left my true aptitude for success behind in my mother's vagina*, she'd told him, *and I'll be damned if I'm not going to go back and get it.* This going back didn't involve her actual mother—she wanted to go to a retreat in the Mojave Desert where gurus would slather her with a mix of silicone lubricant and strawberry jelly then force her to worm her way through a snug foam cylinder ten feet in length. *Yeah,* he'd told her, *you should go for it!* knowing full well she wouldn't have the money to do it after he left. That one he didn't feel quite as bad about as all the others. She already wanted to be robbed.

But he did feel bad. About her and everyone else. He'd provided the rabbit woman with some names, and she'd given him a list of current addresses; if he left now, he could make it to some of the houses before the download happened, if it was going to happen. Before Byron began to hunt him down.

"You're the best thing I've ever done," Jasper said to Hazel, smiling. "Thank you for the opportunity." The competition wasn't very fierce, but it was still a nice sentiment to be able to share with another person.

"You're sure welcome," Hazel said. "I've never had anyone express gratitude for the way my poor decisions placed us both in mortal peril. Really though, thanks for maybe risking your life to maybe save mine." She placed her hand on his, which felt awkward, then leaned in and gave him an even more awkward-feeling hug. He was glad he'd never be in a position where he had to try to con Hazel. She might be harder than most to pretend to fall in love with.

HAZEL WENT INTO THE DINER'S BATHROOM AND DECIDED TO PRACTICE the speech she'd give Byron if the deactivation didn't work. "I'm sorry I didn't fall in love with you," she said to her reflection in the mirror. "I tried to." This was the nicest true thing she could think of to say. Hazel suddenly had an urge to go out with kindness, not as a superiority thing but as a guilt thing.

She didn't know the full extent of the changes Byron wanted to usher into mankind, but they didn't seem like they were going to foster nurturing human connections. Something far larger than her own life seemed about to end. Had she been responsible, even a fraction of a percent, for any of his heart's hardening? If so, she wanted to explain.

Yes, unfiltered Byron would creep out a lot of people. But he was truly a genius. "You know how impressive you are, of course," she continued. "That's what's unfair. You could've married someone who was actually amazed by you instead of someone who just pretended to be. I'm sure many people out there truly would've felt honored to be the inaugural host to all your brain implements. It was a bad match. I knew we were different, but I thought it might turn out all right because my parents were total opposites. They weren't suited to each other at all and fought all the time. To them, compatability didn't matter; they'd committed and they were married and that was their life. Plus they didn't have money. I thought it would be really easy to fall in love with a rich person.

"I know how dumb all this sounds. When I realized I wasn't going to be able to love you, I should've just told you. We hadn't been married long when I realized. Maybe you realized the same thing. Or maybe you wouldn't have cared, but I should've told you. It just seemed crazy to give you up. Everyone told me I was so lucky that I figured I'd start feeling lucky soon. It's not your fault I never did.

"Now I feel like when you find me, you won't kill me," Hazel continued. "You'll just keep me holed up somewhere, or do some kind of brainwashing. But brainwashing feels too easy. I know you want me to be aware of my suffering. Can I at least have a virtual reality pod to while away the time? That is one thing I'll agree with you on. There are many vicarious lives that are preferable to actual ones."

She stood at the sink with the faucet on as the download time neared, just in case it happened and she threw up.

It ended up not happening, but she still vomited. Hazel felt that it would've been inappropriate not to vomit, somehow. The alternative would've been just standing there, looking into the mirror and grinning, and she worried that the general universe might interpret a lack of dramatic action as ingratitude. *Here*, was what Hazel hoped to convey as she bent down next to the faucet, *I'm overflowing with emphatic thanks*.

When she finished, she felt good about the decision. Hazel was not looking to start her new life off on an anticlimactic foot.

22

HAZEL DECIDED TO STAY IN THE TOWN WHERE JASPER HAD DROPPED her off and get a job at the diner because the manager-owner was very mean and bossy and somewhat resembled her mother. This pretend intimacy felt good to Hazel because it was also distant. Mother semblance she could deal with and even right now liked a little. Were her actual mother to resurrect from the grave, she could not work for her. In a restaurant or anywhere else. Even or especially if her mother's second life depended on Hazel being an employee.

She said her only requirement was that she didn't want to work out in the front with people, which she blamed on an anxiety disorder. "Well, it's hotter in the back and you get paid less," her boss warned her. "But you come in the back door in the morning, so you can show up to work looking like anything." Hazel couldn't decide if this was a commentary on her present appearance or not.

"You can just roll out of bed and walk up. The cook staff sure does. They're always hungover. One morning the dishwasher, Pierre, kept scratching at himself, his private self, and finally went to the bathroom, then we heard him laugh. When he pulled down his underwear, a used condom fell out. He'd gotten so drunk the night before he didn't even remember having sex. These are your colleagues if you work in the back. Good luck and God bless."

She asked if she had to fill out paperwork. "I can pay you cash but I'll pay you a lot less. It's nothing personal. I'm running a business. If you're that desperate it would be irresponsible of me, from an economic standpoint, not to take advantage." Hazel agreed; she was grateful not to have to lie on the forms or make up a formal name.

What should her name be, Hazel wondered, if she were to rename herself appropriately? Maybe "Oh Well"? Or "Should Have Tried"?

Except when the manager asked her what her name was, she panicked and said, "Hazel."

Everyone called her boss the Big Cheese, but Hazel wanted to be very polite so she tried to treat it like a legal name, with "Cheese" being the surname, and would call her "Ms. Cheese," which always made her boss give her a very confused look.

"Doesn't take much to make you uncomfortable, does it?" Ms. Cheese said to her once by the ice machine. Hazel was looking at a roach on the floor that had been stepped on; its barbed leg was doing an end-game twitch. Warm wind and sunshine were coming through the back door as the produce supplier wheeled vegetables in, and Hazel was thinking about how difficult (if not impossible) it was to keep anything contained—how bad and good always join hard together. Hazel nodded; discomfort was her resting state after all, and Ms. Cheese had walked up to the ice machine and looked both ways and said, "I need a little pick-me-up today," and grabbed the scooper out of the ice machine. She pulled her shirt down and began packing her bra with ice, then handed Hazel the scooper and walked away.

Despite the yelling, Ms. Cheese seemed to like Hazel enough to have designs on fixing her up with her son, who lived in a nearby city but never visited. Hazel tried hard to put these fantasies to rest. "I'm barren," Hazel lied, "and a lesbian, or maybe even asexual, but if I'm even a little sexual it's lesbian, and I'm a practitioner of a radical religion that the government thinks is a cult." "Well, you might not have tons in common," Ms. Cheese said, "but I could see it working."

The steam of the kitchen felt like a form of amnesia, which Hazel liked. She decided she'd recommend working in a restaurant to anyone who was trying to forget everything they'd ever done. All that mattered were the orders, up and out and to-go. Unless she screwed up, it was a near-invisible job—not once did someone picking up an order stop and say, *Who placed these fries inside this Styrofoam container? Could I meet that person? Is that possible?*—and even if she did screw up, it just meant Ms. Cheese coming back and yelling at her. "I should make you go out and apologize," she'd say, "but that wouldn't work because you look so downtrodden. Our wronged customers would end up apologizing to you instead, probably taking the change out of their pockets and giving you any extra money they had and feeling bad about themselves for complaining. 'Don't go in there,' they'd start telling other people, pointing to our diner. 'They screwed up the toppings on my hamburger order, then when I said something, the saddest woman in the world got trotted out from the back. Something in this lady's eyes conveys the expression of an actress starring in a commercial for intestinal discomfort medication, the prescription kind, a woman who's clenching her jaw and gripping her abdomen. When she is making no expression at all, that is still what you see when she looks at you. I went in for lunch and left with a mantle of guilt and gravid unease. Try the pizza joint across the street.'"

But that pizza, Hazel pointed out, really was not that good. "You eat it all the time, don't you?" Ms. Cheese countered. Hazel could only nod. It was still pizza.

Ms. Cheese sighed and kicked a large yellow trash bucket labeled FOOD WASTE ONLY. It rolled a few inches on its tiny wheels. Hazel didn't understand how the wheels on this receptacle could be so little. They were a real win for the small guys. "Melted cheese is a culinary veil," Ms. Cheese said, stepping up to the waste bucket again. "A foxhole where mediocrity can hide." She gave it another kick and a piece of onion skin lifted into the air and floated down to the tile floor right near the drain grate. They both paused to stare at it because it seemed as if it could also be the shed husk of their collective disappointment, something to ponder and mourn.

It reminded Hazel of a tarantula molt display she'd seen once at a natural history museum. The tarantula skins had a disconcerting tempura look about them. They provided no spiritual reassurance. She'd stood in front of the informational tablet that gave a description of the molting process and read and reread it for hours, and become very sad, because it felt like an apt psychic was reading her fortune. Not just her own, but every living thing's. Molting was not easy—the spider didn't eat for weeks and seemed mainly dead and its leg joints began weeping fluid and its stomach went bald. The psychic stress was incredible. Interrupt a tarantula during the molting process and it could die. Afterward its new skin is temporarily so vulnerable that the very insects it consumes, like crickets, can injure it.

The silver lining is that if the spider is missing a leg, the leg can grow back. It will be a smaller, less-functional leg, a sort of spare-tire doughnut situation, but a true second chance.

Hazel wondered if molting, which was kind of like giving birth to your *self*, was more painful than giving birth in the regular way. She remembered her mother telling her how during labor she wanted to die. The pain was that intense. "And I'm no cream puff," her mother reminded her. "That is next level. I kept telling your father to go home and get his gun and shoot me in the head, right between the eyes; I was grabbing his hand and putting his finger on my forehead just so, screaming, 'Here! Here! This is where the bullet goes! Straight into the brain!' And of course the only gun he has is an antique from his grandpa; no ammo at all, doesn't even fire; he felt the need to tell me all this instead of getting the staff to hurry it up with the epidural."

Hazel didn't have this pain for comparison, but she felt an affinity through her own pain and how bad she seemed to be at life. Except that the cause of her own pain was less specific, and she had no idea if she would ever be able to push it out and feel better.

In some ways it was silly how physical the pain seemed, like a big duffle she toted around with her all the time. She often pictured her sadness as an IV cart she had to wheel everywhere she went, its bag dripping a heavy fluid that was keeping her sick instead of making her better. Hazel moved slowly, which sometimes made Ms. Cheese yell, but Ms. Cheese wasn't born yesterday. "In addition to my son, whom I talk about daily, I have five daughters I seldom mention," she told Hazel. "But I'll speak of them now to say that I have six kids, and they were all young at the same time. And sometimes in the grocery store when they'd want something, they'd all lie down on the floor and grab onto my ankle, three on each side, to try to get me to buy it. But instead I'd just walk to the checkout counter and drag them all behind me. It would take about twenty minutes to get ten feet but I'd do it. And well-meaning people in line, men especially, would be like, 'Ma'am? Do you want some assistance with these kids? I can administer punitive slaps to them, or threaten them using the masculine tenor of my voice?' and I'd say, 'No thank you, they'll all let go when we get to the parking lot because the cement will scrape their stomachs.' Because it did. But it took forever to get there, and that's the way you walk all the time, Hazel, and you are a tiny thing, so you must be pulling serious demons. Take a break and slug into the deep freeze if you want; see if you can ice the monkey on your back into submission. Because I need you to refill all the mayo jars before the dinner rush, and if some hustle isn't involved you aren't gonna make it."

Other nights she would hand Hazel a barely drunk milk shake left behind by a customer, one who looked very healthy, Ms. Cheese always stressed, and tell Hazel to drink it in front of her so she could confirm that calories were entering Hazel's body. "I have seen about everything," Ms. Cheese said. "Witnessed the very worst sort of tragedies. But your story I do not ever want you to tell me. I don't want to know what happened. I think it would mess with my head. You are loveless and haunted and I wonder daily if it's bad luck to have you around."

"It's probably not good luck," Hazel agreed. Ms. Cheese filled the empty portion of Hazel's milk shake glass up with aerosol whipped cream.

"I had to fire a kid once because he kept sucking the nitrous oxide out of the whipped cream cans. He admitted he was doing it to get high, that was the *main* reason he said, but he also told me that one weekend he'd done a powerful hallucinogen and had a vision that the gas inside whipped cream cans was actually the trapped souls of dead people who'd been violently wronged. They were trapped in there kind of like a genie in a bottle. If he inhaled them then breathed them out, they could be saved and ascend to the spirit world; if he didn't, they were doomed to power aerofoam dessert toppings then be extinguished forever. I said, in that case, do they grant him a wish when he saves them? Because he needed to go wish for a new job. And he said, 'No, it's more an act of service I'm performing for the dead community.' A real hero, that kid."

This thought depressed Hazel even more all day. Imagine dying only to fall into a spirit trap and get imprisoned inside a can of whipped cream.

ON THE TV IN HER EFFICIENCY MOTEL ROOM (THE OWNER GAVE HER a decent monthly rate), Hazel watched the interviewer lean in and place her hand upon Byron's. The motel where Hazel lived wasn't very clean, but it was next door to a Laundromat, so the air often smelled like dryer sheets. This made everything seem a little fresher than it actually was.

Hazel learned that Byron had reported her "missing and troubled," wracked with grief due to the terminal illness of her father, who also seemed to have disappeared. He was offering an enormous reward for any information. He said he feared she'd been kidnapped due to his financial stature and fame, and that something terrible had happened before the demand could be made. "The search for answers regarding what happened to Hazel is my highest priority," he said, "alongside my responsibilities to Gogol shareholders."

The woman interviewing him was notorious for getting emotional reactions out of celebrities. She'd infamously made the pop star Dolphin Savior break down in tears.

"How are you managing to go on amidst your wife's disappearance?" she asked, scanning Byron's face.

"I describe my work as the technologies business," Byron said. "But what I really sell is access to information." He paused a moment. His pupils reflected the LED stock stream from the face of his watch; it moved across the surface of his eyes like a visible memory. "As Hazel's husband, I am supposed to have more information about her than anyone else does. So the loss is also compounded by all sorts of lesser feelings—humiliation, fraudulence, inadequacy. At the end of the day I have to assume the unthinkable and begin gestures toward moving forward."

"You recently filed for an abandonment divorce. I can't imagine the difficulty of that decision. You brought one of your project managers here with you, Fiffany Leiber." The camera panned offstage to show Fiffany, professional and glamorous, look up from her device and smile. "You've spoken of how grateful you are to be surrounded by such a supportive team. What helps you cope with the day to day? If Hazel isn't found, do you think you could ever find love again?"

"I think Hazel will be found," he said. "I've given up hope that she'll be found alive, but I think she'll be discovered and we'll have answers. I run a company that is all about breakthroughs. What we're technologically capable of one month is often something that would've felt impossible just a few weeks before."

Hazel swallowed and stared at the door bolt. It didn't seem like Byron had moved into a "let bygones be bygones" mind-set.

"And I keep myself surrounded with energized, imaginative

people who aren't afraid to be brave. When you experience loss, the easiest thing to try to fill that space with is fear. All my best employees are fearless." His eyes seemed to dart over to Fiffany for a brief shared glance. "That's a rare thing."

EVERYTHING AT THE DINER TASTED A LOT LIKE FRENCH FRIES. FRY grease was the prevailing flavor note. It was the smell that clung to Hazel's clothes and followed her home. Her bedsheets smelled like fry grease because of the nights she came home and felt too sad to do anything but go lie in bed. Her motel room was a relief because she could walk on all fours. That felt the most natural. In the morning she crawled into the shower and had no idea how she'd ever taken a shower standing upright before. In hindsight, taking an upright shower seemed like running a marathon. There was one small section of tile near the floor that she kept pretty clean with a sponge, because while the water streamed down onto her head she liked to sit by the drain and rest her cheek against the wall there. With the water streaming down she could close her eyes and pretend she was a type of plant. All she had to do was sit there, indefinitely, and sometimes feel water. The drain creeped her out a little—it was hard not to wonder if Byron had found her and placed a camera inside it. Something harmful might come up through its holes one day.

Byron and Fiffany finding Hazel while working together as a power couple and executing her jointly would be even worse than Byron alone killing her. That would be just like middle school, with the popular girl winning once again. It was wrong and gross to still feel like marrying Byron had been an accomplishment, but Hazel did—it had been a win that a weird girl like her technically shouldn't have gotten, according to social rules. Byron's wife should've been Fiffany from the start. But it had been Hazel, and however sick a victory that was, it would be erased if they killed her as a pair and used her murder as a bonding opportunity, like a game of doubles tennis.

It was this thought that made her climb out of her shell a little and go use one of the Internet computers at the library. Of course she couldn't check her e-mail or any other account as her old self. She also didn't want to do a search for Byron or Fiffany or her own name, even though Byron's was probably searched for by hundreds of thousands of people a day; anything that might place her needle in a haystack for one of his algorithms to find had to be avoided. So she just scanned front-page headlines of news sites and gleaned what she could from occasional mentions. Byron and Fiffany were definitely an item now. Had they been together before she'd moved out? Should she care? She supposed it was telling that what saddened her about that thought was not Byron having sex with Fiffany, but an ego sadness. She hated the thought of him having cheated on her with Fiffany while they were still married, being with both of them at once and comparing the two, with Hazel losing in every category. And with Fiffany aware that they were competing while Hazel was ignorant.

Not that she would've traded in her futuristic microfiber sweatpants for silk underwear and tried to swoon and seduce Byron back if she had known. But maybe she would've had a little more pride and awareness, for her own sake. Maybe she wouldn't have snuck gas station candy inside the compound and eaten it in bed and occasionally forgotten the wrapper. Once Byron had rolled over and foil from a chocolate bar had come loose from the sheets and stuck to his cheek. He'd reacted like that scene in *The*

Godfather where the man wakes up to find the severed head of a horse. She'd tried to downplay this indiscretion with comparison to an affair—"At least it wasn't a condom wrapper," she'd joked, but Byron didn't find humor or relief in this statement. "They're different causes of terror," Byron said. "But equal vulgarities."

The other people she really wanted to look up online, Jasper and Liver, didn't exist online. Hazel found herself with no one to try to care deeply about. She didn't want to develop feelings for anyone new in case Byron found her, or them.

She had an idea that one safe way to interact with people would be to make a fake social media account for an imaginary cute pet, like a guinea pig or a puppy. But even this seemed possibly too risky. What if the account became super popular and then was exposed as a hoax, the pictures all borrowed, and a nationwide hunt to find the deceptive human responsible for the account ensued? Maybe one of the biggest fans of the account, pre-exposure, would coincidentally be a librarian at the public library where Hazel used the Internet, and when chat rooms of angry scorned hackers determined the location of the computers where the account was checked and maintained, the librarian would offer to comb through video-security footage, checking against the times of the posts and discovering her. The whole Internet could know who she was and she wouldn't know that they knew until she walked in to do another update and the librarian and a mob were there waiting for her.

Better to just look at cute animal images without making them a deceptive vehicle for interaction with other human beings.

WHEN BYRON AND FIFFANY MARRIED SIX MONTHS LATER, THEIR WED-ding was a far more public, promoted affair than Byron and Hazel's had been. Instead of technology they were actively selling their love story; if the public bought that, they'd buy whatever Byron was going to peddle next.

It was what Fiffany said, or didn't say, that made it so excruciating to listen to her talk in interviews. Every statement she uttered was a sentence Hazel herself could remember saying, some of them highly peculiar in context. Asked where they were thinking of going on their honeymoon, Fiffany said, "When I'm near a pool in a dry bathing suit, I have a phobia of the people whose suits are already wet. I've moved past it but I always have this fear that if I accidentally brush up against one of their arms, my suit will suddenly be wet too, saturated with pool water even though I haven't been in the pool, which seems so frightening to me." "I guess you'd rather not go to a tropical location then?" the reporter said.

Hazel hadn't seen hours of footage of Fiffany speaking—she couldn't bear to watch Fiffany and Byron's prenuptial celebrity interview that appeared to be unilaterally aired and streamed on every major network and Web site—but she didn't need to. She just knew. That had been the agreement that Fiffany had entered into, which was part of Hazel's punishment: the only sentences Fiffany would be able to speak in public were sentences Hazel had spoken to Byron during the context of their marriage.

Why would Fiffany agree to something so messed up, Hazel wondered, to whatever neuroalterations were required for this software to function? Incredible wealth and also celebrity, she supposed. Hazel hadn't wanted these—the judgment of the general public frightened her, plus the general public did not seem to go out of its way to find Hazel fascinating or engage with her—but Fiffany was well received and liked being in the media. And it was clever, the way Fiffany used Hazel's former responses, often meta-

phorically. Maybe it was a fun sort of game for her. Hazel found herself wondering how its mental software worked, if Fiffany thought
an internal question and then got to "see" her possible responses.

Hazel also wondered how Fiffany felt about her, and how much
Fiffany knew about what Byron had done. Maybe Fiffany knew
everything and married him anyway. Maybe she didn't think of him
as evil.

Maybe she just saw Hazel as an idiot. Ungrateful in the extreme.

IT ALL MADE HAZEL FEEL EXTRA LONELY—THE PERSON TRYING TO
kill her had a lover but she didn't. One night she decided to try
an anonymous hookup service. It was dangerous, but her life was
already in danger and she'd spent so many years, her married years
included, not really being touched. Since companionship was out
of the picture, she thought random sex might be the nicest physical
thing she could experience with another person.

The way the service worked was that you called in and gave
a day and a time but no name, and then you chose whether you
wanted to get an address or give one. She gave her real address
since she already lived in a seedy motel. There were no possessions
to indicate her extended stay; they'd just assume she'd rented the
room for the evening. "Is there anything specific I should tell him?"
the operator asked. *Make sure he likes the smell of French fries*, Hazel
thought. She requested someone sober, so there would be more of
a chance that he was as miserable as she was. "As little talking as
possible," Hazel decided. The operator went on to ask what she'd
like to consent to, then recited a long grocery list of activities that
Hazel could say yes or no to ahead of time, including things she
hadn't ever thought about. "Afterward, can your partner use the

bathing facilities?" Hazel thought again of the possible drain camera. "Well, the toilet is totally fair game at all times," she said. "But no shower." Because if Byron was spying on her with a toilet cam, it seemed like the shame was more on him no matter what her guests or activities entailed.

When the guy showed up, he looked normal to the point of obscurity, like an extra in a movie. He was well dressed and Hazel wondered if he would change his mind when he saw her. His consent list was far longer than hers; she was allowed to take initiation liberties, and she figured she should just go for it right away and know immediately if he wouldn't be partaking. So when he closed the door she ran to him like a beloved fiancée returned from overseas, throwing her arms around him and kissing and groping him passionately.

Right from the start she simultaneously wanted it to never end and already be over. She hadn't expected to feel jealous, possessive feelings when they got into her bed—it was an awful bed, but almost immediately she resented having to share it, even though it had been her idea. Though she was comforted by the fact that she'd get to sleep in it alone. For her, an overnight sleepover was a nonconsent item, though she hadn't ruled out the possibility of a tandem nap.

It surprised her how it felt affectionate. She'd always assumed that intimacy required love or at the very least a baseline of shared familiarities, but she decided now that that wasn't the case. The man was kissing her neck and rubbing her nipples with the firm-but-not-hard grope she'd requested over the phone, and she felt incredibly close to him, incredibly thankful for the feel of his skin against hers. He spooned around her, running his fingertips up and down her inner thighs while they kissed and she moaned and writhed, and when she was ready she faced away from him and buried her face in her pillow and the musty linen and the French-fry smell transformed into something deeper and sweeter, and for a moment she escaped herself and all things entirely—her head rose out of the ocean of her life and she took a clear breath of everything beyond her situation before sinking underneath again and opening her eyes.

When they were finished, she found she didn't want to turn around to look at him and realized she couldn't remember his face at all—she hadn't taken a long glance before attacking him with her mouth. The man couldn't secretly be Byron because he was far better at touching and kissing than Byron. But what an awful shock that would be: if the man's mustache ripped off then the skin around his neck lifted up and turned out to be a latex balaclava with Byron's face beneath it. *Hey, gotcha!*

Or on the opposite end of the spectrum, she could turn to find her anonymous lover seemingly at rest, start to cover him up with a sheet then notice a long blade protruding from his abdomen and the spreading pool of warm blood. *Was he bothering you, darlin'?* Liver would ask, drawing the blade back, his right eye coming to life with a few enthusiastic twitches. *Or did I overreact?* And he'd proceed to tell her how he'd tracked her down using mammalian intuitions and techniques that technology could never replicate. And then she'd have to stay with him, since he'd killed someone for her, even though it hadn't been for her at all, really. Kind of like how since Jasper had saved her life, she no longer felt that she was allowed to kill herself. Even though the saving was more about him and she hadn't really wanted to be saved.

What other horrors might she see if she rolled over? Maybe this onetime lover next to her, asleep, but then her mother's very awake ghost lying right next to him, pissed off and ready to talk about it. *Are you kidding me with this casual promiscuity?* Her mother wasn't from New Jersey, but Hazel could see her ghost picking up the accent; it would be a personality fit. *Are you doing this because you're desperate to get pregnant? I know I told you once that I wanted a grandchild under any circumstances, but I've reconsidered. Certainly you will never turn your own life around, but I don't even think you're capable of being a neutral vessel. Even if the baby were whisked away from you at birth, the gravity of your curse would be inescapable. It's not fair to irreversibly doom the young.* Her father, luckily, would never haunt. He'd feel it to be weak somehow. An afterlife form of whining.

Hazel shook her head in horror and felt a hand on her arm. It was warm, human, far better than the cold pinch of her mother's ghost. Maybe it was Jasper, his face contrite, explaining that he had indeed tried to be good but just wasn't; Gogol had caught up with him and it was either he go down or she did, and since he was more attractive, more fun and charming, he felt he had more of a right to life, plus Byron was her enraged ex after all, not his, and then Jasper would pull out a syringe and stick an anti-antidote into her arm and the chip would turn back on and she'd be back to square one.

But it was just the anonymous man, just a squeeze. He got up and left without speaking or saying good-bye. She'd asked for this, but when it happened she felt disappointed. She supposed there was no way to avoid disappointment.

But she didn't feel disappointed overall. She'd just had a pleasant experience. Did that mean that something bad was about to happen? Didn't pleasure always come with a shadow?

For a few weeks afterward she thought of trying the service

again, maybe this time getting a room elsewhere for the night as a precaution. Then on her walk to work, she saw the sign.

Across the street from the diner, in the same plaza as the pizza restaurant, a Gogol store was coming.

It was probably a coincidence?

But what if it wasn't? Was the man from the hookup service somehow connected to Gogol?

Hazel walked up to the storefront's glass, which she knew would have been replaced—it was a spec for all Gogol stores to have windows made with a finish that couldn't be smudged or scratched; when you breathed on it, your breath did not show up. Most disconcerting of all was that it didn't reflect. There was no way to impose your physical human experience on it. Someone could throw a bucket of blood at it (Hazel had actually seen this demonstrated in the lab) and every drop would bounce right off like a miniature red tennis ball. "Incredible!" Hazel had exclaimed to Byron when he'd showed her. She'd acted interested and awed. "It can't be destroyed?" "It can," he'd answered. "But not with items passing consumers will have." This had given Hazel a fantasy of getting one such item, she had no idea what—a diamond drill bit?—putting on a blue wig and going to deface one of the stores, pulling off the disguise at a critical moment and yelling into the security camera: *I hate Byron and I hate Gogol; I am miserable and I want people to know. If you get close enough to him that you can hear his breathing and you really listen, you will find it has a sharp tinkling sound to it, the sound of like really small toenail clippings being scattered over the top of a sheet of ice, rodent nail clippings probably. Anyone who makes that sound when they inhale is a bad person.* But then she would've looked crazy, and Byron would've been awarded some sort of psychiatric guardianship over her, and she never would've left The Hub again.

She couldn't trust that a store opening so close to her job was a coincidence. And she shouldn't have let a stranger come to her hotel room.

Hazel worked her shift like normal, but that evening found Ms. Cheese behind her desk in the office, listening to an AM talk-radio show and soaking her feet in a large bucket that had once held chicken gravy. The show's host was interviewing a woman who'd had a near-death experience and claimed to have temporarily gone to heaven. "There are a lot of TVs up there," the woman said. "Almost everywhere you look there's a TV, and they float in the air alongside you wherever you go. That's one thing I'm looking forward to now about dying. In heaven I'll be able to watch my stories while I stroll down to the bus stop. I'm pretty sure I saw one or two bus stops there. What takes getting used to in heaven is that no one talks; they sing everything. Even the voices on the TV sing. At first it seems like a little much. I thought, 'This could start to get on my nerves.' But everyone's voice was pretty decent. After a while it seemed normal. When I came out of the coma, everyone talking was what sounded strange. My husband and I only sing when we're at home now. I've come to prefer that. It's hard for me to talk to you like this right now, in fact. Talking feels like forcing a smile."

The office didn't have a door, so Hazel knocked on the wall. Ms. Cheese slid her glasses down and looked up with skepticism. "Shit," she said.

"Yeah. I have to leave town," Hazel said. "I'm sorry for the short notice. This has been a great job."

"I am sorry to hear that. You weren't that bright or industrious but you sure didn't have anywhere else to be. I'll miss your sulking face reminding me of all I have to be thankful for. I hope you win your soul back in a bet or something. Let me give you some cash for what you've worked this week, adjusted for the very short notice of you quitting. Do you have any resources? Do you want to take one of those big bags of rice with you? Are you strong enough to carry it?"

Hazel accepted the cash and the rice. Maybe she could figure out a way to duct-tape it to her torso and it could be dual purpose: If someone from Gogol came to get her in the middle of the night, it could serve as a makeshift bulletproof vest. Though it would probably just slow the bullet down enough that it would take longer for her to die, and be a lot more painful. But if they were apprehending her and taking her to another location to kill her, maybe she could reach up under her shirt and slit the bag open and a trail of rice would be left, should anyone try to find her. But there was no one who would.

She left and began to walk, taking the long way home. After a few minutes, she noticed that a man talking on a device was walking behind her. From what she could see in her periphery, his suit wasn't made of Gogol-issued fabric, but he wasn't giving her much space.

Hazel turned down an unnecessary street. The man followed. Her heart began to race.

"Yeah," she heard him say into his device. "Yes. Byron Gogol."

There was a puddle on the ground that she glanced into to eyeball his height. He was tall and muscular. But for Jasper's sake, for what he risked and did, she felt she had to give it everything she had.

Hazel whipped around with the bag of rice and hit the man on the side of the face. His device went flying and hit the ground with a loud crack. She took off running.

She heard him yell out twice as she sprinted off—first for his face, and then for his phone.

But as she passed a large electronics store, she saw that photos of Byron were flashing all over the multiple television screens.

Had something happened?

Something had happened. He would not be looking for Hazel anymore.

23

IN THE MORNING, HAZEL RETURNED TO THE DINER AND PUT ON HER apron. It was right where she'd left it the night before.

"Hey, you!" Ms. Cheese called out from the office. "I know it's you. The quiet way you shut the door and then walk all silent. Like you're a wildlife photographer or something. I assume you're back on a volunteer basis? Will work for patty melts? Ha. Haha. Just fooling. They're doing an AM fryer clean-out. To celebrate your continued employment you can go help scrub the heating coils."

Hearing the news yesterday had been like snorting a drug, some kind of upper that coated euphoria with a firm layer of panic. Mid-afternoon, the line cook Benny noticed Hazel's hands and arms trembling at regular intervals despite the heat of the kitchen. "You know how being tickled too long starts to hurt?" she asked him. "I have felt like that for hours now but without the tickling."

Benny nodded. "Did you know it's impossible to tickle yourself? That's because your brain knows what's up."

"Have you ever taken too much cold medicine—"

"Y-e-s," he said.

"—and had that scalp thing where it feels like needles are connecting your hair to your head?"

Just then, Ms. Cheese entered the kitchen. "Hazel, some guy came in asking for you in the middle of lunchtime rush. 'Does this look like an office building?' I said to him. 'Do you have a noon appointment with Hazel? Did you get an e-mail reminder? I don't think so!' Then he grabbed a pen and wrote out a note on a napkin. Winked at me and then started to leave without ordering a thing. I called out after him. 'There's no return address on this correspondence, *sir*,' I said. 'You expect me to deliver this without a stamp?'"

Hazel's whole body began trembling now, so hard that she worried she wouldn't be able to swallow. She tried speaking, but couldn't. It felt like her mouth was filling up with water. So everything on the news had been an elaborate trick. Elaborate for anyone but Byron. Of course he'd want to fill her with hope just before he came to get her.

"Why are you shaking?" Ms. Cheese turned to the line cook. "Did you give her something?"

He shook his head no and shrugged. Ms. Cheese theatrically lay the napkin down on a cutting board and pinned it down with the tip of a large knife.

"I'm just trying to run a business here," she said. "As you can see, good help is hard to find. Take a moment. Get yourself together. And next time you see this joker, tell him not to drop by during your shift," she said.

Hazel sat down on the floor. That would actually be a great thing to say to Byron just before he killed her or took her away or whatever his plans were: *I'm not allowed to have visitors at work.*

"What does the note say?" she asked Benny.

"It says, 'Now you're free.'" He paused. "Did you just get dumped?"

Hazel stood and reached for the knife. Benny began to move away from her. "Don't act in anger," he said.

She lifted the blade and picked up the note. It wasn't from Byron.

JASPER WAS OUTSIDE WAITING WHEN SHE GOT OFF HER SHIFT. "HUZ-zah!" he yelled. He climbed up on the hood of his car, raised his hands in the air and started yelling again, yipping sounds of victory.

Hazel looked back toward the diner. Ms. Cheese was peeking out through the blinds. Hazel watched a curl of cigarette smoke drift up past the set of scowling eyes.

"Let's go somewhere else to celebrate," she said. "My place? We can watch the news?"

For hours in Hazel's motel room, they pounded beers and took in the media's coverage. There was the leaked video of Byron's death, from The Hub's bedroom security cameras (the ones Byron swore shut off at night when Hazel had first moved in—of course they didn't). It featured Byron and Fiffany in bed side by side, both sleep-helmeted, when Byron sat upright moaning, intermittently gripping at his helmet and his chest. Fiffany removed her helmet and shook out her hair, then tried to figure out what the problem was. Byron couldn't get his helmet off. Something was wrong—it was hurting him.

"This could not have been a malfunction like they're claiming," Hazel said. The story being told was that the helmet wouldn't come off. Due to a software glitch or another technical failure, perhaps it had even been messing with his brain waves. He'd apparently panicked to the point of giving himself a heart attack. "There's no way," Hazel said. "Safeguard after safeguard prevents it. Whatever happened was intentional. Fiffany killed him. He must've realized that right before he died. That she'd outsmarted him."

"Ah. How sweet is that," Jasper said.

It was nice, Hazel had to admit, that the world at large thought Byron's death was due to an error of technology he'd created. But the worst part of Hazel wished this had been the case. "It sucks that he knows he didn't fail, though. At least not in his technology."

"But he's dead. He didn't exactly win."

"You're right," Hazel agreed. "I guess part of me still doesn't believe it. But there's a lot to appreciate here." It was great to watch Byron's escalation of panic in the video: his black-and-white image attempting to break the helmet off by hitting his head against the wall, first standing and then on all fours, knocking his head against the ground until he no longer could. If he was trying to speak actual words, they didn't come through on the recording. Not with the helmet's muffling and Fiffany's supposedly frantic screams. She was a good actress.

Hazel decided to pretend the context of the video was Byron realizing the error of his ways and beating his head into the ground accordingly.

"Do you think it was really someone at the police station who leaked the footage?" Jasper asked. The way he was shoveling peanuts into his mouth made Hazel feel like they were at a movie theater.

Maybe this was true, but the threat of a lawsuit from Gogol would be too scary for most workers to risk it. "I feel like maybe Fiffany had a hand in that too," Hazel said. If so, the act almost seemed like an apology meant just for her.

Jasper raised his bottle in the air. "Hail to the new CEO."

Fiffany was "requesting privacy during this difficult time," but all channels were confirming that she was going to be named as the new CEO of Gogol.

Hazel had had Fiffany all wrong. Fiffany's ultimate pursuit had been the company, not Byron. And in killing him, she'd probably saved the world a little. One of her new VPs was already discussing what speculative changes the company might undergo with her leadership, and none of the projected initiatives included brain melds. She'd likely be bowing out of several of Gogol's weapons contracts and wanted to increase the company's humanitarian initiatives. "She's quite interested in expanding development for art and education technologies," the television said.

"Hail to the new CEO," Hazel agreed.

Later that night, Hazel and Jasper ended up at the small green pool behind her motel. Jasper cannonballed into the water without hesitation. "Second chances," he said when he surfaced. "So what are you going to do now?"

After all the mistakes Hazel had made, it was real magic to be there, in front of a pool and under a sky. "Well. I can make some friends. I don't have to worry about Byron hunting them or burning their house down now."

"I think I want to try having friends," Jasper said.

"What I want to avoid, I suppose, is getting trapped in another emotionally fake relationship where my daily life is a false performance tantamount to self-harm?" Hazel said.

"Yes." Jasper began floating toward the middle of the pool. "Yes, yes, yes."

On impulse, she took off her dress. Jasper lifted his head. "You should get in," he said. "You really should."

Hazel smiled, holding his gaze, then slowly took off her underwear and bra too. "It's not that I hope other hotel guests are looking out their windows and seeing me doing this," she said. "I hope they aren't. I know voyeurism is a thing, a sexual thing, sometimes, and after Byron's surveillance I'm way more into whatever sexual thing is the opposite of voyeurism."

"I think you're naked in public right now," Jasper said.

"Yes. But *Byron* can't see me." She jumped in; the water was bathlike. When she surfaced, Jasper smiled in a way that made her feel playful. "Why don't you get naked too?"

He laughed and slid his boxers off then threw them up on the sidewalk. They landed with a wet slap.

Hazel cleared her throat. "So if we fooled around right now, you'd really feel like you were having sex with a dolphin?"

Jasper gave her an embarrassed shrug and nodded. "It might not be that great for you. If you're into emotional connection and stuff. I kind of go off to another world."

Hazel thought for a moment. "But I wouldn't have to pretend it was great, right?" Prior to Liver, she'd pretended to be in love with everyone she slept with, at least initially, although that never turned out well. Especially not with Byron. When had she so internalized the feeling that if something wasn't great she needed to bridge the gap between reality and idealism with her own manufactured enthusiasm? Her enthusiasm was like one of those faux snow machines at a ski resort. For most of her life it had been churning out synthetic delight. It had basically forgotten the original recipe.

She'd been surprised at how much she'd liked sleeping with Liver: having it be mediocre then *not* acting like it wasn't mediocre. "I'm kind of excited to sleep with people I don't love and not pretend to love them," Hazel admitted. She was looking forward to this: having sex and saying, *That was uninspired but pleasant* or *We have less in common than I thought in a way that makes it more fun to be alone than be with you* or *My needs are opposed to your innate daily habits; let's go try other things separately and then not report back.*

"Me too, actually," said Jasper. "And you know I'm not trying to get your money since you don't have any."

"Plus I'm not interested in loving you at all." Hazel smiled. Their bodies started bobbing toward one another.

When she'd married Byron, Hazel thought she could figure out a way to stand being with whoever would have her; after her childhood she felt fortunate to be wanted by anyone. She assumed that for the right payoff, there were endless situations she could slip into and purport to feel at home. She could feign an interest in anything.

But pretending all the time was a different sort of virtual life, as fake as any of Byron's technological simulations. Her lips met Jasper's, her tongue. "It's starting," he whispered. He closed his eyes and she decided to close hers too—she didn't need to watch him for feedback cues. He wouldn't be looking to her to perform. These were all good things, so Hazel kept kissing him. What she most wanted to do with her second chance, she decided, was never fake anything ever again.

ACKNOWLEDGMENTS

THANKS TO AGENT EXTRAORDINAIRE JIM RUTMAN FOR CREATING THE opportunity to write this book, and to Lee Boudreaux, the book's first fairy godmother.

I could not have written this novel without Megan Lynch. Through her guidance, clarity, and insight, the manuscript became better and more itself with each revision. She understood the book long before it was "there," and was a tireless copilot in helping it arrive. I am so grateful for her editorial genius. Thanks also to Emma Dries, Eleanor Kriseman, Ashley Garland, and everyone involved at Ecco for their fantastic work.

Amy Martin and Julie Nichols generously opened their home to me when I needed a quiet work space; I wrote much of the first draft there. There is no aspect of my life they did not help me with, from childcare to reality television. The second draft of this book was finished at the beautiful Maple Wood Lodge thanks to the generosity of John Fetters and Coleman. I wrote multiple revisions of this book in the home of Birdie and Maile Chapman, who held me together and kept me going in ways I can never repay.

Many writers, artists, academics, and heroes served as critical sources of inspiration throughout the writing of this book, especially Jami Attenberg, Natalie Bakopoulos, Lynda Barry, Kate Bernheimer, Gabrielle Calvocoressi, Jeremy Chamberlin, Dan Chaon, Dave Hickey, Roxane Gay, Lindsay Hunter, Kiese Laymon, Annie Liontas, Carmen Maria Machado, Danielle Pafunda, Jeff Parker, Lee Running, Ralph Savarese, Vu Tran, and Richard Wiley.

At John Carroll University: George Bilgere, Anna Hocevar, Dave Lucas, John McBratney, Phil Metres, Tom Pace, Debby Rosenthal, and Maria Soriano; at the NEOMFA: Mary Biddinger, Mike Geither, David Giffels, Caryl Pagel, and Imad Rahman; at the University of Nevada, Las Vegas: Megan Becker, Olivia Clare, Lynn Comella, Carol Harter, Anne Stevens, Doug Unger, and Maritza White. To all my former, current, and future students—you keep me in love with the process of writing.

To Team Bakoponutt: Amos Bakopoulos, Lydia Bakopoulos, and Sparrow Nutting. No one makes me laugh harder or feel happier. Having the three of you in my life is the best and luckiest part of being me.

And thanks to DB, whose steady encouragement gets me through everything. I'm no good, but I love you.